AMBUSH AT HORSE CREEK

MICHAEL L CLARK

Ambush at Horse Creek

ISBN: 979-8-9871616-6-1 (Paperback)

ISBN: 979-8-9871616-5-4 (Hardcover)

In Memory of

Steven "Stevie" Watson

My Friend and Fellow Bullrider Who was

Tragically Killed While Competing

in an NCAA Rodeo in Arkansas in 1979.

At the Time of His Death, Stevie was

Ranked as the Number One Bullrider in

the Ozark Region.

He Died Doing What He Loved.

This is For You, Stevie!

TRAIL TO ST. JOSEPH

Niagara Falls
NEW YORK
Albany
Buffalo
PENNSYLVANIA
New York
OHIO
Columbus

PONY EXPRESS TRAIL #2

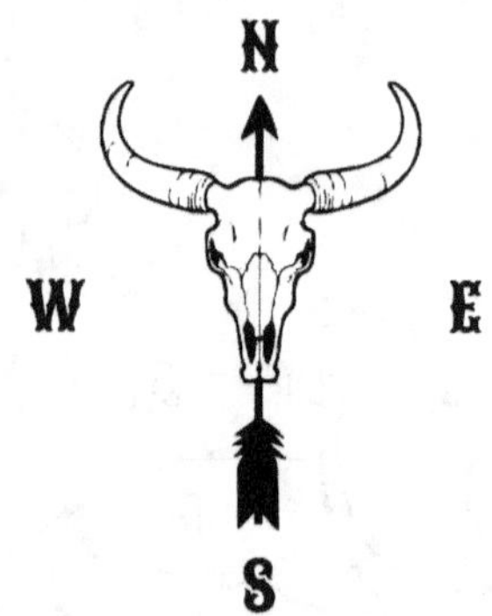

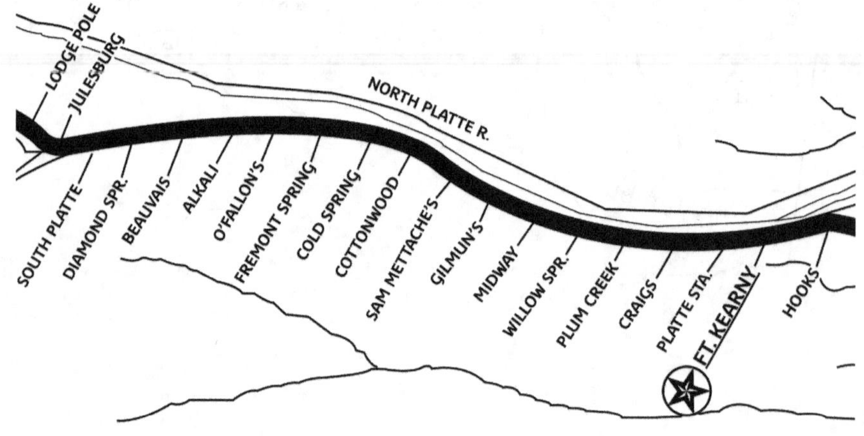

PONY EXPRESS TRAIL #1

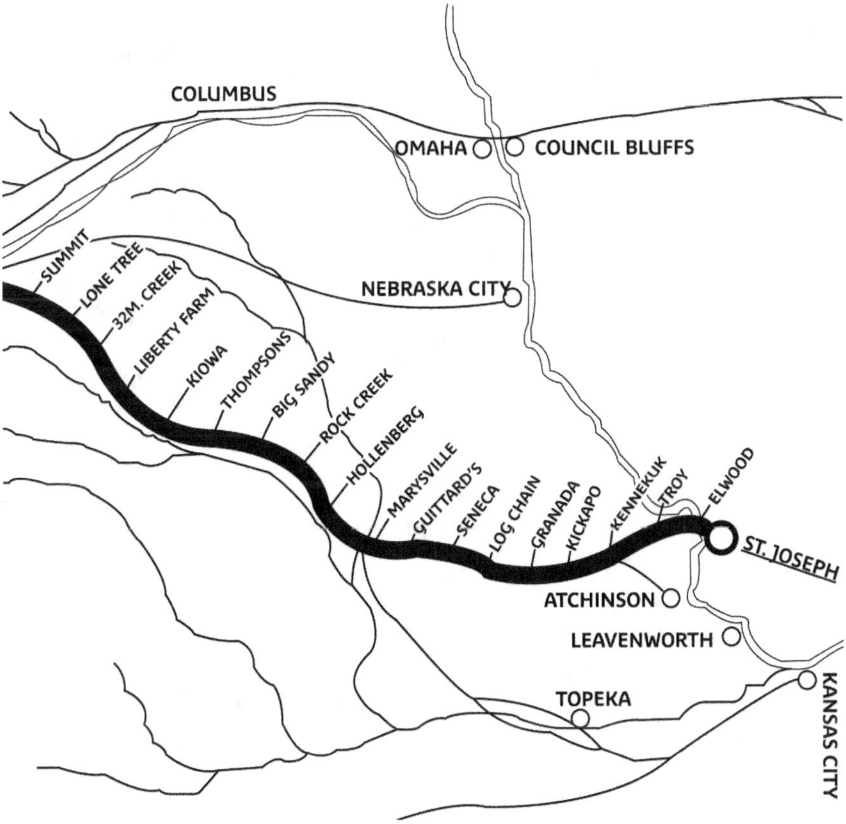

PONY EXPRESS TRAIL #3

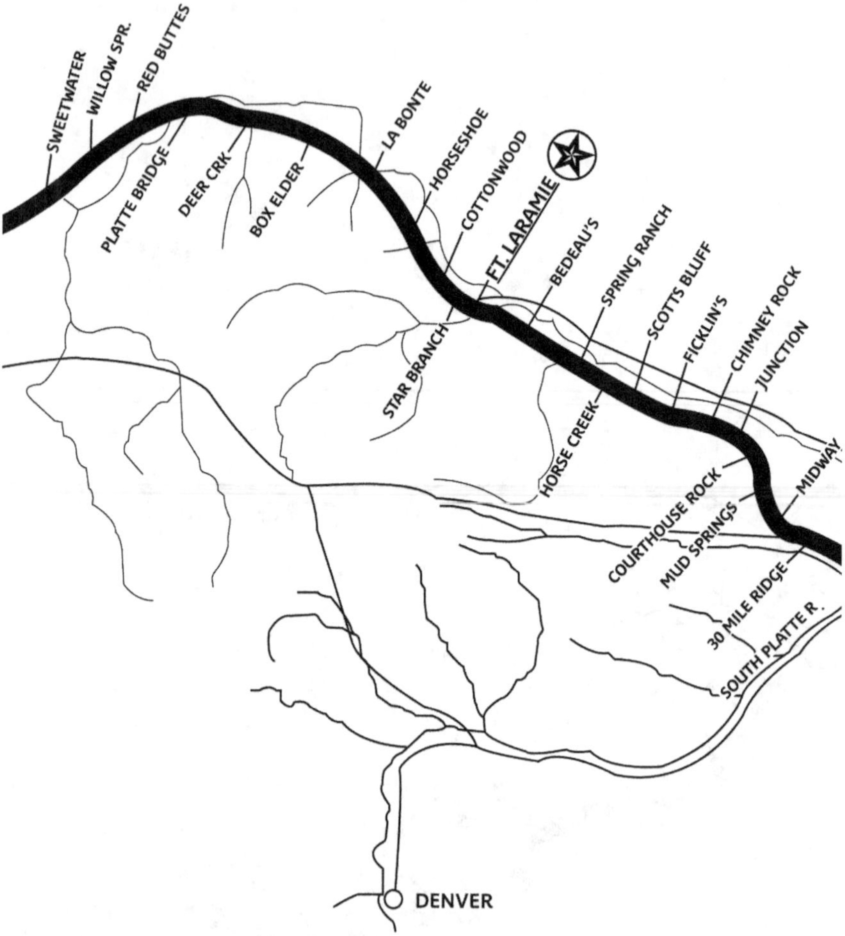

PONY EXPRESS TRAIL #2

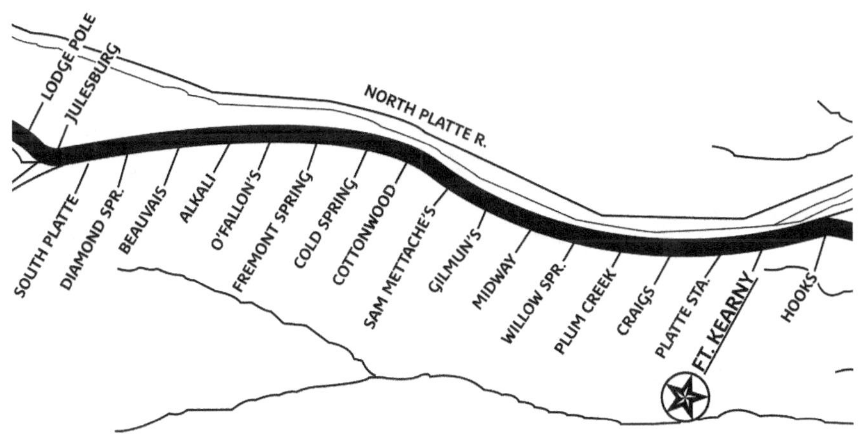

CHAPTER 1

SEPTEMBER 14, 1860

About a mile from Bedeau's as he rode along the Horse Creek, Stevie saw a trail of smoke reaching above the horizon. "*Oh, no!*" he thought. "*Not again!*"

Ficklin's Station had already fallen victim at the hands of the Kiowa, who raided along the trail from Ft. Kearny to Ft. Laramie only five months ago. Ficklin's had just been rebuilt by Russell, Majors, and Waddell, the conglomerate who established the Pony Express in April. Now it seemed Bedeau's Station had also been attacked and burned by the local Indians.

Stevie regretted what he might find up ahead. However, his regret was short- lived as his pony suddenly stumbled, falling head-over-feet and rolling to the ground, propelling Stevie and his mochila through the air. Stevie tumbled to the ground with a thud, landing on his right shoulder and dislocating it. Stevie lay momentarily, trying to decide if he was injured or not. Unfortunately, he couldn't move his right arm without wincing in excruciating pain.

Stevie looked around to find his horse, who was struggling to stand. As the pony finally stood, it was evident that he, too, was in pain. The pony grunted, snorted, and whinnied while favoring his leg. Stevie managed to raise himself to his feet, then walked to the pony to have a look. He felt each of the horse's legs and discovered the pony had broken his right foreleg at the canon bone. Stevie unbelievingly shook his head and rolled his eyes as he said, "Sorry, old man."

Stevie reached with his left hand and took his Colt revolver from its holster on his right hip. He clumsily shifted the gun in an unfamiliar left-handed grip and raised the pistol to the pony's temple. Stevie pulled the trigger and a shot echoed through the open fields. The horse lay lifeless on the ground at Stevie's feet.

Stevie slid the Colt inside his belt behind the buckle, then removed his kerchief and loosened the knot making a sling to carry his lame arm. He slipped the sling over his head and gingerly placed his right arm into the sling. Stevie then walked over to where his mochila had landed, picked it up, slung it over his left shoulder, and began walking toward Bedeau's.

Ten Kiowa braves rode together, heading southeast, when they heard a gunshot in the distance. The clan leader raised his staff while sitting atop his Appaloosa pony to halt his men. They listened to the air as it flowed past them. Finally, the leader motioned for his men to follow as he led them toward the direction from which he had heard the gunshot.

The summer sun beat down on Stevie as he walked along. He grew wearier and wearier as he walked underneath the blazing sunlight. Finally, Stevie stopped next to a stream and lay face down to drink from the creek. He plunged his face underneath the water as it flowed over his head. The cooling waters revived Stevie so he could pick himself up and walk again.

As Stevie continued down the trail, he came upon a small grove of Boxelder trees. He decided to take a short rest under the shade of the trees, so he walked into the grove and sat underneath one of the Boxelders.

Suddenly, Stevie heard something whiz past his left ear and imbed itself into the tree. An arrow had narrowly missed Stevie's head and impaled the tree only inches from his ear. Stevie rolled away from the arrow to find shelter behind his tree, but he was too late. Another arrow flew at him and didn't miss. Stevie felt a sharp pain in his back as an arrow pierced him below the shoulder blade. Stevie gasped as ten riders came out of nowhere, whooping and crying out in their native war yells.

Stevie drew the Colt from his belt and fired with his left hand. The first shot felt awkward and missed its target. So he fired again, hitting one of the Kiowa braves in the chest and knocking him off his horse. Another brave rode directly at Stevie as he raised the Colt again and fired, "Bang!" The bullet hit the Indian in the face, and he fell to the ground.

The remaining braves began riding a circle around the grove of trees, trying to catch Stevie by surprise from behind. Stevie continued to fire at the Kiowa braves as they circled him. Another brave hit the ground eight feet away from where Stevie was hiding.

The fifteen-year-old Stevie Watson was all alone, fighting off grown men who wanted nothing more than to kill him. He hid among the Boxelders and thought about his family living back in St. Joseph, Missouri. He hadn't seen them since he left home to join the Pony Express.

Stevie thought about Ma and Pa, who had brought the family from Albany, New York, seven years ago. Stevie was only eight years old at the time, but he had been mature and responsible for a young boy. His pa had depended on Stevie so often to look after the family whenever he needed to be away.

Stevie's brother, William, was just the opposite. Two years younger and always interested in having fun rather than working. William looked up to his older brother and depended upon him for help.

Stevie thought of Lillian, who was now ten years old, almost a young woman who dearly loved Stevie. Stevie had always looked after Lillian and allowed her to come along whenever possible to participate in any adventure he might find.

His youngest sister, Heather, wasn't born until the family reached St. Joseph. She was now six years old. Heather always wanted to tag along with Lillian, but Lillian was more interested in whatever Stevie was doing.

Stevie suddenly grew homesick. He had been gone from home only six months, and he had always been too busy to think much about home and his family. However, his present predicament changed all that. He now longed to be back home with his family.

Stevie lay in the Boxelder grove, hiding and hoping that one of the other Express riders would come to his rescue. He knew it wasn't likely to happen, though. It might be hours before another rider would come through here.

As the Kiowa closed in on Stevie, he drew his Colt revolver and began firing at them. Bullets flew through the air in one direction while arrows flew toward Stevie. Stevie only carried four extra cylinders of ammunition for the Colt. He knew he would have to make each shot count. However, ten Indians against one Express rider was poor odds.

CHAPTER 2

MAY 3, 1853

The day had finally arrived. The day that Stevie had looked forward to for almost a year. His ma and pa had spent hours at night talking and planning for this day. They had saved every penny they could manage and sold anything no longer needed. Pa had bought a used wagon and traded one of his horses for a pair of oxen. They sold the cabin and five acres situated just outside Albany for twenty dollars.

Pa had looked forward to this day even longer than Stevie. Pa had spent his last ten years working in a tannery just north of Albany, New York, along the Mohawk River. The money wasn't too bad, 75¢ a day. However, Pa longed for more. More land, money, and freedom to do as he pleased. He had heard about land for sale in Missouri that was less expensive than in New York. Jobs could be found, too. Jobs that paid more, even as much as a dollar a day.

They loaded the wagon with all their belongings they intended to bring with them. Ma climbed onto the wagon alongside Pa while Stevie's sister, Lillian, sat between them. Stevie rode Pa's Grey stallion, Jack, while his brother, William, sat behind him. William would turn seven tomorrow. Stevie was eight but would be nine in December.

Steven Henry Watson was the oldest son of Benjamin and Abigail. Benjamin was of Scottish descent. He was born just north of Glasgow but traveled with his parents to America as an infant. He had no memories of his homeland. Benjamin's father also worked at the tannery until his untimely death when Benjamin was only sixteen. It was then left up to Benjamin to care for his mother and younger sister. After Benjamin married, his mother died at age fifty. His sister married a young man who worked at the shipping yard when she was seventeen. Benjamin was red-headed with a fair complexion. He wasn't tall, only about 5' 7" tall. He spoke with only a slight Scottish brogue. With no extended family depending on him for support, Benjamin felt it was the perfect time to move his family west.

Stevie's mother, Abigail, was born and raised in Albany. She, too, came from meager circumstances. Her father worked in a bakery. He didn't make much money, but he was allowed to bring home day-old bread as part of his wages, so there was always plenty to eat. Abigail had long straight, auburn-colored hair. No one could have asked for a more loving mother. She unselfishly cared for her children, sometimes doing without so her children could eat. She was a great teacher, too. She taught Stevie and William how to read and write as well as how to do their sums. Stevie loved to learn. William, however, was less interested in learning and more interested in exploring the outdoors.

Stevie took after his ma; he had dark auburn hair. He was slender in his build but tall for an eight-year-old. He had hopes that someday he would be taller than Pa.

William's hair was more like Pa's. His was a lighter shade of red, and his face, unlike Stevie's, was covered in brown freckles. He was a little chubbier than Stevie, too. But, just as tough. He wanted to do everything Stevie did.

Abigail's parents were there to see them off as they began their journey westward. They weren't happy that their little girl was moving so far away, but they understood. Abigail hugged her parents and lingered in their embrace as tears began to flow down her cheeks. Finally, Abigail extracted herself from her parents and climbed onto the wagon.

So, off they went into the great unknown. The oxen and wagon led the way down the streets of Albany, with Stevie and William following behind on the back of Jack. It was still very early in the morning, so few people were on the streets to observe the tiny caravan as it moved through town. Occasionally, William would catch the attention of a passerby and announce, "We're going to Missouri! We're going to live there!"

People would smile and wave to William as he proudly made his announcement.

The Watson family moved slowly down the road toward New York City. Albany was a little over one hundred and fifty miles from New York City. They would arrive there in a couple of weeks if they made good time.

As they left Albany, the road seemed somewhat lonely. It was quiet, with only the sound of the wagon creaking as it rolled down the street, the clip-clop of Jack's hooves hitting the ground, and the occasional bird chirping high in a tree top. And, of course, William's never-ending barrage of questions.

"Stevie, how long will it take us to get to St. Joe?"

"Pa says about four or five months."

William then asked, "Why does it take so long?"

"Gosh!" exclaimed William. "That's a lot of miles! How many miles have we gone so far?"

Stevie replied, "William, we just got out of Albany. We've only traveled about a mile."

"Well, how many miles will we go today?"

"I don't know," replied Stevie. "It's almost summer, so we'll have plenty of daylight. We could make as many as twenty miles if we don't have any trouble."

William asked, "What kind of trouble?"

"Oh, bad weather, the wagon could break down, we could get attacked by wild animals or even bandits."

"Bandits?" asked William.

Stevie replied, "Don't worry. Pa has his rifle, and I got my jackknife. There ain't no bandits gonna bother us."

"Wish I had a jackknife. Then, I could fight off the bandits too."

"Don't worry," replied Stevie. "You'll get one some day. Maybe even tomorrow."

"Why? What's tomorrow?"

Stevie smiled and answered, "It's your birthday, silly."

"My birthday! Really! How do you know?"

Stevie replied, "Because, today is May 3rd. Your birthday is May 4th."

William asked, "Do you think I might get a jackknife for my birthday?"

"I don't know, William. I reckon you'll find out tomorrow."

The Watson family made it as far as Schenectady before they stopped to camp for the night. Fourteen miles on their first day of travel. They camped on the far side of the town, hoping to avoid unwanted interaction with undesirable people who might be lingering throughout the night. They found a grassy spot near a creek just right for their campsite. Plenty of fresh water and grass for the oxen and horse. Pa staked out the livestock nearby the wagon so they would be in earshot of them in case of predators or unwelcome humans.

Ma started a fire while Stevie and William gathered enough firewood to get them through the night and the next morning. Then, Pa took up his rifle and announced, "I think I'll see if I can find us a rabbit or a squirrel for supper."

Stevie excitedly asked, "Can I go, Pa?"

Pa had a way of telling Stevie no without demoralizing him. "No, son. I need you to stay here and keep an eye on the family for me. I want everyone to be safe while I'm gone. It's important to me, son."

Stevie puffed out his chest a bit and responded, "You can count on me, Pa."

Pa responded, "Good man!"

Ma boiled some beans and potatoes in a pot together and fried some corn cakes in the skillet. She made extra corn cakes so they could have them for breakfast in the morning. Pa returned to camp after an hour of looking for prey, but none were to be had.

After supper, the family bedded down underneath the wagon and said their good nights to each other. Stevie didn't fall asleep right away. He kept thinking about what Missouri would be like. He wondered if they might get to see any Indians on the way there. Stevie hoped that he could get his own horse and maybe a gun so he could hunt like Pa. Finally, the strain of riding fourteen miles overcame him, and he drifted off to sleep.

The next morning, Stevie awoke to the sound of his parents packing up the wagon. He quickly rolled out of his blanket to join them in the packing. Then, Abigail called out, "William! It's time to get up."

William blearily crawled out from under the wagon to join his family. He walked over to Ma, who handed him a corn cake. One bite of the cake woke him up.

"Mornin', Ma."

Ma replied, "Good morning, William. How did you sleep?"

William replied, "Rightly good!"

"William!"

Sheepishly, William said, "Sorry, Ma. I slept very well, thank you."

"That's better," Ma replied. "I'm not raising you to be a heathen. I'm beginning to think that moving to the frontier is a bad idea. I expect you to practice the things that I teach you. Proper grammar and proper manners at all times. Do you understand?"

"Yes, Ma."

William suddenly remembered what day it was. "Ma? What day is it?"

"It's Friday."

William began to worry a little when he said, "Oh. But what is the date?"

Ma replied with an almost undetectable smirk, "Hmm, let's see. I think it's May 4th. Why do you ask?"

Frustrated, William replied, "Oh, no reason. I just feel like I'm forgetting something."

Ma said, "Well, let's see - It's not my birthday. My birthday is in September.

Pa's birthday is in July. Is it Stevie's birthday?"

"No, Ma! Stevie's birthday is in December. Remember?"

Ma smiled and said, "Oh yes. Well I know it isn't Lillian's birthday. Her's was in March. I'm sorry, William. I just can't think of anything important about today." William showed his disappointment as he lowered his head and looked at the ground. He slightly kicked at the dirt in disgust. Ma stepped over to him and knelt. "Silly. I would never forget your birthday. Happy birthday, William!"

Ma grabbed William and held him close, then kissed him on the cheek. "Thanks, Ma! Did you get me anything?"

Ma replied, "I think Pa has something for you. But, don't bother him right now. Wait until he finishes hitching up the oxen."

Once Pa had finished hitching up the team, he walked over to join the others.

He reached down and picked up two pieces of the corn cake. He took a bite and said, "Bacon would sure go good with this."

Ma replied, "Would you settle for salt pork this morning?"

"I sure would!"

Ma pulled out a sack containing a slab of salted pork. Most of the time, she would slice pieces off to fry like bacon, or add a chunk of it to the beans to add flavoring, but other times Pa liked to eat it raw. So she cut Pa a chunk of the pork and handed it to him. He took a bite of the pork and chewed it, savoring the taste.

After a few bites of the pork and corn cake, Pa asked, "Is someone having a birthday today?"

William's face brightened as he looked at Pa. "It's my birthday, Pa!"

Pa replied, "Really? Didn't you have a birthday just last year?

William giggled and replied, "Pa, you say that every year."

Pa reached into his trouser pocket, pulled out a piece of oil-cloth wrapped around something, and then handed it to William. "Happy birthday, Son."

William took the cloth and unwrapped it. Inside was a small jackknife. William smiled as he replied, "Thanks, Pa! It's just what I wanted!"

Ma said, "Now you be careful with that thing. It's very sharp."

"I will, Ma."

By May 19th, the family had traveled one-hundred, fifty-five miles and had found themselves in the middle of New York City. Everyone was in awe of the tall buildings that made up the landscape of this bustling metropolis. However, one building stood out among the others.

"What's that thing, Pa?" asked William as he pointed to a tower near the middle of the city.

"I don't know, Son. Why don't we get a closer look?"

Pa moved the oxen toward the tower that stood in the distance hovering over every other tall building along their path. Row after row of streets lined with large houses and apartment buildings, shops and banks, and many other businesses. They finally came to a sign which read, "Bryant Park." They continued down the street and found themselves at the base of the structure they had been searching for.

The tower had been built from large timbers supported by an iron bracket. Stevie tried to see the top of the structure, but it was so far up that it was nearly invisible. A sign in front of the tower read,

"Latting Observatory. This structure, built in 1853, is the first of its kind in NYC. It stands 315 feet high or 29 stories tall. Open to the public as an observation tower."

Stevie asked, "Pa? Can we go up?"

William echoed, "Yeah, Pa! Can we go up?"

Benjamin looked at his wife, and she replied, "Go ahead. Lilly and I will stay here with the wagon."

Pa took the boys with him to the front of the tower. The closer they got, the taller the structure seemed to be. They followed a crowd of people into the tower and began climbing a seemingly endless staircase. After walking up five or six stories, the boys found a platform that opened up to the outside of the structure. There was a rail around the perimeter of the platform, and people were standing all around it, looking up, down, and in every direction. Stevie cautiously walked to the rail and looked down to see if he could find Ma and Lilly. His head began to spin a little as he moved closer to the edge of the platform. Ma and Lilly weren't there, so he moved to another side of the tower. Finally, there they were, looking up. Stevie yelled down to them, "Ma! Ma!"

He waved furiously to her. Finally, she saw Stevie standing on the first platform, waving to her. She could just barely hear him as he yelled to her. Pa and William came over and waved to Abigail as well.

Stevie asked, "Pa, can we go higher?" Pa replied, "Sure!"

The three of them continued the climb up the staircase. Rather than stopping at the next platform, Stevie continued upward.

"Let's go to the top, Pa!"

They were nearly out of breath when they reached the uppermost platform. Very few people had dared to traverse all twenty-nine floors to get to the top. Stevie stepped out first and was met with a burst of strong wind that nearly knocked him down. Pa and William eventually joined him on the platform. Stevie gripped the rail tightly as he searched for Ma and Lillian. He could barely make out the wagon parked on the side of the street. Jack and the oxen looked like ants from where he stood.

Stevie looked to the north and asked, "Pa, is that Albany?"

Pa replied, "I'm not sure, Son. I guess it could be."

William asked, "Can we see Missouri from here?"

Pa answered, "I doubt it. We'd have to be on the west side to look, but even then, Missouri is just too far away."

CHAPTER 3

Three weeks had passed since the Watsons had left New York City. The month of June brought long days of daylight, allowing the family to travel deeper into the evening hours. Stevie, and especially William, found it more and more challenging to stay awake on the back of Pa's horse, Jack, as they followed behind the wagon. More than once, Stevie caught William before he fell off the horse as he dosed.

On the late evening of June 21st, the family set up camp near a fork in the road. A sign had been raised on the side of the road which read, "Niagara Falls - 15 miles."

Other families were also camping in the area of the fork. Many of them dressed in fine attire of silk dresses and neatly pressed suits.

As Ma set up the campfire, Pa walked over to the nearby lake to see if he might catch supper. This time, he allowed Stevie and William to tag along. When they reached the edge of the water, they discovered others standing at the bank's edge, trying to catch fish as well.

Pa noticed several well-dressed gents were using a fancy rig of a cane pole with a wheel attached near the base. A thin string had been unrolled from the wheel and threaded through eyelets along the length of the cane pole. A hook had been attached at the end of the line with an insect impaled on the hook. The men would draw out a length of the line from the wheel with their left hand as their right hand rocked the cane pole back and forth, toward, then away from the water. With each movement of the rod, the hook traveled farther and farther out until it finally rested on top of the water.

These men were intent on placing their hooks in just the right area on top of the water. But, they never seemed to be satisfied. Instead, they continued the process over and over, without the benefit of a single bite from a fish.

Benjamin, mildly amused, took his Hickory stick to which he had attached a line with a hook at the end. He secured a big fat worm to the hook and swung his line into the water near the bank of the lake. The hook had barely begun to sink toward the bottom of the lake when Pa's line became taut. He pulled slightly against the pressure to set the hook. Pa pulled his line out of the water and found a nice-sized fish hanging from his line. A two-pound lake trout wriggled as Pa moved his line out of the water. Stevie and William cheered as they watched their father swing the fish onto the bank. Pa grinned as he removed the trout from the hook and placed it in a basket to carry back to the campsite.

All the men wearing fancy duds and using fancy fishing gear stared as this poor traveler who had dared to invade their space snatched the first fish of the day.

Pa handed Stevie the pole and said, "Here, Stevie. Your turn."

Stevie took a worm from the can and carefully attached it to his hook. He swung his line into the lake just as Pa had taught him. Stevie felt something tugging on the line but was patient not to pull too quickly. Suddenly, the line went taut again, just as it had when Pa had held the pole. Stevie pulled against the line, careful not to pull too hard. The hook set in the fish's mouth, and Stevie pulled the line toward the bank. William cheered once again as he witnessed his brother catch the next fish. Stevie cried out, "I got one, Pa! I got one!"

Pa said, "Bring him on in, son!"

Stevie moved the pole back away from the bank of the lake and pulled another nice trout out to show the others. Pa picked up the fish and began to unhook it when Stevie asked, "How big is it, Pa?"

Pa replied, "Oh, I'd say it's at least two and a half pounds."

Stevie took the fish from his father and placed it with the other fish in the basket.

William asked, "Is it my turn, now?"

Pa replied, "Sure, son. Do you need help with the worm?"

"No, Pa. I can do it."

William took a worm from the can and carefully threaded the hook through the worm, once, twice, and a third time. As he did so, he stuck out his tongue as if that would make it more manageable for him. His tongue swung from side to side as he moved the worm back and forth, trying to attach it just so. Finally satisfied, William swung the line into the water and impatiently waited.

Stevie instructed, "Now, don't pull too early."

"I know, Stevie!"

The line began to move in the water, but nothing ever pulled against the pole to indicate that a fish was on the line. Finally, several minutes later, Pa said, "William, pull the line back in. Let's check your bait."

William did as Pa had said, and to his disgust, he found the worm was no longer on the hook. Willam let out a long sigh. Pa said, "Here, let me help you with that worm this time."

Pa re-baited the hook, then allowed Willam to try again. They waited together as Stevie encouragingly said, "You'll get one this time, William."

William's line went taut when he screamed out, "I got one! I got one!"

William pulled in the line as he walked back from the lake's edge. Following William away from the water was a trout larger than Pa's and Stevie's put together. They all celebrated William's great catch.

They continued taking turns with the fishing pole for another thirty minutes. Finally, Pa was satisfied that they had enough fish to feed their little clan. As they packed up their things and were ready to return to camp, a nicely dressed gentleman who seemed a little younger than Pa walked up to congratulate them.

"Well done, gentlemen! My name is Paul. Paul Wilson."

He held out his hand to Pa, and Pa took it. "I'm Benjamin Watson. This is Stevie and William."

Paul shook hands with each of the boys as he continued to speak. "May I ask, what were you using for bait?"

William held up the tin can holding their bait and announced, "Worms!"

Paul replied, "I see. Is there any chance you might be willing to allow me to borrow your pole and bait? I'll be sure to bring it back to you unscathed."

Benjamin replied, "Sure! Help yourself. We're camped right over there. When you're finished, just come on by and let us see what you catch."

Paul said, "Thank-you ever so much! I pray I won't be long."

Pa and the boys returned to camp to show Ma and Lillian the fish they had caught for supper. They were excited to have something besides beans and bread for their meal.

Pa showed Stevie and William how to dress out the fish. He first scraped off the scales, then removed the head. He then cut a slit down the belly of each fish to remove the entrails.

Ma rolled the fish around in flour and cornmeal, then fried them up in lard. Finally, she served the fish with some boiled potatoes and made hush puppies instead of cornbread.

The family was in good spirits as they enjoyed their evening meal. Then, just as Ma began to clean up the supper dishes, Paul approached the camp. Pa saw him coming and asked, "Did you have any luck?"

Paul replied, "I did! I caught three nice sized trout thanks to you."

Paul handed the fishing pole and bait can over to Pa and thanked him again. Then he asked, "Are you here to see the falls?"

Benjamin replied, "Falls?"

"Yes, Niagara Falls." replied Paul. "My wife and I are traveling to go see the falls. It's a sort of vacation for us."

Pa said, "No, we're on our way to Missouri. We plan to homestead out there. We hear that the land is cheap, at least cheaper than it was in Albany."

Paul asked, "Is that from where you came?"

Pa replied, "Yeah, we left there about two months ago. We hope to get to St. Joe before winter sets in."

Paul suggested, "You really should consider going to see the falls while you're so close. You may never have another opportunity to see them again. Why don't you drive over with us tomorrow? We can all see them together."

Abigail spoke up and asked, "Can we, Benjamin? It would be something fine for us all to see. I've heard they're the tallest falls in the world."

Benjamin thought for a moment, then replied, "I don't see why not. It might be educational for us all."

Paul replied, "Wonderful! My wife and I will meet you here tomorrow at first light."

CHAPTER 4

As the sun began to peak above the horizon to the east, the Watson family rose to start packing their wagon, preparing for the day-long ride to Niagara Falls. Paul Wilson and his young wife pulled up in a carriage driven by an older gentleman. Another wagon carrying their belongings, followed behind driven by another man.

As they entered the Watson's camp, Paul stepped down to meet Benjamin. "Good morning, Mr. Watson."

"Good morning to you." Pa replied.

Paul said, "I'd like to introduce you to my lovely wife, Anna. Anna, this is Benjamin Watson and his family."

Anna replied, "How nice to meet you all!" Somehow, neither Benjamin nor Abigail thought she was sincere in her greeting. Her mannerisms were a bit snobbish.

Then Paul asked, "Are we all ready to go?"

Benjamin replied, "Let's go!"

The Wilson caravan led the way, with the Watsons following closely behind.

Even though it was late June, the weather felt like a spring morning. The temperature was mild, and a cool breeze was whispering through the tree tops.

They traveled past the town of Buffalo as they wound down the road leading to the falls. Sea birds often swooped past them while hovering over the waves of Lake Erie. The Watsons had never seen the ocean, but Lake Erie seemed so big to Stevie that he couldn't imagine there being a body of water any larger. Large boats could be seen in the distance while smaller craft floated along the banks.

As they rode along, William asked Stevie, "How long will it take for us to get to the falls?"

Stevie replied, "Well, the sign said it was fifteen miles away. So, I guess we should be there by nightfall."

Willam asked, "And why are we going to the falls?"

Stevie answered, "Cause Ma wants to see it. She said it is probably the biggest waterfall in the world."

William asked, "Have you ever seen a waterfall, Stevie?"

"No. I've only ever seen a spillway like the one back home on the Johnson Creek. It only drops about four feet. Ma says Niagara is about three hundred feet high. Maybe more."

"Gosh!" William exclaimed. "You think that's how tall that tower was in New York City we climbed?"

Stevie replied, "Just about the same height. I know one thing's for sure. I wouldn't want to fall off of either one."

"Yeah! Me neither." said William.

Halfway along the road, Benjamin began to have second thoughts about their detour. He hated losing three days on the trail just so they could see a waterfall. He tried to brush the idea out of his mind. He knew it was something Abigail was looking forward to seeing. The children would no doubt find it interesting too. But could it really be all that impressive? Was it worth a three-day delay for them to see it?

When noon approached, they reached the northernmost point of Lake Erie. Finally, the Niagara River came into view. It wound northward for a while before splitting into two branches. They followed the eastern branch of the river for the rest of the day. As the sun began lowering itself below the banks of the river to the west, the falls began to rise above their view to the north. They still had two or three hours left to travel before reaching the falls, but it had already become apparent just how massive and impressive the falls really were. As they continued north, the falls grew taller and taller.

Just before dusk, they pulled into what seemed to be a little village at the base of the falls. Niagara Falls had become quite the tourist attraction in the past few decades. Businesses had sought to take advantage of the draw the giant natural wonder had become. Gift shops, cafes, Inns, and even campgrounds had been erected to handle the needs of the tourists who had traveled great distances to experience the unbelievable sight God had created.

The Wilsons chose to pull up just shy of all the attractions to set up camp along the road. The Watson's pulled their wagon up along beside the Wilsons. Everyone began setting up camp except Mr. and Mrs. Wilson, that is. They left camp duties to their two servants. The young Mrs. Wilson sat on a folding chair nearby and watched everyone work while Paul milled around the area, scoping things out.

Anna Wilson wasn't nearly as friendly as her husband, Paul. She only just tolerated the family she seemed forced to travel with. Anna looked down her nose at the two dirty little boys that worked hard helping their parents set up camp. She barely noticed little Lillian at all as Lillian, too, helped put the camp together.

Anna was born and raised in Manhattan, New York. She was educated at the finest finishing school for girls. She had always had the best of everything and plenty of it. She couldn't understand why Paul would drag her way out in the middle of the wilderness to look at a waterfall. She didn't see the beauty in nature. She only found it annoying. Full of bugs, snakes, and other creatures that made her shiver at the mere thought of them.

Paul, on the other hand, was thoroughly enjoying himself. He loved the outdoors. He enjoyed spending time on the grounds of their vast estate. He loved fishing and hunting. He loved riding horses with his friends as they hunted foxes with the hounds baying in the distance.

Once the servants had finished setting up Mrs. Wilson's tent, she retired to her quarters, where she bathed and changed her clothing for the evening meal. Paul soon entered her tent and informed her he would invite the Watsons to join them for dinner. Anna was shocked by Paul's news and replied, "I'll not have that sort sitting at my table. They aren't even capable of serving at my table. Have you not seen how uncouth they are?"

Paul replied, "I rather like them. They will be dining with us tonight and I expect you to be on your best behavior. On second thought, I expect you to act even better than your best behavior. I want you to be completely accommodating to them."

Anna replied, "I'll do no such thing. If you insist on entertaining that rabble, then I won't be joining you tonight. I'll have my dinner served here."

Paul responded, "On the contrary, my dear. You'll either join me while I entertain our guest or you will confine yourself to these quarters without dinner."

Anna replied, "So be it!", then turned her back on her husband, crossed her arms in disgust, and stared at the tent wall.

Paul left the tent and walked over to the Watson camp. He found Abigail and said, "Mrs. Watson, I was wondering if you and your family would honor me in joining me for dinner tonight?"

Ma replied, "Oh, that isn't necessary. We will make do with what we normally do. Thanks all the same."

"Please, Mrs. Watson! I want so much to have you and your family dine with me. I want to get to know you all much better. Won't you please join me?"

Abigail replied, "Well, I don't want to put anyone out. Mrs. Wilson might not be comfortable with us sitting at her table. We're just common folk with common ways. I wouldn't want to make anyone feel uncomfortable."

Paul replied, "Anna won't be joining us tonight. She isn't feeling well, so she has decided to retire early. So, you see, I could really use you and your family's company tonight."

Abigail hesitantly replied, "Well, I wouldn't want you to be alone, so, I guess we could join you tonight. If, you're sure it's alright."

"Absolutely!"

Abigail returned to her family and prepared them for their dinner with Paul. First, she washed herself and Lillian, and they put on their best dresses for the occasion. Next, she told Stevie and William to wash, comb their hair, and change into their best clothes. Once they met Ma's approval, they, along with Benjamin, walked over to join Paul for dinner.

Paul's carriage driver, Reginald, also served as his butler. The driver of the other wagon, Tobias, was his chef. Reginald was also a talented musician who played guitar for everyone during and after dinner.

The Watson family was quite intrigued with how well-to-do members of society conducted themselves during something as simple as an evening meal. Abigail was nervous about how her family might be perceived at such a fancy feast. However, Paul was a gracious host and helped them all to feel at ease.

The next morning, Stevie's family rose from their sleep much like any other day. Ma prepared a light breakfast while Pa tended the livestock. Ma noticed Mrs. Wilson exiting her tent at one point and tried to acknowledge her with a smile. However, Anna was not interested in even looking toward the Watson's camp.

After breakfast, Benjamin gathered his family and began the trek toward the falls. Benjamin brought Jack along just in case any of the children grew too tired as the day rolled along.

The Wilsons pretty much toured the area on their own. Occasionally they might run into the Watsons at a gift shop or along the path leading to the falls. Stevie and his siblings were fascinated by the shops along the way. Many artisans had set up tents in the area to sell their wares of wood carvings, painted seashells, blown glass trinkets, and other items. More than once, Ma had to remind the children to "Look, but don't touch!".

When they finally reached the falls, it was even more than they had expected. The sound of the water falling at such a great distance and velocity was almost deafening. Stevie and William found themselves yelling at one another when they were only inches apart.

Stevie turned back away from the falls and caught sight of Paul and Anna about twenty yards away. They were standing arm in arm at the edge of the high bluff along the Niagara River. They seemed quite happy together as they watched the water spill over the mountainous falls.

As they turned to walk away, something suddenly went wrong. Anna lost her footing on the ledge. She slipped away from Paul and fell over the side of the bluff. She screamed as she fell. Paul stared in horror as his bride fell away from him. "Anna!", He cried out as he felt her slip away from him. He watched her as she managed to snag hold of a tree root on the side of the bluff that had been exposed due to erosion.

Stevie yelled out, "Pa! Pa! She went over the side! Mrs. Wilson fell over the side!"

Pa turned to find Paul lying face down on the bluff's edge, reaching for something. Pa quickly led Jack over to Paul's location as he called out to his family, "Stay here!"

Stevie ignored his demand and followed along. William tried to follow too, but was snatched back by Ma. When Pa reached the bluff, he turned and found Stevie behind him. He didn't have time to scold him. Instead, he decided he would use him. "Get up on Jack!"

Stevie did as Pa said. Benjamin grabbed a rope hanging from Jack's saddle and tied a loop in one end. He handed the other end to Stevie and said, "Dally off this end and tie it tight. I'm going to have you lower me over the edge so I can reach Anna!"

Stevie nodded his head in understanding, wrapped his end of the rope around the saddle horn with two loops, and then tied it off so it wouldn't slip. He then waited for Pa's instructions.

Benjamin walked to the edge to find Anna and found her hanging on for dear life, screaming hysterically. "Help me! Somebody, help me!"

Benjamin stepped into the loop and positioned it just under his shoulders, around his chest. Pa then turned to Stevie and said, "Back up until the rope is tight. Then lower me down easy!"

Stevie again nodded, then turned Jack around and pushed him forward until the rope no longer held slack. He then turned Jack to face Pa. Slowly, Pa backed off the bluff's edge trying not to slip while Stevie moved Jack forward one step at a time. Anna yelled even more desperately as dirt began to fall upon her while Benjamin began his descent down the cliff. Her grip began to loosen and she started to panic. "Help me!" she cried out hysterically.

Stevie encouraged the horse as he lowered Pa down the cliff. "Up, Jack. Whoa! Up, Jack. Whoa, boy!"

Benjamin slid down the cliff, slowly making his way to Anna. He tried to stay over to the side of where Anna hung so he wouldn't pelt her with rocks and dirt. It seemed the harder he tried, the more debris fell on top of Anna.

Benjamin continued to climb down until Stevie and Jack had reached within ten feet of the bluff. Paul raised his hand to Stevie and said, "Hold it! He's reached her!"

Stevie held Jack steady, not allowing him to move either forward nor backward.

Benjamin found himself hanging from a rope three hundred feet from the bottom. He tried not to look down or think about what could happen if his plan failed.

"Anna! It's me, Benjamin Watson. I'm going to get you out of here, okay?" Anna cried out, still hysterical. "Please, please! Don't let me fall!"

"I won't, Anna. You're not going to fall."

Benjamin reached over to Anna trying to wrap his right arm around her waist.

Her grip was slipping from the tree root, but she tried not to let her grip relax. Suddenly, the root became dislodged from the dirt that held it in place. Anna slipped downward two feet and screamed as she fell. Benjamin quickly snatched her by the hand as she began to fall.

Benjamin said, "Alright, Anna. I've got you. You can let go of the tree root. I won't let you fall."

Anna continued to cry, "I can't! I can't!"

"Look at me, Anna! Look at me!"

Anna forced herself to look at Benjamin. She saw his dark brown eyes. They were fearless. She suddenly found comfort and then courage. Her grip on the root loosened, then released completely. She wrapped her free hand around Benjamin's hand, then wrapped her arms around Benjamin and held on tightly as he lifted her up to him. She sobbed into his chest.

Benjamin looked up and called out, "Pull us up!"

Paul turned to Stevie and said, "He's got her! Pull them up!"

Stevie slowly and easily pulled back on the reins and coaxed Jack to move away from the ledge. "Back up, Jack. Back up."

The horse slowly and steadily stepped backward, pulling Benjamin and Anna up over the side of the cliff.

A crowd had gathered around with all the commotions, and they began to cheer with delight as they witnessed Benjamin and Anna being drawn back to safety. As soon as they made it back to the top of the cliff, Paul grabbed his wife and held her in a tight grip nearly cutting off her breath.

Men and women gathered around Benjamin and Stevie to congratulate them for a job well done. Benjamin slowly worked his way back to Stevie and said, "Good job, Son! I knew you wouldn't let me down!"

Stevie felt more pride in his father's words than he had ever felt before. Ma and the other children came forward through the crowd and hugged Benjamin and Stevie, congratulating them, too.

Paul began to escort his wife back to the campsite when, she stumbled and nearly fell. She was feeling faint and was no longer able to walk. Paul picked Anna up into his arms and carried her back to her tent. The Watsons followed closely behind, concerned for her well being.

When Paul reached Anna's tent and carried her in, he found Abigail had followed him. "Let me take care of her, Paul. She needs rest. I'll help her change into her bed clothes and let her rest."

Paul conceded and said, "Thank you so much Abigail. You and your family have been so kind to us. If it hadn't been for Benjamin and Stevie, I'm sure I would have lost her."

Paul then turn and left Abigail to attend to Anna's needs. As he exited the tent, he found Benjamin holding Lillian in his arms while Stevie and William stood next to him.

"Benjamin, I don't know how to thank you! You, too, Stevie! I'm forever in your debt."

Paul shook both Benjamin's and Stevie's hand as he continued to share how grateful he was to them.

CHAPTER 5

The next day, the Watsons packed up their wagon and proceeded down the trail that followed along Lake Erie. By the end of the first day, they were back to where they had been just two days earlier. They camped at the same place and fished in the same spot as they had before.

The following morning, they moved farther down the trail toward Cleveland. They drove along the edge of the giant lake for days and days. Occasionally, they met storm clouds along the way, which slowed their progress. However, the lake provided them with fresh water, fish, and at times recreation. The temperature was still reasonably warm. At least warm enough for Stevie and William to go swimming whenever they were allowed. Ma looked at it as a way for the boys to get a bath without complaining.

Occasionally, Pa would see game watering along the edge of the lake. However, most of the time, they were too far in the distance for him to get a shot with his muzzle-load rifle. He badly wanted to buy a new rifle that would shoot cartridges instead of the lead balls like his old rifle shot. However, money was hard to come by, so he would have to wait until after they reached St. Joseph and found work.

Halfway to Cleveland, the Watsons met a group of Ottawa Indians along the trail. At first, Benjamin was cautious about meeting a party of Indians on their journey. But when he saw it was only a family of indigenous people rather than a war party, Pa's mind eased a bit.

The leader of the group walked up to Benjamin's wagon and raised his hand in greeting. Pa raised his hand in greeting also.

The man was a little taller than Benjamin. He wore buckskin leggings which showed half of his bare legs. A leather cloth hung around his waist both in front and back. He was bare-chested except for the strand of beads and animal teeth that hung around his neck. The man carried a staff that Benjamin assumed could be used for protection and a walking stick. The man began to talk to Benjamin in broken sentences of English.

The Indian pointed to himself and said, "Me, Pontiac!"

Pa returned the gesture and said, "I am, Benjamin."

Pontiac repeated the name slowly, "Bin-ja-min."

Pa nodded in approval.

Pontiac then asked, "You have wees-kee?"

Benjamin pondered what the man was trying to ask. He suddenly realized what Pontiac was asking and replied, "No. I have no whiskey."

Pontiac grunted as he looked over the wagon. He figured there must be something in there worth trading for. He then asked Benjamin, "We trade?"

Benjamin was a little nervous. He didn't know what they might be able to trade. Everything they owned was needed. He certainly didn't want to trade something important away for a handful of trinkets. However, he thought trading might be a suitable way of maintaining good relations with these people. Even though it was just a family, not much different from his own, they were better armed and more capable of overtaking the Watsons if they had that intent.

"What do you want to trade?" Benjamin asked.

Pontiac replied, "I want gun."

Benjamin was taken aback by Pontiac's response. He only had one rifle. Although it wasn't perfect as rifles go, it was a rifle. Then Benjamin got an idea.

"I don't know." he said as he lowered his head and looked at the ground. "This rifle is very valuable."

Pontiac questioned, "Val-u-ble?"

Benjamin then clarified, "It's worth a lot. Much money. What would you trade for it?"

Pontiac motioned for one of his sons to bring some items forward as he spoke in his native Ojibwe tongue. A boy of about fourteen brought a buffalo rug forward and lay it on the ground in front of his father. Pontiac then placed a tomahawk on the rug.
Benjamin tried to keep from laughing at the unbelievably meager offering that had been made. Instead, he looked up at Pontiac and shook his head as he said, "No, no trade."

Pontiac turned to his clan and spoke again. Two more boys

approached carrying two more buffalo rugs. Pontiac then looked at Benjamin to see his reaction to the addition of the offering.

Benjamin looked up at Pontiac again. This time he raised one side of his mouth and shook his head to indicate his disappointment. "No. Sorry. It's just not enough."

Pontiac was desperate for the rifle. What did this white man want? Did he expect him to trade his wife and his children? Then, he called out to another son in the back of the formation. The boy was in charge of the horses. When Pontiac called to him, the boy refused and said something back to his father, making Pontiac angry. Pontiac yelled once again to the boy and beckoned him forward. Ashamed and disappointed, the boy walked forward. With him, he brought a black and white painted pony. It was a filly that Benjamin estimated to be two years old.

"*Now we're talking!*" Benjamin thought to himself but held his countenance steady so that Pontiac could not read his face.

Pontiac presented the horse, then pointed at everything that lay on the ground and said, "All for gun!"

Benjamin sighed before walking over to the filly to take a look. He opened the horse's mouth and checked his teeth. As Benjamin suspected, the filly was only about two years old. He walked around the filly, feeling his legs and checking his hindquarters. The filly was absolutely beautiful, but Benjamin wouldn't let on that he thought so.

Benjamin looked up at Abigail, who still sat atop the wagon, and saw her slightly shake her head. Benjamin then walked over to Pontiac. He looked to the ground while shaking his head, then said, "Deal!".

Then he shook Pontiac's hand. Benjamin handed Pontiac the rifle. Pontiac then asked, "Bullets?"

Benjamin then replied, "Yeah, bullets and gunpowder."

Pa walked to the wagon and brought out a leather pouch containing lead shot and two powder horns nearly full of gunpowder. He handed them to Pontiac, who raised his rifle to the sky and yelled a warrior's "Whoop!"

Pontiac's family cheered with him as they gathered around to look at the new gun. Then, Benjamin led the filly over to Stevie and handed him the lead rein as he said, "You take good care of her, son."

Stevie was shocked as he replied, "Pa! For me?"

Pa replied, "I think you're old enough to have your own horse, now."

"Thanks, Pa!"

The two families parted ways. As Benjamin climbed back onto the wagon,

Abigail was slightly upset.

"Benjamin? What are we going to do about game while we're traveling?

What about protection?"

Pa replied, "Ma, that rifle was worthless. It doesn't shoot straight and if someone was to attack us I'd only be able to get one shot off. What good's that gonna do. Just make'm madder than all get out. We'll get a better rifle somewhere down the road. But for now, look how happy that boy is."

Over the next few weeks, the trail became monotonous. Stevie felt like he was seeing the same group of Pine trees along the bank of the lake and the same boats fishing off in the distance day after day.

It now seemed that storms were an everyday event. They didn't last all day, at least not every day, but they were pretty intense. First, heavy rains pelted the family as they trudged through the muddy terrain. Then, one day produced nasty lightning storms.

Two days later, the rains ceased. The sun came out and began to dry the trail. The birds were singing again, and everything seemed to come back to life. Then, however, death came too. As they continued on the trail, buzzards could be seen gliding above the trees in the distance. It was noon the next day before they saw what the giant black vultures were eyeing.

Pa pulled up the wagon just shy of where the remnants of a

wagon sat on the side of the trail. The wagon was smoldering after having burned for what appeared quite a while.

Pa said, "You all stay here while I have a look."

Benjamin hopped down from the wagon and walked over to the burnt wagon. Buzzards were on the ground eating from a half-devoured horse carcass that had been burnt to a crisp. Four figures lay under the wagon. Two about the size of adults and two children. They were all burnt beyond recognition. What must have been their belongings were scattered throughout the camp. Some were partially charred, while other items were in perfect condition other than remaining wet from the storm.

Benjamin gathered what was still of use; an iron skillet, a coffee pot, a saddle and bridle, and something else. He froze as he spotted what could only have been a God send. There on the ground lay a slightly weathered rifle. It was a muzzle-loader like his old gun. But it was newer. Benjamin couldn't believe it. He continued to look around for any survivors, but he found no one. Finally, he gathered all the items and returned to his wagon.

Ma asked, "What do you think happened?"

Benjamin replied, "My guess is lightning struck during that last big storm. It killed four people, two of them children by the looks of it. Killed their horses and burned their wagon. I gathered up what I thought could be useful. Everything else is all burned up."

Abigail noticed something in Benjamin's right hand that he held slightly behind his back. "What do you have, there?"

Benjamin looked up and smiled at her as he presented the item to her. "Ma! Looks like the Lord has provided for us again. It'll need some cleaning up and oiling, but it's a good rifle. All we need is some more shot and powder."

Abigail smiled, looked to the sky, and responded, "God be praised!" Pa then said, "We'll go ahead and make camp here."

Ma asked, "Why so early? We've barely gone four miles today."

Benjamin replied, "Did you forget? There were some unfortunate folk over there who were struck by lightning and died. They'll need burying."

Abigail exclaimed, "Oh, my word, yes! God bless their

souls."

While Abigail began setting up camp, Benjamin grabbed the pick ax and shovel from the wagon and walked out to find a suitable place to dig four graves. First, Stevie and William unhitched the oxen from the wagon and staked them out to graze nearby. Next, they unsaddled the horses and picketed them out to graze as well. Then the boys walked over to see if they could help their pa.

Stevie asked, "Pa? Can we help?"

Pa answered, "Well, lets see. How 'bout after I get the dirt broken up, you two can take turns scooping out the loose dirt."

"Sure, Pa!" they said in unison.

Pa swung the pick up over his head and down to the earth to break apart sections that could be managed with the shovel. He staked out a section in his mind where he intended for each grave to lay. When he broke up a rectangular area for the first grave, he began digging out the loose clumps of dirt and grass within the rectangle. As he dug deeper and deeper into the soil, he allowed the boys to take turns scooping out the loose dirt. It would have taken him less time to do it himself, but he knew the boys could learn more by doing than just watching. If he had made them sit and watch the whole time, they would eventually get bored and want to find something else to occupy their time.

They had finished about an hour before dusk. Ma had taken the time to find some old blankets she used to wrap the burnt bodies in so they could be handled more easily. Abigail and Benjamin carried the bodies to the gravesite and lay them to rest.

The Watson family gathered around the open graves to pay their respects. Ma handed Pa the family Bible. He opened it to Psalm 23, and read. As he read the scripture, his family joined in reciting the words they had been taught and memorized.

Then, Pa prayed. "O Lord, we present these poor souls to you for safekeeping. We don't know them, Lord, but you do. Help us, Lord, to remain faithful to you in all that we do; in the way we treat others in this world, in the way we treat the creatures you created, and especially in how we treat those of our family. Help us always to love one another. Amen!

CHAPTER 6

Supplies were dwindling for the family. After fourteen weeks of traveling, they finally reached Cleveland. Pa decided they had better buy enough supplies to get them the rest of the way to St. Joseph. So, they pulled up to the first dry goods store they saw.

Benson's was located just inside the city limits of Cleveland. Pa pulled the wagon up in front of the store and tied the oxen to a hitching rail. Stevie and Willam tied the horses in front of the livery stable next door to Benson's. The boys now rode their own mounts. The saddle Pa had found along the trail was put on the Pinto so Stevie could ride his own horse. William rode atop the ever-dependable Jack by himself.

The family walked into the dry goods store together and was immediately greeted by Mr. Wallace Benson.

"Good day, folks! Can I help you with anything?"

Pa replied, "Yes, Sir. We need to stock up on a few supplies. My wife here has a list for you."

Abigail handed Mr. Benson the list she had made. Wally looked it over.

> Flour
> Cornmeal
> Lard
> Salt
> Baking Powder
> Coffee
> Molasses
> Bacon

After Wally read over the list, he asked, "Are you folks headed out west?"

Benjamin replied, "We're headed to St. Joseph, Missouri. We began a couple of months ago in Albany, New York."

"Well now, that's a fair piece. No wonder you're ready for supplies. I'll get you fixed right up."

Benjamin then asked, "Do you have any gunpowder and lead shot for my rifle?"

"Sure! Have a look over in that corner, there. You should be able to find whatever you need. Just let me know once you've decided and I'll measure out whatever you need."

"Thanks!" said Benjamin.

Pa walked back to the area mentioned by Wally and looked at the firearms he had on display. Several pistols of various sizes and makes lay in a glass case. Accessories like powder horns, gun holsters, leather belts, and the like were in another case next to the guns. Five long rifles were hung on the wall behind the cases. Large barrels and small kegs of black powder were stacked against the back wall.

After Wally filled Abigail's order, he returned to check on Benjamin. "Did you find what you were looking for?"

Benjamin asked, "How much for two of those powder horns filled with powder and a small bag of lead shot?"

Wally replied, "Well, lets see. The powder horns and powder will run six bits each. I can let you have the lead shot for two bits per pound."

Benjamin asked, "Have you tallied up my wife's list yet?"

Wally said, "Let's go do that now."

Wally mumbled to himself as he wrote down a number next to each item on Abigail's list. Then he added the numbers together and wrote the total at the bottom.

"Looks like everything on the list will run you $3.50."

Benjamin quickly figured in his head how much he could afford for the lead shot and powder.

"Give me two of the powder horns and three pounds of shot."

Wally added the total to Abigail's list and then said, "Alright, that'll be $7.50." Pa pulled out his poke containing their money and counted out $7.50. He then noticed three pennies in his hand that seemed a bit out of place. "Mr. Benson, do you have any penny candies?"

Stevie's and William's faces lit up with anticipation at Pa's question. Store-bought candy was rare in their household. They might receive a stick of candy at Christmas, but rarely any other time of the year.

Wally walked to another counter near the front of the store

and presented four jars of stick candy. "Anything in these jars is two for a penny."

Pa looked down at his children and said, "Alright, each of you can choose two pieces of candy."

The boys quickly approached the counter and picked the candy sticks they preferred. Then, Ma walked Lillian to the counter and helped her pick out two candy sticks. Ma then said, "Children, what do you tell your Pa?"

They all said in between tastings of the sweet sticky candy, "Thanks, Pa!"

Pa paid Mr. Benson for the goods, then loaded them into the wagon. They had plenty of daylight left, so they left Cleveland, heading down the trail once again.

From Cleveland, they turned south, moving away from Lake Erie. They had grown quite used to having fresh water and fish at their beck and call. But, unfortunately, the trail now would be less likely to be so accommodating.

The trail was about the same as they had traveled before. However, there seemed to be more traffic along the way. Almost daily, the Watson family met someone going in the opposite direction. Some were friendly; others were not so friendly. However, the farther down the trail they traveled, the fewer travelers they met. On several occasions, they saw wagons constructed to carry prisoners. Almost always, those prisoners were black.

The "Fugitive Slave Law" had been passed in 1850. This law favored slave owners throughout the country. So, anyone who gave assistance to slaves who fled from their owners or impeded their capture, were subject to prosecution by federal law. Most citizens of Ohio, many of whom were Quakers, opposed this law and often violated it.

Five days after the Watsons left Cleveland, they camped next to a creek just outside a town called Lexington. After supper, Ma gave the children their lessons. Arithmetic was the subject for tonight. Stevie loved arithmetic. He was a natural at adding and subtracting in his head. Even three-digit numbers seemed to give him little trouble. He knew all of his times' tables from zero to twelve. He was good at reading too. Ma had him read aloud from the Bible nearly every night. Of course, he had trouble with some of the names. But so did Ma and Pa.

After everyone had gone to bed, Stevie was awakened by a stirring in the creek. He thought it might have been some big fish splashing around or maybe a critter playing in the water. He raised his head to see if he could spot anything. The moon was only at half phase, but there was enough light for him to see the silhouette of a small figure exiting the creek.

Stevie continued to watch as the figure moved closer to their camp. The horses began to rumble as the stranger approached. Finally, Stevie decided to get a closer look. He rolled out of his blanket and crawled out from under the wagon. Stevie knelt behind the rear wheel of the wagon. The back gate of the wagon had been left open where Ma had prepared and served supper earlier that night.

Stevie quietly watched as a dark boy tip-toed toward the wagon. When the boy reached the back of the wagon, he searched the tailgate for something to eat. Ma had wrapped the remaining cornbread sticks in a cloth napkin and left them for their next morning's breakfast.

Stevie saw that the boy was about his size. He wore a torn shirt and ripped pants that were held up with a rope tied around his waist. His hair was uncombed, and stood up on top of his head about three inches high.

The boy snatched up the cornbread and quickly slipped into the brush heading north away from the creek.

Stevie wasn't sure what he should do. Should he wake his parents? Should he go after the boy? Stevie chose the latter. He quietly moved through the brush in the direction the boy had traveled. About twenty yards from where his family was peacefully sleeping, Stevie found the boy. The boy was quickly shoving bits of cornbread into his mouth. He didn't notice Stevie until it was too late.

The boy froze in place when he saw the white boy peeking at him through the tall sage grass. Stevie spoke, "Hey, don't be afraid. I won't hurt you. What's your name?"

The boy swallowed the morsel of cornbread still rolling around in his mouth and replied, "Elisha. What's yourn?"

Stevie replied, "I'm Stevie. Whatcha doing way out here all

alone?"

Elisha replied, "Me and my daddy done run away. Masta Henry chased us with the dawgs, but we got away. Then, two days ago, somebody seen my daddy runnin' through a field and shot him. I guess they didn't see me cause I's so little."

Stevie asked, "Where you going to?"

"Canada! Daddy said we'd be safe there. We supposed to meet a man in Lexington who was gonna take us. Do you know how far Lexington is?"

Stevie replied, "It's right over there," pointing to the north. "We passed it earlier while we were traveling."

Elisha looked over his shoulder northward to see if anyone might be lying in wait for him. "Well, I best be goin' then."

Elisha handed Stevie the napkin and quickly jumped into the brush, where he disappeared from Stevie's sight. Stevie walked back to his family's camp and crawled back under the wagon. He spent the next sleepless hour contemplating whether or not he should tell Ma and Pa.

The following day, Ma rose to prepare breakfast. She fried up some bacon and cooked biscuits in the dutch oven. When Stevie rose, he greeted Ma with a sleepy, "Mornin', Ma."

"Good morning!" she replied. "Did I hear you get up during the night?"

"Yes, ma'am. I thought I heard something."

Ma continued interrogating Stevie, "I left cornbread here on the tailgate last night. It was supposed to be for our breakfast this morning. Did you eat it?"

"No, Ma!" replied Stevie. "We had a visitor last night. I saw a boy run through here. He snatched up the cornbread and took off that away."

Stevie had no choice but to tell his Ma everything.

"I followed him and caught up with him. He was shoving in that cornbread quicker than a jackrabbit. When I asked him who he was, he said his name was Elisha. He was a runaway slave, Ma! He said his Pa got shot a ways back. He was trying to make it to Lexington. Some people there were going to help him get to Canada."

Ma listened impatiently, then asked, "Stevie, are you making that up? Did you really talk to a runaway?"

"Yes, Ma!"

Benjamin approached them, leading the oxen. He intended to hitch up the team so they could begin their journey.

"What's this all about?" he asked.

Ma replied, "Stevie's just been telling me how he talked to a runaway slave boy last night. The boy stole our cornbread that we were going to have for breakfast this morning."

Pa asked, "Is that true, Stevie?"

"Yes, Pa."

Pa's face went stiff. He sighed, then said, "Both of you listen. Don't say any more about this. Not even to the little ones. William's liable to run his mouth off to a stranger about it not knowing what kind of danger he has put us in. But, Stevie, you know it's against the law to help runaway slaves, don't you?"

"Yes, Pa."

"We can't get involved in any of this business. We could all end up in jail if word got out. We just need to mind our own business and keep out of it. You understand?"

"Yes, Pa."

Ma then said, "Well, let's finish getting packed and get out of here. Somebody could be looking for the boy."

She finished the biscuits and bacon while Stevie and Pa finished with the livestock. Ma passed out bacon and biscuit sandwiches to everyone as they prepared to drive away.

Pa was vigilantly searching the area as they drove along, searching for anyone he thought might be hunting runaway slaves. Stevie found himself doing the same. He kept looking backward, then from side to side. Finally, William noticed and asked, "Whatcha looking for, Stevie?"

"Oh, nothing."

"Are you sure? You look like you're looking for something." replied William.

Stevie said, "No. I'm just loo..."

Suddenly, Stevie heard the sound of horses galloping behind him. He turned and saw five men on horseback racing toward him. Stevie kicked his Pinto and encouraged him forward to where Pa was driving the wagon.

"Pa! Pa! There's riders coming up behind us! They seem to be in an awful hurry!"

Pa leaned his face over the side of the wagon to look behind. He saw what Stevie had described.

Stevie asked, "What do we do, Pa?"

Pa replied, "Nothing, son. You keep quiet and let me do the talking, you hear?"

"Yes, Sir."

Benjamin pulled up the wagon to the side of the road and waited for the men to catch up with him. It didn't take long. The riders burst in on the Watsons like their tails were on fire.

As the men pulled up, Benjamin noticed that one of them wore a badge indicating he was some form of law enforcer. Benjamin jumped down from the wagon to meet the men. Benjamin looked up to the men still mounted on their horses and said, "Good day to you."

The man wearing the badge was a rugged individual. He seemed to be a little older than Benjamin. He wore a bushy mustache that was as black as a coal. "Who are you people and where are you heading?"

Pa replied, "I'm Benjamin Watson and this is my family. We're moving to St. Joseph, Missouri from Albany, New York."

The lawman then said, "I'm Marshal Luther Staggs. These are my deputies. We're looking for a runaway slave that we've been tracking for days. We got his daddy but the boy got away. Have you seen him?"

"No, Marshal. I haven't seen anyone other than my family since we left Cleveland."

The marshal said, "Mister, we found where you camped last night. That boy's tracks led right up to your camp. Are you sure you haven't seen him? You know it's against the law to help runaway slaves."

Benjamin replied, "Yes sir, I know. But I'm telling you the truth. If he came to our camp it was either while we were sleeping or after we left. I haven't seen any boy other than my two right here."

Staggs then asked, "If you're telling the truth, you won't

mind if we look in the back of your wagon, will you?"

"Marshal, I don't mind if you look in my wagon as long as you and your men don't damage our property."

Staggs looked at his men and motioned for them to check the Watson's wagon for anyone who might be hiding. Two of the men climbed into the back of the wagon and began throwing items out onto the ground. The other two began searching through the things that had been expelled from the wagon.

Benjamin protested, "I told you to be careful with our things!"

Staggs ignored Benjamin. Benjamin looked up to Abigail and nodded to her. Abigail reached into the floorboard of the wagon and picked up the rifle, and threw it to her husband. Benjamin caught the gun and cocked it seemingly in one motion as he held the barrel of the gun to the side of Stagg's head.

"Mister, I'm not going to tell you again. You tell your men to be careful with our things or they're gonna need that spatula over there to pick your head up off the ground. Now, I'm a law abiding man. I teach my family to obey the law. You can search the wagon all you want but you're not gonna find no runaway slave boy in there."

Staggs responded, "Do you think you can get us all with that rifle? There's five of us. You've only got one shot in that gun."

Benjamin replied, "One shot is all I need to take you down."

Benjamin then reached up, took the marshal's revolver from its holster, and said, "I'm guessing I can take out the other four with your pistol if I have to. Now step down off that horse and get over there with your men."

Staggs did as Benjamin instructed.

"You men get out of that wagon and get over here with the others."

The men complied, and soon Benjamin had them all lined up in front of him. Then Benjamin said, "Stevie, you and William pack the wagon back up. You men start removing those gun belts, carefully, and lay them on the ground over here next to this horse."

Everyone did as Benjamin told them. He now held his rifle in his left hand and pointed at the men, while the pistol was in his right hand also pointed at them. They were all careful to do as they were told.

"Stevie, come over here and collect these guns and throw them in the back of the wagon."

Stevie did as Pa had told him.

Then, Benjamin told the men, "Now, shuck off your boots and toss them to the wagon."

Staggs protested, "What are you planning, Mister? You know you're causing yourself a heap of trouble, don't you?"

Benjamin said, "I'm just giving me and my family a head start. We'll leave your horses and all your gear up the trail a ways. Once you've caught up and retrieved your gear you'll have a decision to make. Are you gonna come after me and my family, or are you gonna try to pick up the trail of that runaway? Now, one more thing. Stevie, get a long piece of rope out of the wagon."

Stevie found a length of rope about eight feet long and brought it to Pa. Benjamin handed Stevie the rifle and said, "Keep it pointed at them, son. If they try anything, shoot the marshal."

Benjamin took the rope and tied one end around the wrist of Staggs, then to the man standing next to him. He continued down the line linking each man's hands behind their backs, then to each other until they formed a circle with each man facing outward. They wouldn't be able to move quickly, but they could move. Only, some of the men in the back would have to walk either sideways or backward.

"Boys, get their horses and tie them behind the wagon."

Stevie and William tied the horses in a string formation behind the wagon, then got up on their horses and prepared to ride. Benjamin said, "You men will find your mounts and your gear up the trail about five miles from here. Good luck to you."

Benjamin climbed aboard the wagon and pushed the oxen forward, leaving the troubled lawmen behind.

CHAPTER 7

The Watsons were a little anxious as they drove on down the trail. Abigail was incredibly nervous about their plight. They had never encountered trouble with the law before, and she was concerned that they might be arrested should these men catch up with them. "What are we going to do?" Abigail asked Benjamin.

"We're going to drop their things off about five miles down the road. We'll find a suitable place where their horses will have access to fresh water. Then, we'll put as much distance between them and us as we can."

Abigail asked with a crack in her voice, "What if they catch up? What will they do to us?"

Benjamin replied, "Now, Abigail. Don't you concern yourself with such. You can't allow yourself to worry about what might not ever be. I've got a few tricks up my sleeve that will make it difficult for them to find us. Don't worry, woman."

They continued down the road, saying very little after that. William had his own set of questions for Stevie.

"Stevie, do you think those men will come after us?"

"Oh, they'll come after their horses and their guns. But, they've probably got more important things to do than chase us all the way to Missouri."

William thought back to when Pa had those men at gunpoint. "Do you think Pa would've killed them? I mean, if he had to."

Stevie replied, "I'm sure Pa would do whatever it takes to keep us all safe. He's not going to let anything happen to us."

William then asked, "What was it like?"

Puzzled, Stevie asked, "What was what like?"

William then said, "Holding that gun on those men. What did it feel like?"

Stevie replied, "I was scared. I didn't want to pull that trigger by accident, but I didn't want those men hurting us either."

William thought, then asked, "Could you have done it? Could you have pulled the trigger?"

Stevie then replied, "I don't know. I was pretty scared, but

I think that if those men had tried anything like trying to get that handgun away from Pa, I think I could have done it. But, I'm glad we didn't find out."

William replied, "Me too."

About an hour down the trail, Pa pulled up the oxen and beckoned Stevie and William forward. As the two boys reached the front of the wagon, Pa said, "William, trade places with me. You and your ma are going to continue ahead while Stevie and I go on up ahead and scout a place to leave their horses."

The young boy moved Jack up next to the wagon so William could climb directly onto the wagon from the back of the horse. Benjamin then stepped off the wagon onto the back of Jack.

Pa said, "You all just keep moving down this road. It won't be hard to follow our tracks."

As William moved the oxen forward, Pa reached over and grabbed the ax that hung on the side of the wagon. He then looked at Stevie and said, "Grab the lead on that first horse, and we'll take them with us."

Stevie managed to untie the lead rein from the string of horses by making a quick tug on the end, then followed Pa down the road at an easy gallop. All the horses stirred up a cloud of dust as they moved away from the wagon. William squinted trying to keep the dirt from settling in his eyes.

Pa and Stevie continued down the trail at a steady pace for about an hour. Benjamin finally found what he thought would be a suitable place for his plan. "Hold up!"

They stopped at a place on the trail along a creek bank. A big Elm stretched out over the creek, providing plenty of shade. Smaller trees surrounded the area near the stream, but off to the South were open plains. It was as if God had placed an oasis there right in the middle of this dusty, lifeless, deserted place.

Pa said, "This is what we need. This is perfect."

Stevie asked, "Perfect for what, Pa?"

"For a diversion. We're going to lead those men to this spot. They'll find their horses and gear, but they won't know which way we went once we're finished. Stevie, lead those horses down to the creek and let them drink a bit. Then, hobble them all so they can't move away from this spot."

"Okay, Pa."

While Stevie watered the horses, Pa began chopping down a couple of small trees that stood near the Elm. Stevie was a little puzzled at seeing his pa chop down the trees but decided not to question him just yet.

Once the horses had finished drinking, Stevie led them away from the creek. He took out his pocket knife and cut short lengths of rope to use in hobbling the horses. They would be able to walk, but not very easily. This would help confine the horses to this location without depriving them of any movement altogether.

When Benjamin finished cutting the trees, he and Stevie returned on their horses and headed back to meet with the wagon. They rode for about forty-five minutes before they found the wagon moving toward them. Pa pulled up to rest the horses and waited for the wagon to catch up. When the wagon finally caught up to Pa and Stevie, Pa called out, "Are you alright, William?"

With a massive smile on his face, William replied, "Never better, Pa!"

Pa returned his smile, then said, "Well let's keep moving."

Two hours passed before the Watsons finally reached the spot near the creek where the horses were waiting. Benjamin stopped the caravan and said, "Alright, this is where things get a little interesting. William, I want you to turn the wagon that way (as he pointed south) and keep going until I tell you. Stevie, get their gear out of the wagon and put it with their horses."

"Alright, Pa!"

William pressed the oxen forward and turned them south away from the creek. Pa got off his horse, then tied a length of rope to each of the trees he had previously chopped down. He handed one rope to Stevie and then remounted his horse with the other rope in hand.

"Stevie, we're going to follow the wagon and erase the trail with these trees by dragging them through the dirt. Let's move a little to the west first, then turn back and fall in behind the wagon. That way, those men will think we're heading south when they see the wagon wheel tracks."

Stevie nodded to his Pa and followed his lead. They moved forward for about an hour, then veered over and moved into line with the wagon tracks. As they followed the wagon, Benjamin erased the left side of the tracks while Stevie followed on the right side. When they both looked back, they saw Pa's idea was successful. All the wagon wheel tracks were being erased except the ones they wanted the men to see.

They continued south for about an hour. Then, Pa called out to William and told him to turn right and move back toward the original trail. "Keep the sun on your left shoulder, son!"

Benjamin and Stevie continued to erase the tracks for another mile, then cut the trees loose and left them behind.

Marshal Staggs and his group slowly walked together down the trail, searching for their horses. His men moved along with him quite clumsily since three of them were forced to walk either backward or by shuffling their feet from side to side. Finally, after an hour of this tiresome activity, the man directly behind Staggs, whose name was Bill asked, "Marshal, what makes you think those people will leave our horses and guns up ahead?"

Staggs replied, "He didn't seem the type that would lie to me. All he wanted was to keep his family safe. So I see no reason not to believe him."

Bill then said, "Well, I hope you're right. It's starting to get a little thirsty out here."

Staggs said, "It'll get a little less thirsty if you keep your mouth shut!"

Four hours later, the muddled mass of men found themselves in sight of their loyal steeds. The horses were scattered a bit, munching on outcroppings of grass along the edge of the creek. Then, with a hint of satisfaction, Staggs exclaimed, "There they are, boys!"

The men shuffled their feet more quickly now, moving anxiously while anticipating their freedom from their bonds. But instead, they found their gun belts lying under a giant Elm tree beside the creek. "Alright, boys. We need to have a seat so that I can get my knife out of my gun belt."

They clumsily fell to the ground as they attempted to sit.

Staggs ordered, "Sikes, hold onto that belt while I get my knife."

Staggs retrieved his knife from its sheath that hung from his gun belt. It was a sharp, six-inch bladed knife with an elk horn handle. Staggs carefully inserted the knife between the rope around his left wrist and the skin of his forearm. Next, he slowly began sawing through the fibers of the grass rope. It only took a minute for his left hand to be set free. Staggs then proceeded to cut the bonds of the other men.

Once they were free, they rounded up their horses and cut off the hobbles from their horses' feet. When everyone had freed themselves and the horses, they mounted up and waited for the marshal to give them instructions.

Bill finally asked, "Which way are we going, Marshal?"

Staggs checked the ground for tracks. He spotted a set of wagon wheel tracks leading to the South. When Staggs looked south, he saw that the tracks continued as far as he could see. He looked to the west but saw no tracks leading that way. Luther pondered why the tracks would lead to the South. Watson had told him they were going to Missouri. Were they taking a different route, trying to throw the lawmen off their tail?

"We're moving south. We'll follow these wagon tracks. I think they're trying to throw us off their trail."

Staggs led his men south, following the wagon wheel imprints that had been left in the dust. They continued for about five miles until the tracks ended. Then, the marshal said, "You men, spread out. Look for tracks leading away from here."

They split into five directions, looking for any sign of where the Watson family had gone. They found nothing. The tracks seemingly just disappeared. Eventually, the men all met back at the position where the tracks had ended. Sikes asked. "What do you want to do, Marshal?"

Staggs replied, "Well, I hate to admit it, but, looks like we've been outfoxed. I see no sense in us spending anymore time looking for them. We'll head back to Lexington and see if anyone has seen the boy. Maybe we can pick up his trail. He's worth more to us than a bunch of homesteaders anyway."

CHAPTER 8

SEPTEMBER 3, 1853

As they packed up to leave, Abigail began feeling sick to her stomach. Just before climbing aboard the wagon, she braced herself against the wagon wheel and bent over to vomit. Benjamin came upon her and asked, "Are you alright?"

"Yes. I guess I ate something that didn't agree with me. I'll be fine."

Abigail climbed onto the wagon and sat Lillian in her lap. Benjamin climbed up the other side and prepared to drive the oxen forward.

The Watsons continued their travels, moving westward, then southward, and found themselves in Columbus, Ohio, by September 3rd. Columbus was much larger than Benjamin had anticipated. It had been designated the capital of Ohio only recently, and the city was a buzzing metropolis. Benjamin wanted to get his family out of the busy city as soon as possible. He feared a place with this many people would produce unwanted challenges.

People were in an uproar throughout Columbus. Many of the population could be seen with copies of a newspaper in their hands. Individuals were arguing throughout the area, and from what Benjamin could gather from the fragments of conversations, it had something to do with the new fugitive slave law.

It took nearly an hour for the family to move through the streets of Columbus and find themselves on the western outskirts of town. September meant shorter days which meant fewer miles that the family could safely travel each day. However, Benjamin wanted to remove his family as far away from Columbus as possible. Unfortunately, dusk had overtaken the evening skies before Benjamin could find a suitable campsite to settle down for the night.

The family was well practiced in setting up camp now. The boys knew their job was to locate and gather enough firewood to last the night. Pa took care of the livestock and kept an eye out for any game that might wander into the sites of his new rifle. Ma, of course, prepared the evening meals and readied the bedrolls for the family. Three-year-old Lillian was of little help; however, Ma made her feel important by allowing her to help with meal preparations.

Ma started the fire to prepare the family's supper while the boys continued to search for firewood. After caring for the livestock, Pa set out to search for game. He found a game trail that led him easterly away from camp. He found signs of rabbit, possum, and deer along the path.

Stevie and William rambled through the woods in search of suitable firewood. There were fallen trees all around them. It looked as if a small tornado had come through the area recently and cleared out a section of trees. However, small sticks of broken branches suitable for firewood could be easily found.

William decided to climb onto one of the larger fallen trees that rested in the woods. He walked along the tree as if he were a tightrope performer.

Stevie called out to William, "Be careful, William. Ma will skin me if you fall and get hurt."

William ignored his older brother as he continued to walk along the side of the tree. Suddenly, William's foot slipped on the edge of the tree. He lost his balance and fell from the tree into a briar patch twelve feet below. He screamed as he fell. Stevie looked up from where he had been gathering wood and saw that his brother no longer stood atop the fallen tree.

"William!" he cried out.

No one answered. Stevie scrambled forward to the tree where he had last seen his brother. He climbed the end of the fallen tree, which still lay on the ground. Stevie called out again, "William!"

Stevie heard a groan below him about twelve feet down. A small gorge lay beneath the tree's middle. The gorge was filled with briars and Ivy and all sorts of vines.

Stevie crept carefully along the tree length as he searched for his brother. The groaning continued as Stevie crept forward. Finally, Stevie caught sight of a slight movement in the gorge. There lay William at the bottom, unable to move.

Stevie called out, "William! Are you alright?"

William only moaned, and his head rolled back and forth

from his pain. Stevie called out, "Don't worry, William! I'll get Pa!"

The light of the sun had all but vanished, making it difficult for Benjamin to see the path any longer. He was finally forced to turn back and walk to camp. Halfway up the trail, Benjamin balked and listened. Voices whispered upon the wind. He couldn't quite make it out. The wind picked up slightly and kissed his face as he finally heard, "Pa! Pa! Come quick!"

Benjamin sprinted back toward the camp, his mind racing. "*What's wrong?*" he asked himself. Benjamin jetted back and forth, avoiding obstacles within his path. He leaped over fallen trees and ducked under low-lying branches. The sound of the voice grew louder and louder. "Pa! Pa!"

Finally, he reached the clearing where his family had set up camp. Benjamin now recognized the voice. It was Stevie. "Pa! Over here!"

Benjamin turned and saw Stevie waving his arms in the air, trying to get his pa's attention. Benjamin ran to Stevie and asked, "What is it?"

Stevie replied, "It's William, Pa! He's hurt."

Benjamin followed Stevie into an area off the trail. Trees grew closely together here. Some had fallen after being uprooted from some recent storm. Movement through the trees was strenuous, but Benjamin moved forward as he heard William crying in the distance. Benjamin was anxious about what he might see when he found Willam. "Stevie, what's wrong with William?"

Stevie replied, "He was climbing over one of the big trees and slipped. He fell and hurt himself."

Benjamin finally reached the tree where his youngest son had fallen. He climbed over the big Walnut tree that had been uprooted. On the ground, Benjamin found William lying in a gorge filled with briars and vines, his shirt soaked in blood.

Benjamin assessed the situation momentarily and said, "Stevie, go back to camp and get a rope and a blanket. Tell your ma to come."

As Stevie ran back to the camp, Benjamin carefully began the descent into the gorge. The thorns of the briars ripped at his skin. He barely noticed them, however, as his only concern was getting to his son and getting him some help. When he finally reached William, Benjamin found things to be much worse than he had anticipated. William lay on the ground surrounded by the briars. Blood was collecting on the front of his shirt. Benjamin was confused by the amount of blood he was seeing. There was too much blood for someone who had been pricked by briars, no matter how many thorns had pierced their body.

Benjamin knelt by his son and lifted the boy's shirt to find out why. There was his answer. Benjamin's heart leaped in his chest. The blood rushed from his head, and he felt himself wavering. He shook his head and talked himself out of fainting.

William had fallen onto the broken end of a green tree branch about two inches in diameter. He was bleeding, but not as much as Benjamin would have thought from such a severe wound. Then, he realized that the branch that had traveled through William's body was plugging the hole it had made. Benjamin knew that once they removed the limb from William, he would probably die from blood loss. Benjamin sat and pondered what he must do to save his son.

Stevie called out to his pa as he returned with the rope and blanket. "Pa! I'm back! Do you want me to climb down and help?"

"No, Son! I need one more thing. Go get the bow saw. I need to cut a branch down here before I can move William."

Stevie said, "Okay, Pa! I'll be right back."

Moments after Stevie left the fallen tree, Abigail appeared over the side of the tree and called down to her husband. "Benjamin? How is he?"

Pa replied, "Not good, Abigail! I need to cut him free from this tree down here before we can move him."

Tears began to run down Abigail's cheeks. She couldn't see William, but she knew he must be in bad shape. She held Lillian in her arms as she looked over the edge into the gorge. Abigail hugged Lillian tightly, trying to comfort herself.

Lillian didn't understand but had no choice in the matter. Finally, Lillian cried out, "Ma! You're hurting me!"

Abigail cried harder as she replied, "I'm sorry, Honey. I didn't mean to harm you."

Stevie finally arrived with the saw. He tied one end of the

rope around the handle of the saw and lowered it down to Pa.

"Here it comes, Pa!"

Pa called to Stevie, "Do you think you can come down and help me, Stevie?"

Stevie replied, "Sure, Pa!"

Stevie carefully lowered himself over the edge of the gorge and slid down the side of the twelve-foot gorge to land beside his pa. Stevie, too, endured the skin-ripping pain of the briars as he slid down the gorge wall.

When he reached the bottom, Pa said, "Good, Son. Now help me roll William over just enough to get this saw under him."

Stevie picked up on William's right shoulder very gently. As he did, William began to cry out.

Pa said, "It's okay! But, Stevie, hold him right there while I cut this limb loose."

Benjamin carefully moved the bow saw into place beneath William's shoulder. He moved the saw back and forth against the limb, creating a slot as he sawed. Moments later, the tree limb broke free, and William's body rolled into Stevie, causing him to slip slightly down the slope of the gorge. Pa caught the boys before they could fall any farther.

Benjamin called up to Abigail, "Honey, can you tie one end of the rope around a good sturdy tree, then toss us the other end?"

Abigail did as Benjamin instructed. Once she had secured the rope around a Dogwood tree that stood nearby, she tossed the other end down to her husband.

Pa said to Stevie, "I need you to shimmy up and give your ma a hand. When you get up there you're gonna need to help her pull us up."

"Yessir, Pa."

Stevie quickly climbed up the rope hand over hand and soon reached the top. Benjamin tied the rope around his waist, then lifted William's body up on to his shoulder. Then he called up, "Alright, pull us up, easy!"

Abigail and Stevie slowly and steadily pulled against the rope, trying to lift Pa and William out of the gorge. Abigail braced herself by stepping against the backside of a tree. She wrapped the rope around the back of her waist, keeping the rope taut, while Stevie pulled with all his might helping his pa climb out of the gorge. Daylight was entirely gone as they struggled to fish Pa and William out of the gorge.

When Benjamin finally reached the top, Abigail saw the stub of the tree limb protruding from William's body. She gasped as she asked, "Is he okay?"

Benjamin replied, "Well, he's alive. But we've got to get him to a doctor. Stevie, run ahead and saddle up Jack for me."

Stevie sprinted back to camp and saddled up the old gray stud. Pa carried William over his right shoulder and held the saw in his left hand as they walked back to camp. Ma followed behind, carrying the rope while Lillian tagged along behind.

When Pa and Ma arrived back at camp, Jack was ready to ride. Pa mounted up on Jack while still carrying William over his shoulder. Then he said, "I'm headed back to Columbus to find a doctor. You all stay the night here and come back in the morning. Set up camp on the outside of town and wait for me. As soon as I can, I'll come find you."

Benjamin then looked to Stevie and said, "Stevie, you take care of your ma and Lilly. I'm counting on you, son."

"I will, Pa!"

Benjamin kicked Jack forward at a canter as he rode back to Columbus.

CHAPTER 9

It was nearly midnight when Benjamin arrived back in Columbus. The streets were all but empty. Only the local taverns and bars were still operating. Benjamin searched the streets for any indication that a doctor might be found. Finally, he found a man walking down the street who seemed slightly intoxicated. The man wobbled as he walked. Benjamin approached the man, who had a half-smoked cigar hanging from his lips.

"Excuse me, Sir. Can you tell me where I might find a doctor?"

The drunkard looked up at the stranger sitting astride a tall gray horse. "A doctor, you say?"

The man raised his right hand to point out the direction of a physician in the area. However, his body wouldn't cooperate and spun him around as he searched for the location he hoped to find.

"Doctor Wyatt lives over there. He operates his business in an office just below. You'll find his name displayed on a sign above the door, just there."

Benjamin said, "Thanks!" as he rode away from the man while searching for the location of Dr. Wyatt's office.

Benjamin searched the storefronts as he slowly walked his horse down the street. It was about twenty yards from where he had met the drunkard. A sign was hanging above the doorway reading, "Dr. James Wyatt, M.D."

Benjamin dismounted carefully, trying not to disturb William, who had fallen asleep while slung over Benjamin's right shoulder. Benjamin approached the door and knocked. The streets were quiet here, away from the bars. Benjamin feared he might wake everyone in town if he knocked too loudly; however, William urgently needed medical attention. Benjamin knocked much harder, but there still was no answer. Finally, Benjamin began feeling desperate, so he rapped on the door more furiously and constantly until he saw a light come on in the upper room.

A window opened above Benjamin, and a voice called out, "Who is it?"

Benjamin stepped back from the door and looked up to see a man about thirty years old staring out of the opened window.

Benjamin called up to the man and said, "I'm Benjamin Watson. My son has had an accident and needs the help of a doctor. Are you the doctor?"

"I am. Name's Dr. Wyatt. I'll be right down."

Moments later, Dr. Wyatt opened the door and allowed Benjamin to enter his office.

Wyatt pointed to a table in the middle of the room and said, "Lay him down there so I can have a look."

Benjamin carefully lay William on the table. As he did, William began to moan in anguish while still sleeping.

The doctor asked, "What happened to him?"

Benjamin replied, "He was out gathering firewood for our camp. He was walking along atop a fallen tree, slipped and fell about twelve feet. He landed on a broken tree branch that went through his shoulder. I cut it loose with my saw and brought him here to find a doctor."

Wyatt asked, "What made you decide to leave the branch in him?"

Benjamin replied, "Well, I was afraid if I pulled it out, he might bleed to death before I could find a doctor."

Wyatt replied, "You did the right thing, Mr. Watson. He would already be dead if you had decided to pull that limb from his body."

Benjamin asked, "Well, can you help him?"

The doctor said, "Sure. The location of the stick is ideal. If it had been anywhere else, it would probably have damaged his lungs or his liver or maybe even his heart. We'll get the branch extracted and then I'll cauterize the wounds to keep them from bleeding. He should be completely healed in a couple of months."

Dr. Wyatt started a fire in a stove in the corner of the room. Unfortunately, it took a while for the fire to get hot enough to heat the cauterizing irons he intended to use to close up William's wounds.

Wyatt asked Benjamin, "Have you ever seen a wound cauterized, Mr. Watson?" Benjamin replied, "No. I haven't."

"Well you're about to see it now. It's the only way we can

close up the wound and kill any bacteria that might already be living inside your son's wounds. The first thing, however, is to get that stake out of his shoulder."

The doctor had Benjamin hold William down against the tabletop with his body hanging slightly over the edge so that the stake protruding from the back of his body slumped over the edge of the table. Then, just as they prepared to remove the branch from William's shoulder, a woman stepped into the room and asked, "Is there anything I can do to help?"

It was Dr. Wyatt's wife, Mary. She had just walked down the stairs from their living quarters and was still pinning up her hair as she entered the examination room.

"Mary, this is Mr. Watson and his son, William. Help us hold the boy down while we remove this piece of wood from his shoulder."

Mary walked over to the left side of William's body and grasped his left shoulder to pin him against the table. Benjamin held William's right side down as the doctor gripped the piece of wood with both hands. Wyatt looked at Benjamin and said, "Ready? On three. One...two...three!"

The doctor pulled upward with a quick and steady jerk while Mary and Benjamin struggled to keep William's body pinned against the table. It took a few seconds for the stake to finally allow itself to work free of William's body. William screamed in pain, crying as he had never cried before.

Once the stake was free, Mary quickly blocked the wounds with a towel to help slow the bleeding. Dr. Wyatt walked to the stove, removed the cauterizing iron from the fire, and brought it over to the table. Mary removed the towel from William's shoulder so the doctor could stick the hot iron into the wound. William screamed again as the hot poker was placed against and into the wound. The pain was too much for William. He screamed and cried until he fainted. Once the doctor was satisfied with the cauterization of the front side of the shoulder, he had Benjamin turn William over onto his stomach so the back side could be burned as well.

Once the wounds were cauterized, Dr. Wyatt applied a salve to the burns made of Lavender oil and other medicinal herbs. He then wrapped William's shoulder and placed his right arm in a sling.

Dr. Wyatt told Benjamin, "He should sleep for a while, now. We'll watch and make sure he doesn't run a fever. It's probably best if he doesn't move for a while. Do you have other family, Mr. Watson?"

Benjamin replied, "My wife, another son and a daughter."

The doctor asked, "Are they here in town?"

"No. They're about half a day's ride west of here. They're supposed to meet me here tomorrow."

Wyatt offered, "Well then, why don't you rest on that bed in the corner? Your son will be fine for now. I'll check on him later. If he wakes or if he displays any symptoms of pain, call for me."

Benjamin replied, "Well, I'm not sure I remember how to sleep in a bed. It's been a few months since any of us have slept anywhere cept on the ground."

The doctor said, "Well, give it a try. We'll see you in the morning."

Doctor Wyatt and Mary excused themselves and climbed the stairs back to their living quarters. Benjamin sat on the bed that sat in the corner of the room. He hadn't realized until then just how tired he was. First, Benjamin decided to remove his boots; then, he laid his head down on the feather pillow that looked so inviting. As soon as he managed to pick his feet up and swing them onto the bed, he fell asleep.

Abigail awoke just before dawn. She hadn't slept well all night. She lay in her blanket and worried all night long about her youngest boy. She prayed that God would ease his pain and help him survive his tragic accident. Then, before the sun had fully risen above the horizon, she got up and began packing for the trip back to Columbus.

Stevie heard her and knew she was anxious to get going, so he rose from his bed roll and helped her pack up the wagon. They ate a cold breakfast that morning to get an even earlier start. Stevie hitched up the oxen, then saddled his horse. Lillian was still asleep, so Ma placed her in the wagon behind her and let her continue her dreams.

Rather than follow the wagon as he had most of their trip, Stevie rode alongside the oxen so he could talk to Ma from time to time. Stevie could tell Ma's mood was tense. No doubt, she was worried about William. Stevie remembered his little brother; how he looked lying in the bottom of the gorge with blood covering the front of his linen shirt. Stevie's stomach turned over at the memory.

Hours passed slowly as the wagon rolled up the trail heading back to Columbus. Finally, just before midday, Ma pulled up the oxen just west of Columbus when she found what she thought would make a suitable campsite. There was a small creek nearby where they could gather fresh water. In addition, large trees would provide shade during the day as the sun beat down upon them. Stevie took care of the livestock while Ma unloaded the cooking gear from the back of the wagon.

Just before noon, Pa rode into camp. Stevie was so excited to see him but became worried when he saw that William wasn't with him. Stevie cried out, "Pa! Is William okay?"

Benjamin looked down from his horse and replied, "William will be just fine. He's back with the doctor for now."

Abigail met Benjamin as he dismounted and asked, "How bad is he hurt?"

Benjamin replied, "He's got a hole through his shoulder that the doctor had to cauterize. Doc says he'll be sore for a long time, but he'll be just fine."

Then Abigail asked, "Can I see him?"

Benjamin said, "Yeah, I'll take you to see him after I get something to eat."

Ma heated up a pot of beans and fried some potatoes for their lunch. Typically, they would eat a cold lunch, but Ma felt like celebrating since the news about William was good.

As Pa ate his lunch, he contemplated what to do about the camp while he took Ma to see William. He hated the idea of packing everything up and carrying it all into Columbus. It would take too much time, and driving the wagon back into Columbus would take longer. The oxen could only move at a slow pace. It would be less time-consuming if he and Ma could ride the horses into town.

"Stevie? Do you think you could look after camp while I take your ma into town to see William?"

Stevie thought for a moment. He knew what Pa was asking was a huge responsibility; however, the thought of being left alone at camp scared him a little.

"I guess so, Pa. When would you and Ma be back?"

Pa replied, "Don't worry, son. We'll be back before nightfall."

Stevie asked, "What about Lillian?"

Pa replied, "We'll take Lillian with us. You won't have to worry about her. Just take care of camp and make sure nobody steals anything. I'm going to leave the rifle here for you. You be careful, though. I don't want you getting yourself hurt while we're gone."

Stevie asked, "What if someone does show up, Pa. What should I do?"

Benjamin paused, then took Stevie aside to speak to him privately. "Son, don't shoot anybody with that rifle unless you have no other choice. But if you find yourself in a situation where you need to defend yourself, you shoot them. And if you shoot them, shoot to kill. Aim for their chest. You'll have a larger target and they'll be less likely to do you harm. Do you understand, son?"

"Yes, Pa."

Chapter 10

Benjamin and Abigail mounted up on the horses along with Lillian. Abigail rode the Pinto and carried Lillian with her on the front of the saddle. As they turned to ride away, Abigail said to Stevie, "Be careful, son. We won't be long."

Stevie waved to them as they rode away. He then took the rifle from the wagon and checked it to make sure it was loaded and ready if needed. Finally, satisfied with his inspection, he stood the gun against one of the wagon's wheels while he worked around camp.

Stevie gathered firewood for the night. He didn't stray far from camp as he searched for the wood. He kept his eyes peeled and his ears alert for anyone who might ride toward their camp. He kept the campfire going without burning too much of the wood he had gathered. He didn't want the fire to go out. He knew it would be harder to start a new fire from scratch.

Once he had gathered enough firewood for the night, Stevie thought he might walk down to the creek and try his hand at fishing. He thought some nice brook Trout would be tasty for an evening meal when his family returned. So Stevie dug up some worms he found under a dead fallen log and placed them into the can Ma had opened for their lunch of beans and potatoes. Stevie took the fishing pole his pa had made, from the wagon, along with the can of worms and the rifle. He walked only a short distance from camp to the edge of the creek and found a nice shady spot to sit and relax as he dipped his line into the water.

It wasn't long before Stevie spotted a nice big Trout swimming close to his line. Stevie watched the fish float nearer and nearer to the worm that dangled from his hook. Then, the line went taut, and Stevie snatched the pole upward to set his hook in the fish's mouth. The fish wriggled furiously, trying to free itself from the sharp hook that had snagged him from freedom.

Stevie pulled steadily against the pole and walked backward to bring the fish up to the bank. He finally managed to drag the fish onto the grassy area underneath Stevie's shade tree. It was a nice two-pound Trout. Stevie was pleased with himself. He looked forward to serving it up for his family at the evening meal, along with any other fish he might be fortunate to catch.

Stevie unhooked the fish and carried it up to the camp to place in a pot of water he had left nearby the fire. He carried his rifle in his free hand while he walked back to camp, leaving the fishing pole to rest by the creek bed.

As he got nearer the campsite, he noticed the faint sound of hoof steps. Stevie stopped to listen. The steady beat of a horse's gait could be heard moving closer and closer. Stevie knew it couldn't be Pa. There had not been enough time for Pa to ride to Columbus and back to camp already. Pa had only been gone a couple of hours.

Stevie dropped the fish into the pan of water, then slowly took cover behind the wagon to spy on whoever might be approaching his camp. There, in the distance, riding from the east, was a lone rider. Stevie watched in silence as the rider came closer and closer.

The rider was thin and not very tall. He wore a wide-brimmed hat that had seen better days. The stranger had pale blue eyes, almost the color of ice, that bulged so severely they looked like there wasn't enough room in his sockets to hold them. His nose must have been broken a few times because it sat crooked on his face. What few teeth he had were crooked and stained from years of chewing tobacco. He rode a Palomino mare.

As the rider came closer, the hair on the back of Stevie's neck stood up a little. A shiver ran down his backbone. The stranger looked around as he rode into Stevie's camp. He spotted no one. He started to dismount when a thin young voice called out to him. "Hold it right there, mister. Don't get off that horse."

The stranger searched for the source of the voice, then said, "I was just hoping for a cup of coffee. I don't mean no harm."

"Ain't got no coffee!" Stevie's voice sang out.

The rider then said, "Well, how 'bout. . ."

"Ain't got any of that neither."

The stranger was a little perplexed by the young voice that called out to him.

What would a child be doing out here all alone? It didn't matter. A single child wouldn't be any test for him. He was a seasoned gunfighter and thief. One small boy wouldn't be a problem. The stranger doubted the boy even had a weapon. He slowly drew his pistol as he began once again to dismount. "Listen, boy. You don't sound like you could be much more than six year old. Now, why don't you come out from where you are so we can talk peaceful like?"

The stranger heard the crack of a rifle being cocked to fire, so he froze in his tracks. He continued to search the area and then began walking slowly toward the campfire, away from his horse.

"Come on out, boy. I ain't gonna hurt cha none."

Stevie then asked, "Then why have you drawn that pistol?"

Stevie's voice gave the stranger a clue to where he was hiding now. The stranger looked toward the wagon as he said, "This is just for my protection. I wouldn't hurt a piss ant."

The stranger caught a glimpse of Stevie standing behind the wagon and quickly raised his pistol to fire. His gun went off as Stevie simultaneously fired the rifle. Smoke from both weapons billowed through the air. The stranger's horse jumped back but didn't run away. Stevie felt his face stinging just above his right eye as his body fell backward toward the ground. Stevie lay on the ground, unable to move temporarily. For a moment, he thought he might be dead. He finally realized he was breathing too hard to be dead. With widened eyes, he slowly sat up to see where the stranger might be. When the smoke finally cleared, Stevie saw the stranger lying on the ground near the fire. Stevie crawled to his feet. He took time to reload the rifle before moving any closer to the body that lay before him. He cocked the rifle again before slowly inching toward the man's body.

Stevie took his time. He looked for any movement from the stranger. The man didn't appear to be breathing, but Stevie wasn't taking any chances. Stevie saw the man's pistol lying apart from his body as he got closer. Stevie walked slowly over to where the gun lay on the ground, bent over, and carefully picked it up. Stevie then noticed the large bloody hole in the stranger's chest. Stevie began to tremble. He had never seen anyone die before. When he realized that he had killed the man, Stevie began to weep. He wasn't sure why. Was it because he had killed someone, or was he just scared from being alone? Stevie was overcome with emotion as his knees buckled. He slumped down beside the body and stared into the distance. He didn't see anything; he didn't hear anything. He was just numb.

Abigail, Benjamin, and Lillian arrived at the doctor's office around two o'clock. Benjamin introduced Dr. Wyatt and his wife, Mary, to Abigail. Abigail asked, "How is he, Doctor?"

Dr. Wyatt said, "Oh, he's doing fine. He's very sore from the trauma his body received, but I expect a full recovery."

Benjamin then asked, "Doc, while we're here, would you mind taking a look at Abigail? She's been vomiting a lot. She can't seem to keep her breakfast down."

Wyatt said, "Of coarse. Mrs. Watson, would you follow me into this other room so we can take a look?"

Abigail protested, "It's really nothing. Benjamin is making it sound worse than it is."

Dr. Wyatt replied, "That's alright. Lets just make sure there's nothing for you to worry about, shall we?"

Abigail followed Dr. Wyatt and Mary into the other room, while Benjamin and Lillian went in to visit with William.

Benjamin asked, "How you feeling, son?"

William responded, "I'm mighty tired, Pa."

Lillian climbed onto William's bed and lay next to him. She put her arm around William to comfort him. William smiled at his little sister's gesture.

It wasn't long before Abigail and the Wyatt's came into the room to join the others. Ma knelt down at William's bedside and asked, "How are you, William?"

"I'm fine, Ma. I'm ready to go to St. Joseph, though. When can we leave?"

Ma replied, "That will be up to the doctor. When he says you can ride, then we'll be on our way."

William's family stayed with him for a couple of hours before heading back to camp. Although Abigail worried about leaving William behind, she was more concerned about getting back to Stevie who had been left alone at the camp.

As they began the trip back to camp, Benjamin asked Abigail, "Well, what did the doctor say?"

Abigail was focused more on Stevie as he asked the question. "Hmm? Oh, He said I'm fine, or at least I will be in about seven months."

Benjamin was puzzled by her answer. "What do you mean, seven months?"

Abigail replied, "That's how long before the baby gets here."

Benjamin smiled at Abigail and shook his head in unbelief. "Are you going to be able to travel, then?"

Abigail replied, "Don't worry. I'll be fine."

About an hour before dusk, Benjamin, Abigail, and Lillian rode back into camp. Benjamin noticed the Palomino grazing nearby and thought it strange. Then, he looked around to find Stevie. There, his son sat next to the motionless body of a stranger. Benjamin quickly dismounted and ran to Stevie. Stevie didn't move. He continued to stare into the distance. "Stevie? Are you alright?"

Stevie didn't answer.

Abigail asked, "What's wrong, Benjamin?"

Benjamin replied, "I think he's in shock."

Benjamin knelt beside Stevie and touched his shoulder. Slowly, Stevie came back to consciousness. He saw Pa and began to cry again. Pa grabbed his son, held him tightly, and said, "It's okay, son. You're alright."

Stevie murmured between his tears and sniffles, "I had to, Pa! I had to! He was going to kill me!"

Pa replied, "I know, son. I'm proud of you. You didn't do anything wrong. Some men are just mean spirited and need a good killing."

Stevie asked, "Will I go to jail?"

Pa said, "No, son. We're headed to St. Joe and you're coming with us. We'll take care of this here fella and be on our way as soon as we can get William back."

Benjamin picked a spot suitable to bury the stranger. He and Stevie worked together to get the body buried before it got too dark. They didn't bother to mark the grave once they had covered him over with dirt. Eventually, the stranger would be forgotten by every-one; everyone except Stevie.

The family did little talking during and after supper. Stevie was exhausted, so he went to bed directly after he had eaten. He was afraid he might not sleep because of the memories of the day; however, no sooner had he stretched out on his bedroll than he fell asleep.

The next morning, Pa rose early. He was anxious to retrieve William so they could continue their trip west. Stevie heard Pa as he prepared to leave, so he rose too. Stevie found Pa rummaging through the stranger's belongings. He didn't have much in the way of possessions. However, Benjamin found a piece of paper with a drawing of the man's face. It was a wanted poster, and it had the likeness of the stranger's face. Benjamin read the notice: Wanted for murder and theft. Billy Hayes. Also known as Bug-eyed Bill. Reward, $100.

Benjamin showed it to Stevie and asked, "What do you think, Stevie? Should we dig him up and take him to town to claim the reward?"

Stevie replied, "Pa, if it's all the same to you, I'd rather not see his face again. It ain't worth a hundred dollars for me to dig him up."

Pa said, "I have to agree with you. How 'bout we take claim to his horse and gear instead?"

Stevie replied, "Sure, Pa."

They looked through the rest of the gear. Billy's gun belt and gun were particularly interesting. The weapon was a 1851 thirty-six caliber Navy Colt revolver. It had been well cared for. Stevie asked, "Can I have the pistol, Pa?"

Benjamin thought for a minute, then replied, "Tell you what, son. We'll store it away. It will be yours when you're old enough to earn the money to buy ammunition for the gun."

Stevie was a little put off by his pa's answer, but he knew it was best he not argue the matter. So they wrapped the Colt and gun belt up in a blanket and stored it in a trunk inside the wagon.

Benjamin saddled Jack, and the Palomino then headed back to Columbus to pick up William. Before he rode away, Pa turned to Stevie and said, "You and your ma go ahead and pack the wagon. Head on out to Indianapolis and William and me will catch up with you as soon as we can."

"Okay, Pa." Stevie said as he waved goodbye to Pa.

CHAPTER 11

An hour later, Benjamin rode into Columbus. The city was already busy with people walking from shop to shop. Residents of the town met on the street and exchanged greetings and conversations.

Benjamin found the doorway to Dr. Wyatt's office and residence and pulled up his horses in front. He tied the horses to a hitching rail, then walked inside, where he found Mrs. Wyatt cleaning in the front area of the office.

"Good morning, Mr. Watson." she greeted him.

"Good morning, Ma'am. How's William doing?"

Mary replied, "He's much better today. He sat up this morning and ate all of his breakfast."

Dr. Wyatt came down from the living quarters to greet Benjamin. "Good morning!"

Benjamin replied, "Good morning, Doctor. Do you think he's well enough to ride today? We're anxious to get back on the road."

Wyatt balked at Benjamin's suggestion and said, "Well, I don't know . . ."

Benjamin interrupted the Doctor and said, "Doc, it's important we get back on the trail. We've still got at least a month of traveling before we reach St. Joseph."

Dr. Wyatt sighed, then said, "Well, if he promises to take it easy I think he'll be fine. Make sure he keeps that sling on for at least two weeks. If he starts to run a fever again, find a doctor and let him have a look. He might have an infection."

Benjamin smiled as he replied, "Thanks, Doc! For everything! How much do I owe you?"

Dr. Wyatt asked, "How does two dollars sound?"

Benjamin reached into his pocket, pulled out two silver dollars, handed them to the doctor, and said, "Thanks again."

Benjamin retrieved William from the next room and got him ready to ride. William walked outside to find two horses waiting for them; the grey stud and a new Palomino he had never seen before.

"Who's horse is that, Pa?"

Benjamin replied, "She's a new little filly we picked up along the way. We couldn't pass her up. What do you think?"

William replied, "She sure is pretty, Pa!"

Benjamin said, "Yes, she is. How 'bout we call her, Pretty Girl?"

William smiled and replied, "Yeah, that fits her just fine."

Benjamin picked up William and placed him on the back of Pretty Girl, then mounted Jack so they could ride together out of town.

William rode the Palomino with a massive smile on his face. Finally, he felt free to be back outside in the fresh cool air. The sun was at their backs as they trotted out of Columbus in search of the wagon carrying their family west. William's shoulder hurt when he bounced in the saddle, but he didn't mind. He was glad to be heading back to meet with the rest of his family.

Two hours passed before Benjamin and William spotted their wagon in the distance. They continued toward their family at an even trot. Then, suddenly, Stevie heard horses coming up behind them. When he turned to see who it might be, he was overcome with joy at the realization that William and Pa had arrived.

"Ma! It's Pa and William!"

Abigail pulled up the team of oxen to a halt, then climbed down from the wagon to spot the approaching riders. Ma was so happy to see her youngest boy as he rode atop the Palomino.

"Welcome back, William! Are you feeling alright?"

William smiled as he replied, "Just fine, Ma! I'm sure glad to be out of that hospital bed."

Ma asked, "Are you alright riding that horse or would you like to lie down in the wagon?"

William replied, "I'm okay, Ma. If I get too tired, I let you know."

The Watson family continued their journey westward. Pa had tied Jack up behind the wagon and rode up front with Ma and Lillian. A couple of hours later, William had decided he was tired and wanted to lie down in the back of the wagon. No sooner had he lay down than he fell off to sleep.

Every day the family continued westward. It became routine for William to start each day on horseback, then later in the day, he would take a break and ride in the wagon. Finally, after ten days, the Watsons rode into Indianapolis.

Once again, they loaded up on supplies but moved quickly onward to avoid the big city as much as possible. Stevie noticed as they rode through the town that many of the people dressed the same. The women wore dark blue dresses with white collars and white bonnets on their heads. The men wore dark blue trousers, light blue shirts, and black wide-brim hats. Stevie asked about the strange people. Pa replied, "They are Amish. They come from Europe, somewhere near Germany. Most of them speak German or some language much like German. They keep to themselves most of the time. They don't much care for 'outsiders.' We had some who lived near Albany, but most of them settled around Pennsylvania, I think."

Stevie asked, "What do you mean, outsiders? You mean people like us that live outside?"

Pa chuckled as he answered, "No, people who live outside of their faith. Their beliefs."

Stevie asked, "Well, what do they believe?"

"I don't really know, son. Like I said, they keep to themselves. I've never spoken to any of them before."

Thirty-five days after leaving Indianapolis, the Watsons arrived at the Mississippi River as it flowed just east of Hannibal, Missouri. When they arrived, they discovered a long line of wagons lined up in front of the river.

Abigail asked her husband, "What is it, Benjamin?"

Benjamin replied, "I'm not sure. Why don't you and the children wait here. I'll ride ahead and check things out."

Benjamin climbed on the back of Jack and rode ahead to see if he could gather information about the line that had formed ahead of them. Benjamin arrived at the bank of the river ten minutes later. When he arrived, he found a large boat docked nearby. The vessel had two large smoke stacks near the middle of the boat. Black smoke billowed from the top of the smoke stacks. Benjamin saw what must have been nearly fifty slaves loading and unloading the ship. Others were directing and loading wagons and livestock onto the vessel so that they might be transferred across the river.

Benjamin saw a small shed-like structure near the boat with a sign that read, "Tickets." He approached the stand where others had gathered. He found a sign on one side of the shed that gave ferry prices for crossing the river.

> Morning Ferry Departs at 10:00 a.m.
> Evening Ferry Departs at 3:00 p.m.
>> Tickets:
>> People - 25 ¢
>> Livestock - 50 ¢
>> Wagons - $2.00
>> All other cargo: SEE FREIGHT MASTER

Benjamin stood in line to see about purchasing tickets for his family to cross the river. But unfortunately, he stood in line for nearly thirty minutes before he was able to talk to an agent.

The agent was a short stumpy man who wore glasses on the end of his nose. He wore a striped shirt and a waistcoat. He spoke to Benjamin, asking, "May I help you, sir?"

Benjamin replied, "I need to see about getting across the river. I've got five people, three horses, two oxen and a wagon. How much will that cost me?"

The agent replied, "That will be $4.75."

Benjamin asked, "How long until we can get on the ferry? It looks like there is quite a long line ahead of us."

"The ferry only leaves here twice a day. It can carry four wagons with livestock aside from the regular cargo it carries daily. So, it will depend on how many people are ahead of you."

Benjamin asked, "Is there another way to cross the river?"

The agent replied, "Swim. Only I wouldn't recommend that. The river is quite swift and quite dangerous."

Benjamin furrowed his brow at the agent's humor as he dug into a pocket to retrieve the $4.75 for the tickets. The agent then passed Benjamin a slip of paper with the number of people, livestock, and wagons written upon it that Benjamin intended to cross over the river.

Benjamin checked the ticket, then raised his hand to the man and said, "Thanks!"

The agent replied, "You're quite welcome."

As Benjamin rode back to his family, he decided to count the wagons lined up in front of him. By the time he returned to Abigail and the children, he had counted thirty-six wagons. He showed Abigail the ticket he had purchased to get them across the river, then told the family what to expect the next few days.

He said, "They only make two trips a day. Each trip they can carry four wagons. I counted thirty-six wagons in front of us."

Stevie quickly calculated in his head and said, "That means we won't be able to cross until the fifth evening."

Abigail smiled and said, "That's right, Stevie! Your math skills are very good."

Every day at 10:00 and 3:00, the family had to pack up the wagon and move it forward in line. The rest of their time was spent repairing their wagon, preparing meals, gathering firewood, and searching for food sources.

William spent his time elsewhere. He made a friend. The family who occupied the wagon in front of them had a boy the same age as William. The two of them spent all their time together. They pretended to ride stick horses. They made pretend campfires by gathering stones and making a circle with them. They placed small sticks inside the ring to act as their campfire. They found large smooth rocks that were nearly shaped like potatoes that they cooked on their imaginary fire. The boy's name was Angelo. His parents were Italian immigrants traveling west to make a home for themselves in California. They had heard that the weather would be ideal for growing grapes, which they intended to plant to produce wine.

Angelo's father was Antonio Sangierri. He was a short man with a dark complexion who spoke with a strong Italian accent. Among the supplies they carried in the back of their wagon were clippings of grape vines that they intended to plant when they reached California. Antonio babied the plants, ensuring they had plenty of water and nutrients to survive the long trek to the Pacific coast.

William asked Stevie to play with them as the boys played their make-believe games. "Come on, Stevie! Don't you want to play with us?"

Stevie always replied, "No thanks! I've got work to do."

Stevie spent all his time shadowing Pa, learning everything he could from him. Pa showed him how to care for the horses properly. He showed Stevie how to clean their feet and put shoes on them. What to feed them and how much. Stevie helped with the wagon repairs and the daily moving of the wagon and stock, which was done twice daily.

Pa was very proud of his son. He was glad to see Stevie taking such an interest in learning to care for the family's needs. Pa and Stevie would go hunting together and sometimes fishing to supply the much-needed protein each would need to survive.

The fifth day finally came, and William had to say goodbye to Angelo. Angelo and his family were the last wagon loaded on the morning ferry to cross the Mississippi.

After the Sangierris loaded their wagon onto the steamboat, Angelo ran to the back of the ship to wave to William. Angelo and William exchanged waves until neither could see the other anymore.

William was downtrodden as he slowly walked back to his wagon. He found himself standing next to Ma as she began preparing lunch. William looked at the ground as he kicked the dirt.

Ma asked, "Did you say goodbye to Angelo?"

William didn't answer. He only continued to kick the dirt.

"William, you know there will be other boys to play with when we reach St. Joseph."

William continued to look at the ground when he replied, "Not like Angelo. He was the best friend I ever knew."

Ma replied, "I know, son. But, you are very young. You have plenty of time to find and make friends. You don't have to have just one you know. The more friends you make, the more you will have. Why don't you think of something else right now. Just think, we are about to get on a large steamboat to cross the largest river in our country. Now won't that be something to experience?"

William only shrugged his shoulders in response, then walked away.

At 1:00 o'clock, the steamboat returned to the dock, and the crew quickly began unloading cargo and preparing to load for the next shipment. There weren't any wagons to unload, so it didn't take long to ready the ship for the next crossing. Stevie sat atop his Pinto, who he had decided to call Dusty, waiting for the signal from the freight master to come aboard. William rode the Palomino while Jack remained tied behind the wagon. Pa, Ma, and Lillian sat on the wagon, waiting for their time to be loaded upon the steamboat.

It only took the crew forty-five minutes to unload the cargo from the ship. The freight master then gave a signal for loading new cargo and passengers to begin boarding.

The freight master finally pointed at Benjamin and beckoned him forward. Pa slowly moved the wagon forward. The freight master asked to see Pa's ticket. Pa presented the ticket to the freight master who looked it over, counted the people and animals, then waved Benjamin forward.

The oxen were unsure of walking across the wooden gangplank, but Pa managed to move them over without incident. The boys followed along behind the wagon. A crewman directed Benjamin to a spot at the far end of the boat. The wagon was finally halted at the bow of the steamboat. A crewman chocked the wagon's wheels with wooden wedges so it wouldn't move either forward or backward during the trip across the river.

Three other wagons were brought aboard and lined up behind the Watson's wagon. Each wagon was secured with wheel chocks, and the livestock were all tied to keep them from moving about on the ship.

The cargo area was filled with cotton bales, sacks of grain, and crates of various sundry. William and Stevie dismounted and met their family at the railing on the bow of the boat. They had a clear view of the river in front of them.

It wasn't long before Stevie heard the bell clanging to indicate the time. Three rings meant it was 3:00 o'clock; time for their journey to begin across the river. The boat whistle blew as steam escaped from its pipes. Stevie heard the paddle wheel start to turn as the boat surged forward. The Watsons all stood together on the bow as they watched the front of the ship move quickly through the deep dark waters of the Mississippi. Cold wind from the river blew through their hair and onto their faces as the boat continued forward. Stevie felt exhilarated as he searched ahead for the far side of the river.

White birds flew around the steamboat as it moved forward. Occasionally one of the birds would swoop down into the water and dive below. Then, a few seconds later, the bird popped out of the water and swam around.

The sun shone on their faces as they approached the western bank of the river. Thirty minutes after they left port, they arrived on the other side. The Captain and his helmsman steered the steamboat into port, moving the starboard side into the dock for disembarkation.

The family moved back to the wagon and the horses and prepared to unload. They were directed to turn right to use the gangplank leading ashore. Pa moved the oxen forward onto the gangplank and off the steamboat. Once ashore, they moved toward a town that sat before them only a short distance away. A large white painted sign stood near the entrance of the city that read, "Welcome to Hannibal, Missouri."

Chapter 12

Hannibal was a growing metropolis that had gained city status only eight years before the Watsons' arrival. It was named for a hero of ancient Carthage. The city's population had multiplied since its establishment in 1819. A town of about thirty residents had quickly grown to the now well-established city of nearly three thousand citizens.

In 1846, John M. Clemens and his associates established the Hannibal and St. Joseph Railroad. Clemens was the father of well-known author Mark Twain. The Hannibal and St. Joseph Railroad was the westernmost railroad in the United States until the completion of the Transcontinental Railroad.

As the Watsons drove through Hannibal, they heard the train whistle blow as it began its departure from the depot. The Watsons passed by the depot as the train pulled away.

William asked, "Where is it going?"

Pa replied, "Well, since the railroad is called the Hannibal and St. Joseph Railroad, I imagine it's on its way to St. Joseph."

William then asked, "Why can't we just take the train to St. Joseph?"

Pa explained, "Well son, we probably could. Except, when we got to St. Joseph we wouldn't have any money left to buy land." "How much does it cost to ride the train?"

Pa pointed to a sign on the side of the train depot that listed ticket prices. "One ticket cost $1.35 and we would need five tickets. Plus, the cost of hauling our oxen, horses, and the wagon. We'd be flat broke by the time we arrived in St. Joseph."

William looked to Stevie and asked, "How much does that add up to?" Stevie looked at the sign posted on the depot. It indicated the cost for livestock was $2.00 each. Heavy freight costs $5.00 each. It quickly added up in his head, and he replied, "It would cost us $21.75. That's more than we got for selling our house back in Albany."

William exclaimed, "Gosh! All that money to ride a train?"

Stevie replied, "Yep!"

William said, "I guess we best keep riding our horses then."

The family found a spot on the western side of town to camp for the night. It was a pretty little spot by Hannibal Creek.

William asked, "Do you think we might run into Angelo and his family on the way to St. Joseph?"

Ma replied, "It isn't likely. They have a five hour head start on us."

Pa said, "If Angelo's pa is smart, they'll lay up in St. Joseph for the winter. They've got a long way to go to get to California. I wouldn't want to get caught in the mountains during the winter."

William replied, "Well, maybe they will. Maybe they'll be in St. Joseph when we get there. I'd like that. Angelo is my friend."

Pa smiled at William and said, "Maybe so, son. Maybe so."

Just after dusk, the family heard a commotion coming from town. A mob was forming and began moving outside town toward the Watson's camp. Nearly one hundred men, some carrying torches, had gathered and started making their way outside Hannibal on the western side.

Stevie asked, "What is it, Pa?"

Pa replied, "I don't know, son. But I think I need to find out before they get too close. You stay here and watch over your ma and the young ones."

Benjamin saddled up Jack and quickly rode toward the mob while still keeping his distance. Benjamin discovered that some of the mob were carrying a man out of town on a rail. He had been doused with tar and covered with feathers. The man screamed in pain and terror as his captors proceeded out of the city limits. Benjamin asked one of the onlookers, "What's he done?"

The man replied, "Some I'tallion feller. He was caught harboring a runaway slave in the back of his wagon."

Benjamin had a bad feeling in the pit of his stomach. He decided to get closer. He moved Jack slowly through the crowd to try to distill his fears. Finally, he was able to get within twenty feet of the captive man. He still couldn't make out who he was. However, the man covered in feathers and tar recognized Benjamin sitting astride the tall grey stallion who stood above the crowd.

"Signore! Signore, Watson! Please! Find my family! Help

them, Signore!"

Benjamin's fears were confirmed. The man who was about to be lynched was Antonio Sangierri. Benjamin's heart sank. His eyes began to water as he saw the father of William's friend with a noose wrapped around his neck being lifted onto a horse . The other end of the rope was looped over a tree branch of a large Elm and then tied off around the tree's trunk.

Men were jeering and raising their torches as they called out, *"Hang him! Hang him! Hang him!"*

Someone led the horse out from underneath Antonio's body, leaving him to dangle, convulse, and finally die. The crowd cheered to see that the deed was done. Then, one by one, the crowd began to disperse and make their way back into Hannibal.

Benjamin decided he needed to find Antonio's family if he could. So he turned Jack and rode quickly back into Hannibal. Benjamin searched the streets, looking down every side road along the way. Finally, thirty minutes into his search, he found them. He heard the crying of children and a woman and followed the wails until he was led to a back street. There they sat, huddled together around their belongings that had been scattered while the men had ransacked their wagon.

Benjamin slowly approached the family, then dismounted. "Mrs. Sangierri? It's me, Benjamin Watson."

She looked up to see who was talking. Her face was soaked with tears. Her two children were curled up under her arms as she sat on the ground.

"Signore Watson?"

"Antonio asked me to take care of you and your children. Is your wagon alright?"

Maria Sangierri asked, "You have seen, Antonio? You know where he is? Is he alright?"

Benjamin only shook his head in response.

Maria cried even harder, now. She was in despair. What would she and the children do without their father and husband?

Benjamin repeated, "Is your wagon alright?"

She replied through sniffles and tears, "Si, but all of our grapes are gone. Destroyed."

Benjamin instructed her, "Let's get your belongings back into the wagon and get you out of here."

Benjamin helped the Sangierris quickly load the wagon with all their clothing, trunks, and kitchen utensils that had been scattered and tossed aside. He then helped Mrs. Sangierri onto the wagon along with the children. Benjamin tied Jack to the back of the wagon, then climbed up to drive them out of town.

Benjamin drove them down back streets to avoid the crowds of people coming back to town from the lynching. He made a wide loop once he left Hannibal to avoid the tree where Antonio's body hung. He wanted to spare Antonio's family the horrid memory of his tar and feathered body hanging from a tree.

It was very late when Benjamin arrived back at camp. He helped Mrs. Sangierri settle in for the night, then went to find his bedroll. Abigail awoke as he crawled into bed. She asked, "Is everything alright?"

Benjamin answered, "Wake me early in the morning. I'll tell you all about it, then."

The next morning, Abigail woke Benjamin as she prepared to start breakfast. Then, as she began mixing corn cakes, she asked him, "Well, what happened last night?"

Benjamin pointed to the Sangierri's wagon, which Abigail had not yet noticed. "They ran into some trouble in Hannibal yesterday. It seems that they were hiding a runaway slave on their wagon. Someone found out about it or spotted him, then things got crazy. Men ransacked the wagon destroying all their grape vines. They captured Antonio, then tarred and feathered him. When I came across the mob outside town, they were getting ready to hang him. He saw me and asked me to take care of his family."

Abigail was shocked to hear Benjamin's account of what had happened. "Is Mrs. Sangierri alright?"

Benjamin replied, "As you can imagine, she's pretty distraught. I'm sure she's wondering what will become of them."

Abigail asked, "Will they travel with us?"

Benjamin replied, "As far as I can see, they've got two choices. Travel to St. Joseph with us, or go back east from wherever they started. What do you think?"

Abigail said, "We can't abandon them. I'm afraid they wouldn't survive without our help."

Mrs. Sangierri emerged from her bed, looking around to see where she and her children had been brought. Abigail spotted her and walked over to speak with her. Maria Sangierri was a thin and frail woman. Her black hair was normally tied back in a bun, but now it hung freely over her shoulders. Her dress was wrinkled from lying in the back of her wagon bed, surrounded by her children.

"Mrs. Sangierri, I made some breakfast. Would you and your children care to join us?"

Maria replied, "Please, call me Maria. Si! Thank you much. I don't know how much of our food is still in the wagon."

Abigail said, "Bring your children over when you're ready. We have plenty."

A few minutes later, Maria and her children, Angelo and Lisa, joined the Watson family at their campsite. They all ate corn cakes in relative silence. Angelo was seven years old, the same age as William. Lisa was four, just a year older than Lillian. After breakfast, the children wandered off to play. However, Stevie remained with the adults.

Benjamin asked Maria, "Do you know what you intend to do now that Antonio is gone?"

She replied, "No, Signore Watson."

"Please. Call me Benjamin, and this is Abigail."

Maria began, "Signore Benjamin, we do not know what to do. Antonio was the one who wanted to go to California to plant the grapes. We do not know anyone in California."

Benjamin asked, "Do you have someone back east who can help you?"

"No. We have no famiglia there. Only in Italy. We do not have enough money to go back to Italy."

Benjamin asked, "Do you have any money for supplies to

get to St. Joseph? That's where we're going. You can travel along with us."

Maria replied, "Si, we have little money. We hid it in the wagon so the men, they not find."

Benjamin offered, "Why don't you travel with us, then? We can stop at the next town and get any supplies you need. Then, when we get to St. Joseph, maybe you can find a place close to us to live. We can help you get started."

Maria said, "Oh, grazie Signore! Thank you!"

The little caravan traveled together for the next four days before they found a town where Maria could replace her supplies. Monroe City was a small community with friendly folks who seemed eager to help those who traveled through their little town. Maria found what she needed at the dry goods store to give them enough to make the trip to St. Joseph. The Watsons also stopped into the store to look around in case they discovered something they might need for the last leg of their journey.

Stevie wandered around near the entrance of the store. As Maria began to pay for her goods, Stevie observed the transaction. The store clerk tallied her order and said, "That'll be five dollars, ma'am."

Maria looked shocked at the price of such a small amount of food. She asked, "So much money for so little food?"

The clerk replied, "Yes ma'am."

Stevie walked over and asked politely, "May I see the bill please, Mrs. Sangierri?"

Maria handed Stevie the bill. Stevie quickly added up the total of items on the bill.

5 lbs flour	35 ¢
1 lb coffee	25 ¢
1/2 lb baking powder	15 ¢
5 lbs lard	20 ¢
2 lbs salt	25 ¢
2 cakes soap	50 ¢
5 lbs corn meal	45 ¢
10 lbs dried beans	75 ¢
Total:	$5.00

Stevie looked to the clerk and politely said, "Excuse me, sir. I think you may have made a mistake in your addition. The total should be $2.90 not five dollars."

The clerk quickly became irate. "There's nothing wrong with my adding, young man. Who do you think you are, coming in here and telling me I don't know how to add. Now, you turn right around and get out of my store."

Stevie didn't move. He knew he was correct, and he wasn't going to let this man bully him. Benjamin heard the commotion and slowly began to walk over to the clerk's counter as Stevie said, "I'm not going anywhere, Mister until I help Mrs. Sangierri buy her supplies."

Maria held out a hand full of coins and waited while Stevie counted out $2.90 and laid it on the counter in front of the clerk. The clerk protested and said, "Hold on there! I told you five dollars. Not a penny less."

Benjamin arrived and said, "Let me see that bill."

Stevie handed Pa the bill and waited while Benjamin tallied the purchased items.

Benjamin asked the clerk, "Mister, do you make a habit of overcharging people like Mrs. Sangierri who might not understand our money system? Because by my calculation this comes to $2.90 just like the boy says."

The clerk sneered at Benjamin, then gathered up the change lying on the counter. Then Benjamin handed the bill to the clerk and said, "Now, mark her bill paid in full. We wouldn't want you telling the law that she walked out of here without paying."

The clerk used a rubber stamp to mark Maria's bill paid, then handed it back to her. Maria said, "Grazie!" as she walked out with her supplies.

CHAPTER 13

Three days after leaving Monroe City, the little wagon train found themselves camping next to a rather large lake. After setting up camp, Benjamin took Stevie, William, and Angelo to the lake to try their hand at fishing. They found a suitable spot on the southern shore underneath a Willow. A mockingbird entertained them with her songs while the boys baited their hooks to begin their hunt for the slippery prey. Benjamin noticed a large grey bird standing in the water just east of their location. He pointed it out to the boys who watched the Great Blue Heron as it waded knee-deep in the water. The bird stood very still as it eyed its target beneath the water. Then, suddenly, it darted its bill under the water's surface and snared a fish. The Heron greedily gulped down the fish, flapped its wings, and flew away.

William turned to Pa and said, "I wish I could do that."

Pa asked, "What? Catch a fish in your beak?"

William replied, "No! Fly!"

Benjamin nodded his head with approval.

The boys spread out along the bank and dipped their lines into the water allowing the baited hooks to sink below the surface. Benjamin found a soft spot among the moss that grew under the Willow. He sat down and reclined back on one elbow. He didn't bother to bait his hook. Benjamin decided to let the boys do all the work as he relaxed and watched.

It was early October, and the leaves in the trees were beginning to change color from bright shades of green to the gold and orange hues of autumn. The evening wind rustled the leaves, causing them to fall from the sky like snowflakes in winter. Benjamin allowed his eyes to close as he listened to nature all around him. He thought of Albany. No doubt, they would have already had their first snow by now. Benjamin was grateful to be away from the harsh winters of New York. No doubt, St. Joseph would have its own obstacles to deal with, but he was delighted that the winters there would be a little shorter than they had been in Albany.

After an hour by the lake, the boys caught two trout and four catfish. Benjamin rounded up the boys and led them back to camp. Ma and Maria were starting to prepare supper when the men arrived back at camp. Benjamin helped the boys clean and dress the fish so that they could be cooked. Abigail seasoned the fish with salt and pepper, then rolled them in flour and cornmeal before frying them in a pan of lard. Maria had never seen fish prepared in such a way and was intrigued by Abigail's choice of preparation.

Since the two families were traveling together, Abigail and Maria had decided it made little sense to have separated meals, so they prepared their meals collectively. Maria made Italian-style bread to eat with the meal, while Abigail boiled potatoes and onions to go with the fish.

It seemed much like a holiday to the camp to be able to relax next to the lake. The mild weather grew cooler as the night approached, but not so much that they couldn't enjoy the night by the campfire.

Maria brought out a mandolin from the back of her wagon, and she played and sang an Italian tune. The Watsons listened intently while not understanding the words. However, they understood the mood of the song. It was a lonesome and sad song of love fading away through absence.

The next day, the wagons continued their trek westward. Thirteen days later, they found themselves on a hill overlooking a large town beside a river. It was the Missouri River. The same river the Lewis and Clark Expedition had traveled so long ago while searching for a passage to the northwest. Benjamin decided to camp outside of town, since they still had at least five miles to travel before reaching St. Joseph. Benjamin decided they would be better off waiting and leaving in the morning.

They all set up camp as usual and sat by the fire eating their supper while staring into the west. The warm glow of lantern lights could be seen throughout the town. When the wind blew just right, the campers could hear voices echoing through the valley, wafting up to their level.

When the group bedded down for the night, none of them except Lisa and Lillian was able to sleep. The anticipation of finally arriving at St. Joseph kept them awake. Benjamin began to worry.

What would they do if there was no land to buy? Maybe the price of land was not as cheap as he had been led to believe. The town's folk might not like them coming in to set up a homestead. He had heard of homesteaders in various towns who had been unwelcome, even driven out and forced to keep moving. Would that happen to them? Benjamin continued to agonize over his doubts until he slowly drifted off to sleep.

The next morning, everyone packed up the wagons and proceeded down the hill. Excitement floated in the air all around them as they grew nearer to the town. St. Joseph began to take shape as they moved closer. Individual buildings developed before them. They saw houses, shops, a bank, a livery stable, and more. Once they rode into town, Benjamin stopped a man walking down the street.

"Excuse me, sir. Can you please tell me where the land office is located?"

The man was an older gentleman. He wore a suit with a derby hat. His face carried a white handlebar mustache under his nose. The gentleman replied, "Yes, sir. Just keep going down this street until you get to Angelique Street. Turn left on Angelique and the land office will be half-way down on the right."

Benjamin replied, "Thank you, sir!"

The gentleman tipped his hat to Abigail as their wagon pulled away.

As the small caravan moved down the streets of St. Joseph, Benjamin noticed that many of the streets seemed to be named after people. Angelique, Edmond, Sylvanie, Charles, and many others. They saw people walking up and down the boardwalks that lined the streets. Ladies were wearing beautiful store-bought dresses with matching hats as they assembled in front of the dress shops in town. Gentlemen greeted one another as they met, entering various offices. It was almost like being back in Albany, except the buildings were more rugged.

Benjamin turned their wagon down the street the older gentleman had instructed him to take. He and Abigail checked the sign of every building on the right, looking for the land office. Finally, they saw a sign reading, "First Title and Land Office of St. Joseph,

Missouri." Benjamin noted that it was conveniently located next door to the First National Bank of St. Joseph.

Benjamin pulled the wagon up in front of the land office, and he and Abigail hopped down to enter the office. "Stevie, you and William stay here and watch the wagon and keep an eye on your sister."

Stevie replied, "Yes sir, Pa."

Benjamin and Abigail walked into the office and were greeted by a tiny bell that rang above their heads as they walked through the door. Then, as they stepped inside and closed the door, the bell rang again.

A portly gentleman greeted them as they entered. He was balding but wore extremely long mutton chop sideburns on each side of his face. He was so large he evidently found it very difficult to breathe. The Watsons could hear him as he took every breath.

"Good morning! I'm Morris Reynolds. How may I help you, folks?"

Benjamin replied, "I'm Benjamin Watson and this is my wife, Abigail. We've just arrived from Albany, New York. We're hoping to find some land for sale here near St. Joseph that we can buy and set up a small farm, maybe twenty acres."

Mr. Reynolds got a curious look on his face when he heard Benjamin say his name.

"Did you say, Watson?"

Benjamin replied, "Yes sir, Benjamin and Abigail."

Morris fumbled through papers on his desk as he said, "Hmm. I think I have something for you. It arrived last month."

Benjamin, baffled, said, "Really? I can't imagine what . . ."

"Yes! Here it is!"

Morris picked up an envelope that had been hiding under the clutter on his desk.

He opened the envelope and pulled out a letter. There was another envelope inside the first envelope, which he handed to Benjamin.

"This one is addressed to you, but let me read this one to you before you open that one."

Benjamin took the envelope from Morris and stared at the

inscription. It was addressed to Benjamin Watson and family of St. Joseph, Missouri. Benjamin was puzzled as he looked at the envelope in his hand while Morris began to read.

"It is addressed to the Manager of the Title and Land Office of St. Joseph, Missouri. It reads:"

Dear Sir;

I request that you help me with a transaction in purchasing property in your area. I have arranged for funds to be transferred into your account at the First National Bank of St. Joseph to cover the land purchase cost and any fees that might incur in the transfer of title. Any funds left over should be given to the individual whose name is written on the second envelope.

The property should be suitable for farming and have living quarters to house atleast five people. I will leave any other specifics to you.

Thank you for your attention to this matter. I trust you will see it through for me.

Sincerely;

Paul Wilson, Esquire

Benjamin looked at Mr. Reynolds, confused as he asked, "What does that mean?"

Morris replied, "My dear sir, you and your family have been awarded a very nice property by this Paul Wilson. Is he a friend of yours?'

Benjamin replied, "Well, sort of. We met on the trail back at Niagara Falls. His wife got herself in a pickle when she fell over the side of a cliff. My son and I rescued her. We pulled her out before she could fall to her death."

Morris said, "Well now bless me! I'm standing in the presence of a true hero. It is my pleasure to help you, Mr. Watson. I have picked out an ideal property for you. It was once owned by an older couple who moved here from Pennsylvania. It has a nice big house, and a barn that both sit on forty acres just outside of town. Most of the land has been cleared, but there is also timber on the property. There is also a creek that runs through the property that feeds into the Missouri River. How does that sound?"

Benjamin and Abigail looked at each other and smiled as they sighed.

Abigail exclaimed, "Oh, it sounds wonderful! When can we see it?"

Morris replied, "Just as soon as we finish signing the deed. It will all be yours."

Mr. Reynolds searched for and found the deed, then presented it to the Watsons for their signatures. He used a rubber stamp to seal the deal with the land office's emblem, then signed his name to the deed. He then pulled out a large book and recorded the deed inside the large ledger. Morris then took out a banknote and made it out to Benjamin for twenty dollars.

"This is a bank note for the funds leftover from our transaction. You can take this next door to the bank and either open an account in your name for it to be deposited into, or you can simply cash it."

Benjamin and Abigail couldn't believe the good fortune that had found them. They both thanked Mr. Reynolds and shook his hand before exiting his office.

Suddenly, Benjamin thought of something. "By the way, how do we find our property?"

Morris replied, "Turn your wagons around and head back to Edmond Street. That's the main street that brought you into town. Take a left and follow Edmond out of town. You'll travel about two miles and see the entrance to the place. The sign reads, Parish Place. The Parish's owned it before they both died of influenza. There's a big white house near the entrance. You can't miss it."

Benjamin said, "Thanks again, Mr. Reynolds!" as he walked out the door.

CHAPTER 14

As Abigail and Benjamin exited the land office, they paused in front of the wagon where the other travelers had gathered. As usual, William was the first to speak, "Well, did you get some land for us to buy?"

Benjamin tried to contain his excitement as he replied, "No, son. We didn't buy any land."

After a long pause, he continued, "Someone bought us some land, though!" Everyone exclaimed, "What? Who? How?"

Benjamin waved his hands, trying to quiet everyone. Then, when the questions subsided, Benjamin explained, "We have a letter here that I hope will explain."

Benjamin opened the envelope addressed to him and began to read aloud:

Dear Watson Family;

Anna and I wanted to express in some small way how much we appreciate the kindness, generosity, and courage you displayed while communing with us on our trip to Niagara Falls.

Anna is incredibly grateful to Benjamin and Stevie for saving her from certain death. She and I will never forget you.

We wanted to offer a gift to help you set up your new life in St. Joseph. I have contacted the land office there and transferred enough money to purchase a suitable home to meet your needs and get you started on your new life in Missouri.

We pray you are all doing well, and we hope someday we may meet you again.

With kindest regards,
Paul Wilson

William asked, "What does that mean? Do we have some land?"

Pa replied, "Mr. Wilson bought us a farm a couple of miles outside of town. There's forty acres and a big house. It's all ours!"

The cheering began again. William and Stevie threw their

hats into the air as they yelled, "Yahoo!"

Finally, Stevie asked, "Can we go see it?"

Pa replied, "Just as soon as I go cash this check at the bank. Mr. Wilson sent us an extra twenty dollars to help us get started."

Benjamin walked into the bank and found it to be impressive. It looked to him more like a fine hotel than a bank. There was fine furniture in the lobby where customers could sit while waiting to be assisted. There were two teller windows where gentlemen wearing suits stood behind iron bars as they helped customers. Behind the wall of bars was an office where the bank's president managed the bank's affairs and a large safe next to it.

There were no other customers there when Benjamin walked in, so he moved to the first teller's window.

"I'd like to cash this check please."

The teller looked at Benjamin over a pair of spectacles that rested on the end of his nose. He then examined the check and found it to have been written against the Title and Land Office. The teller said without emotion, "Yes, sir. Just a moment please."

The bald little man walked back to the president's office and disappeared. When he returned, he was following another man who now held Benjamin's check in his hand. The bank president was a tall, thin man who wore a fine pin-striped suit of dark blue. He had a long slender nose and long sideburns that were closely trimmed. He walked up to Benjamin from behind the window and said, "My name is Lawrence Martin. I am the president of this bank. I understand you would like to cash this check?"

Benjamin replied, "Yes, that's true."

Mr. Martin asked, "Are you new to our fair city?"

Benjamin answered, "Yessir, we just arrived in town today. We have just signed a deed that makes us the new owners of the Parish Place."

Lawrence raised his eyebrows in surprise. He didn't feel that someone of Benjamin's dusty and ragged attire could afford such a fine place like the Parish Place.

Lawrence suggested, "Well then, wouldn't you like to open an account with us? We have fine facilities here to keep your money safe."

Benjamin said, "No, thanks. We're going to need all of our cash to get things up and going on our new farm."

Mr. Martin suggested, "Well, maybe we might interest you in a loan to help get you started. We offer excellent rates."

Benjamin replied, "If it's all the same, Mr. Martin, I don't like to be beholding to anyone. We'll make do with what we have. We always have. If you wouldn't mind just cashing that check, then I'll be on my way."

Martin disappointedly gave Benjamin a wry smile and then said, "Certainly. However, if you decide later on you want to talk with us about a loan, feel free to come back. I would be happy to help you."

"Thank you, Mr. Martin."

Lawrence Martin returned the check to the teller and returned to his office. The little man counted out twenty dollars in paper money and handed it to Benjamin. Benjamin folded the cash before putting it into his shirt pocket. He said, "Thanks," and then he walked out of the bank.

Benjamin found his family and the Sangierris waiting outside in anticipation. William spoke first as usual, and asked, "Pa, can we go to our new house now?"

Benjamin responded, "Oh, I don't know. I thought we might all go and have some lunch before we leave town. What do you think?"

Everyone responded in gasps and comments of delight. None of them had ever eaten in a restaurant before.

Benjamin said, "I noticed a place just up the street we could try. Something in there smells mighty good."

Everyone loaded up and drove back toward Edmond Street. The place Benjamin had in mind was at the corner of Edmond St. and Angelique. They parked the wagons just outside so they could keep an eye on their belongings while they dined.

A sign above the restaurant read: Simmons Restaurant. When they entered the establishment, the two families were amazed at how many tables and chairs there were. A lady wearing an apron and carrying two plates of food saw them as they entered. "Have a seat anywhere. I'll be right with you."

Benjamin directed his crew to two tables that were empty near the door. He wanted to be able to keep an eye on the wagons while they dined. They pulled two tables together and rearranged the chairs so both families could sit together. As they sat down at the table, Benjamin noticed a chalkboard sign that read:

Menu Ham Steak Fried Taters Beans Biscuits
Apple Pie 75¢

The lady in the apron came to their table and greeted them, "Howdy, folks! Name's Alice. You folks new in town?"

Benjamin replied, "Yes. We just bought the old Parish Place. We plan to go out there after we've had a bite to eat."

Benjamin then introduced his family. "I'm Benjamin Watson and this is my wife Abigail. These two boys are our sons Stevie and William, and the little one is Lillian."

Benjamin then introduced Maria's family. "This is Maria Sangierri and her two children, Angelo and Lisa. They're traveling with us. Are you the owner?"

Alice replied, "Yessir! Me and my ma, that is. She's in the back cooking. My son is back there, too. Warshin' dishes. Well, nice to meet you all. I hope you like it here in St. Joe. Now, can I fix you up with some vittles?"

Abigail replied, "Yes please. It smells wonderful."

Benjamin said, "I noticed that many of the streets seem to be named after people."

Alice replied, "Yessir! Joseph Robidoux was the founder of St. Joe. He had eight children and named most of the streets after them. Angelique was his second wife."

Benjamin nodded his understanding to Alice.

Alice said, "Well the menu is limited. What we got is what you get. We ain't fancy, but we'll fill you up. Today it's ham. I'll bring out enough for all of you and you can serve yourselves. You want coffee?"

Alice looked at each of the adults as they replied with a nod. Then, Alice said, "I've got sarsaparilla for the youngens if you like."

The children's faces lit up at the word. None of them had

ever had sarsaparilla, but they knew what it was. Abigail looked at Benjamin for approval. When he nodded his head, Abigail replied, "That would be wonderful. Thanks!"

It wasn't long before Alice arrived carrying a tray with three cups of hot coffee and five bottles of sarsaparilla. First, Alice set a cup of coffee on the table in front of each of the adults, then a bottle of sarsaparilla in front of each child. Then she smiled at each child and said, "You youngens don't drink those up before you get your food. You won't want anything to eat if you do."

Stevie and William looked at Ma, waiting for her approval to drink from the bottle of the fizzy drink. Abigail then said, "You can take a sip."

Each child reached for their bottle and carefully lifted it to their lips. When Stevie tasted the fizzy concoction for the first time, it brought a sensation to his body he had never experienced before. The combination of the rooty, sweet flavor mixed with the bubbly sensation was unlike anything he had ever known. He liked it.

Abigail asked Lillian, "May I have a sip?"

Lillian offered the bottle to her ma and said, "Here, Ma!"

Abigail took a sip and allowed it to linger in her mouth before she swallowed. "Mmm, it taste a little like root beer. I had root beer once when I was a little girl."

Maria decided to try a sip of Lisa's drink. She lifted the bottle to her mouth and took a swig. Unfortunately, it wasn't what she had expected. The bubbles burned her mouth and nose, and when she swallowed the liquid, it caused her to hiccup. Maria displayed a sour look on her face as she exclaimed, "Non Buono!"

Maria sat the drink back on the table, picked up her cup of coffee, and drank, trying to remove the unwanted taste from her mouth. The children all giggled at the look on Maria's face.

Alice quickly arrived with four platters balanced on her arms. She set the first platter down. It was piled high with fried potatoes. The second was a large bowl of pinto beans. She then placed a huge platter of ham onto the table, then a basket of hot biscuits right out of the oven.

"There you go folks! I'll be back later with your apple pie. Can I get you anything else?"

Abigail replied, "No thank you, Alice."

As Alice walked away, Abigail began scooping potatoes, beans, and ham onto her children's plates. It all smelled and looked so delicious. The ham steaks were huge slabs of pork about a quarter inch thick. Abigail cut them into smaller portions before placing them onto the plates. Abigail then passed the platters to Maria so she could serve her children. Once all the children were served, the adults fixed their plates, then passed the basket of biscuits around so everyone could have one.

For a long time, nothing was said. They were all too busy consuming the tasty food set before them. The only noise to be heard was the conversations of the other guest in the room and the scraping of knives and forks against the plates of food.

Alice showed up with a whole apple pie she had cut into eight slices. She left it with Abigail, who then served everyone at her table. The pie was still warm from the oven. The combination of the apples, cinnamon, sugar, and baked dough was irresistible, even on full stomachs.

Once they had finished eating their pie, Alice brought their bill. "I hope you all enjoyed your meal and will come back soon."

Benjamin replied with a deep breath trying to relieve his full stomach. "Thanks! It was so good!"

Benjamin looked at the bill and saw the total was $6.50. Benjamin reached into his shirt pocket and counted out seven dollars. He left the money on the table as they all got up to go. Alice waved to them as they exited the restaurant.

Chapter 15

The Watson/Sangierri clan loaded up into their wagons and began the trek to Parish Place. They turned left on Edmond St. and continued out of St. Joseph. Along the way, they saw a dry goods store, a blacksmith shop, a livery stable, and the train depot where the Hannibal and St. Joseph Railroad terminated.

As they rode southward, they discovered the Missouri River to their right. There was a large dock next to the river where all-sized boats could be seen moored. It was much like they had seen while crossing the Mississippi River, only on a smaller scale. Cargo was stacked next to the docks waiting to be loaded onto ferries to be carried to the west. A ship's bell could be heard now and again as the families continued to drive toward their new home.

As they exited St. Joseph, they saw a sign just outside of town that read, Kansas City 55 miles. There was evidence that the south road had been well traveled. The road's surface was well-compacted from the many travelers who had followed this route from St. Joseph to Kansas City. Along the way, Benjamin and his family saw several small homesteads. Most of them had very tiny homes like the one the Watsons had lived in while in Albany. Occasionally, children could be seen either playing or working at their respective homes.

The road seemed to travel parallel to the Missouri River all along the way. The Watsons witnessed many craft of various sizes floating down the river heading toward Kansas City.

It took less than an hour to see what they were finally searching for. A meadow opened before them as the road began to bend eastward. In the middle of the field sat a white-framed house. A trail exited the south road and led to the structure. Hovering high above the trail entrance was a large log sitting atop two vertical posts. A sign hung from the horizontal log that read, Parish Place.

The Watsons lingered for a moment at the entrance of their new homestead. Although it was only forty acres, the land seemed to stretch out before them for miles. Benjamin finally said, "Well, what are we waiting for?"

He then pushed the oxen forward toward their new home. The meadow was a bit overgrown from neglect. Sage grass cropped up amid the tall grassy meadow. As the wagons went down the path, quail began to fly out from under their cover. Benjamin began to think, "If only I had a shotgun. Quail would be nice for supper."

Finally, they reached the house. It was even larger than they had expected. It wasn't a mansion by any means; it stood only forty-five feet wide at the face and moved back to about twenty-five feet. However, it was two stories high. There were two large chimneys, one on each end of the house. Benjamin noticed that the creek ran close to the home. He suspected there might be a springhouse at the stream. That would allow them to keep meat and milk chilled during the warmer weather months.

The families pulled up in front of the house and got down from their mounts to inspect the home more closely. Everyone seemed to be in awe of the size and design of the house. A large wooden porch covered the expanse of the home's front. Two porch swings hung from the rafters on the western end of the porch. They faced each other, creating a cozy little space for friends and family to visit together.

Everyone walked up the porch steps and entered the home's front door. Abigail gasped when she saw and realized the house was fully furnished. At the entrance stood a wide staircase leading to the bedrooms on the second story. Abigail turned left from the entry and found a large dining area with a table and chairs large enough to seat ten people easily. Abigail passed through the dining area and found the kitchen. Again, she gasped when she realized how huge it was. There were cabinets along the walls, countertops underneath them, and a large cast iron stove that vented into one of the large chimneys. Abigail exclaimed, "Benjamin, what will I do with all this room? I've never seen a kitchen so big!"

They found a trap door in the floor against the wall. Benjamin pulled up on the handle to reveal what might be underneath. Just as he had expected, he found a cellar. Benjamin climbed down the steps into the cellar and saw the spring house at the far end of the structure.

"Looks like we've got a spring house underneath."

Abigail replied, "Oh, that will be wonderful!"

At the back of the kitchen was a door that led to the backyard. There was another covered porch, but not nearly as big as the front porch. A washtub and scrub board were set up for washing clothes. They returned to the entryway and passed through to the next room. It was a parlor. There were two couches and four armchairs scattered throughout the room. The other chimney was situated on the west wall. A large oak mantel rested above the fireplace. A doorway led to a bedroom at the back of the parlor. When Abigail opened the door, she found a large decorative wooden bed frame. On the bed was a feather mattress. Abigail couldn't resist. She had to lie on the mattress and test it out. "Oh, Benjamin! It's so comfortable!"

Benjamin smiled at everything his wife had to say. He was happy that she was pleased.

Finally, they walked up the stairs and found three more bedrooms. Each of them was pretty much identical in decor. Each had a comfortable bed, a dresser, and a chifforobe.

Abigail turned around and asked Maria, "Which one of these bedrooms do you want?"

Maria was shocked. She couldn't believe Abigail would offer her a place to stay in this beautiful house, much less give her a choice of rooms.

"You want us to stay here?" Maria asked.

Abigail replied, "Well, of coarse. Where else would you go? There's more than enough room for you and your children here. Angelo can room with the boys and Lisa can share a room with Lillian. What do you think?"

Maria replied, "Signora Abigail, you have been so kind. We do not want to be a burden to you. We can find another way."

Abigail said, "Don't be silly, Maria. You are now a part of our family. If you decide you no longer want to live here later on, that's fine. You can build your own house if you like, right here on our land. Or, you can continue to live here with us. Either way, you are a part of our family."

"Gratzie, Signore! Grazie!"

Maria decided to take the eastern bedroom so the sun would wake her in the morning as light entered through her window.

Daylight quickly faded, so the Watsons and the Sangierris unloaded their belongings from the wagons and put them away in the house. Lillian and Lisa were placed in the middle bedroom so they would be close to Maria should they need anything during the night. The boys moved into the west bedroom. All three boys would have to sleep in one bed for the time being. Later, as they got older and larger, the Watsons would install smaller single beds so each boy could sleep alone. With a new baby on the way, there might be a need for either an extra bed in the girls' room or four single beds in the boys' room.

While the women set up things in the house, Benjamin and the boys went out to check the barn and tend to the livestock. They moved the wagons into a field near the barn, then unhitched the oxen and Maria's mules. All the stock was placed in a pen just outside the barn on the far end. As they were loosed into the pen, Jack and the other horses ran and bucked enjoying the freedom of not being tied to a tree or a hitching rail. Maria's mules ran around braying at the top of their lungs. The oxen enjoyed the freedom as well. They sparred with each other, bumping heads and pushing each other back and forth.

Benjamin climbed a ladder that led up to a loft area. There, he found hay still being stored from previous seasons. The hay was a bit old, but it would be fine until other arrangements could be made. Benjamin found a pitchfork and began tossing the hay down into the pen. All of the livestock didn't seem to be too picky about it. They all gathered around the pile of hay and began eating.

Satisfied that the stock would be alright for the night, Benjamin gathered the boys, and they all began unloading tools and equipment from the wagon to store in the barn.

Benjamin discovered while unloading their equipment that the previous owners had left many tools and other items behind. He even found bags of grain and seeds for planting. Unfortunately, many of the grain bags had been damaged by rodents, but Benjamin found a grain bin made of wood that was full of grain untouched by rats or mice.

Daylight faded quickly, so Benjamin led the boys back to the house, hoping that supper might be ready. As they walked back to the house, crickets were chirping, bullfrogs were croaking from the creek bank, and quail were calling to one another, *"bobwhite! bobwhite!"*

Benjamin and the boys reached the back porch of the house and found a wash pan sitting on a stand with soap and a towel. Abigail had set it up for them to use before entering the house. Benjamin washed his face, arms, and neck, then dried off with the towel.

"Okay, boys. It's your turn."

Each of the boys imitated Benjamin in the washing regimen. They passed the towel to each other to dry themselves and followed Benjamin into the house. Abigail caught them at the door and instructed, "Leave your dirty shoes at the door. We just swept in here."

Benjamin pulled off his shoes and placed them against the wall out of the entryway of the door. Again, the boys did as he did. Next, they entered the dining room and found supper waiting for them.

As Benjamin entered the room, he asked Abigail, "Where should we all sit?"

Abigail replied, "Why don't you sit at the far end. I will sit on your right, then Lillian and William. Stevie, you sit at this end. Maria, will you sit on Benjamin's left, then Lisa, and then Angelo."

They all took their places at the table and waited to be served. Then, finally, Benjamin said, "Well, I think it would be fitting to give thanks for how we've been blessed before we eat."

Everyone bowed their heads as Benjamin began, "Dear God, we are so grateful for the way you have blessed our lives in allowing us to come to this place and make a new life for ourselves. We ask that you continue to bless us as we work together to make this farm a success. Bless Maria and the children in the loss of their dear father and husband along the way. But thank you for blessing us with their presence in our lives and as a new part of our family. We give you all glory, Father. Amen!"

Everyone repeated, *"Amen!"*

Maria and her two children crossed themselves in the manner that Catholics do. William noticed it and asked Angelo, "Why do you do that?"

Angelo looked a little embarrassed as he eyed his mother

for help. Abigail said, "William, it is a sign of their faith. They are Catholic and as part of their religion, whenever they pray they finish by saying to themselves, 'In the name of the Father, Son and Holy Ghost', as they make the sign of the cross."

William then asked, "Why don't we do that?"

Ma replied, "We just don't. Our religion is different from theirs. But, if you want to cross yourself after praying and recite the words, that's fine. Just understand what you are doing as Maria does. She understands that Jesus died on the cross for us and she honors his memory by doing so. Don't do it just because it looks fun. That's not what it's all about. Understand?"

"I think so, Ma."

After supper, they all gathered in the parlor to relax. Ma pulled out the family Bible and said, "Stevie, will you read for us?"

Stevie took the large book and turned to the page marked with a fabric bookmark. The marker led him to John chapter nineteen, the crucifixion of Jesus. As Stevie read, everyone listened intently. Although the Watson children had read about the crucifixion many times, it was as if they were hearing it for the first time with new ears. Maria's eyes watered as she listened to the reading. She wiped her tears away with her handkerchief. William noticed and asked, "Are you alright, Miss Maria?"

Through tears and sniffles, she replied, "Si, I am alright. I have not heard God's word read in a very long time. It is good to hear them again."

Curious, William asked, "Don't you have a Bible of your own?"

Maria answered, "No, Piccolo (*Little One*). Only the priest read God's holy words. Therefore, God speaks to us through the priest."

William had more questions he wanted to ask, and Abigail knew his questions would go on forever if she allowed them. So instead, she interrupted William and said, "Maria, maybe there will be a church in St. Joseph you can attend."

Maria replied, "Si, Signora Abigail. I hope so."

CHAPTER 16

Stevie awoke the next morning as sunlight breached the darkness of his room. William lay next to him, and Angelo was next to William. Stevie extracted himself from the bed, trying not to wake the younger boys. Stevie pulled off his nightshirt and dressed for the day.

He heard pans rustling in the direction of the kitchen as he approached the staircase. Once Stevie reached the bottom of the stairs, he made his way into the kitchen. There he found Maria and Ma already busy making breakfast. As Stevie entered the kitchen, Ma said, "Good morning, Stevie! How did you sleep last night?"

Stevie replied, "Not bad I guess. William kept stealing the covers and Angelo was snoring. But, I managed to get a little sleep."

Ma walked over, rustled Stevie's hair, and then said, "Would you mind bringing in some more firewood, please?"

Stevie replied, "Sure."

He walked out the back door, down the porch steps, and walked to the woodpile just a few feet away. There were two different piles of firewood. Some were cut to fit the giant fireplaces, and some were cut in shorter links and split into small pieces to fit in the stove. Stevie selected several sticks from the second pile and brought them into the kitchen for Ma.

Stevie set the arm full of wood onto a rack next to the stove. Then, he walked out to get more wood. He made several trips outside before the storage rack was full. He hoped it would be enough to last all day.

Stevie then asked, "Have you seen Pa yet?"

Ma replied, "I think he walked down to the barn to check on the stock. Why don't you walk down and tell him breakfast will be ready in about fifteen minutes?"

Stevie replied, "Yes ma'am."

He walked to the barn to look for Pa. When he reached the barn entrance, he saw hay falling to the ground at the far end of the structure. He knew Pa would be in the loft tossing hay down to the livestock. Stevie climbed the ladder up to the loft and found Pa steadily working at scooping up hay with the pitchfork and dropping the hay down to the animals.

"Pa, Ma says breakfast will be ready in fifteen minutes."

Benjamin looked back to see Stevie standing behind him. Pa replied, "Okay, son. Let's go!"

When Benjamin and Stevie arrived, breakfast was already on the table. Ma had prepared biscuits in her new stove along with fried potatoes and bacon. They all sat down at their places and began eating when Abigail said, "I sure wish we had some eggs. Do you think we could get some chickens?"

Benjamin replied, "I think we should be able to find someone willing to sell some chickens. How many do you think we'll need?"

Abigail pondered how many eggs she might need to feed this bunch in a day. "Well, I think we could get by with maybe twenty laying hens."

Benjamin said, "Alright. What else do we need?"

Stevie spoke up, "How about a cow?"

"Yes," replied Abigail. "We need fresh milk."

William wasn't going to be left out. "Can we get a dog?"

Benjamin asked, "What would you want with a dog?"

William shrugged his shoulders and said, "I don't know. I just want one."

Benjamin smiled at William and said, "Well, I don't see why we can't have a dog. As long as you're willing to take care of him. Maybe he could help keep away the varmints that might come after the chickens."

William's face lit up at Pa's reply.

Benjamin said, "I think I'll take a ride around the place this morning. See how the land lays out. Figure out what we might do with it. We could grow crops or raise cattle or horses. I'm not sure we could raise a lot of cattle on forty acres, but we could at least grow enough beef for ourselves."

Stevie asked, "Can I ride with you, Pa?"

"Sure, son. After that, we might ride into St. Joseph and see about getting your ma some chickens and a cow."

After breakfast, Pa and Stevie walked to the barn to saddle

their horses. They led Dusty and Jack out of the pen and then saddled them. They mounted the horses and rode to the front of Parish Place to begin inspecting their property. Barbed wire fence ran the length of the north end of the property except for the gap that allowed passage to the road. They began riding east, looking for the marker that signified the property's eastern boundary. They followed the fence line until the fence took a sharp right turn heading south. The terrain made a slight upward slope as the fence line continued. After riding nearly fifty yards, they reached a wooded area on the property. They had to slow their pace as they weaved between trees while continuing to keep the fence line in sight. The wooded area was filled with Pines and other varieties of Evergreens. Red Leafed Maples were scattered about as well as Dogwood and Crapes. Poplars were plentiful too.

Eventually, the fence line began turning slowly westward. The trees receded and then were absent as they continued to ride. Finally, Benjamin and Stevie came to the end of the fence row as it stopped at the Missouri River. The river was the western boundary of their property. A river tributary formed just a few yards from where the fence terminated. This was the creek that traveled past the barn and to their home, where the spring house was located.

Most of the land was pretty level. Level enough to plant crops anyway. The woods engulfed most of the land that sloped. The Watson's arrival so late in the year meant it was too late to plant fall crops like wheat, oats, or barley. Instead, they would need to begin soil preparation for the coming spring. Benjamin decided he needed to add a plow to the growing list of items to purchase for the homestead.

As he and Stevie rode back to the barn, Benjamin noticed that the supply of firewood was not nearly enough to get them through the winter. So, Benjamin dismounted at the woodshed to measure how much wood was still available. The wood shed measured sixteen feet wide and six feet tall at the highest point of the roof line. So, firewood could be stacked four feet high without any trouble. The shed also measured eight feet deep from front to back. So, Benjamin figured he could store four cords of firewood. Unfortunately, there was only about a rick of wood stored in there now, so he and the boys would need to get busy cutting wood.

Benjamin said to Stevie, "You ready to ride into town? We need to pick up some things for your ma."

"Yessir, Pa."

Benjamin then said, "Well let's hitch up the wagon. We'll need it for some of the supplies we'll be buying."

They rode back to the barn and hitched up Maria's mules to the wagon after putting the horses back in the pen.

The two of them drove the wagon down to the road that led back to St. Joe and rode back into town about an hour later. Their first stop was at the livery stable.

Johnson's Livery was located on the left side of Edmond Street. It was a large barn with three large rail fence corrals behind it. Inside the barn were ten stalls, a large tack room, and a smaller room where Avery Johnson slept.

Avery Johnson was a man of about forty years. He was completely bald on top. Every hair on his head seemed to gravitate to the tops of his ears and downward. His beard was snowy white, which made him look much older than forty. He had dark brown eyes and a long pointed nose. He was uneducated but still managed to run a business.

Benjamin pulled the wagon up to the barn then he and Stevie walked in to find the owner.

Avery saw them and walked forward to greet them. "Howdy! What can I do fer ya?"

Benjamin replied, "My name is Benjamin Watson. This is my son, Stevie. We just bought the old Parish Place."

Johnson said, "Well, nice ta meet ya! I'm Avery Johnson. I own this here establishment."

"Mr. Johnson..."

"Call me Avery."

"Avery, I was hoping you could help us find some of the things we're going to need to get our farm up and running."

Avery replied, "Sure! I know just about everybody round these parts. Just let me know what you need and I'll see what I can do."

Benjamin said, "The first thing we need is some laying hens.

We haven't had eggs since shortly after leaving Albany."

"Albany?" inquired Avery.

"New York," said Benjamin.

Avery replied, "I see. How many chickens are you wantin?"

Benjamin said, "My wife says we'll need at least twenty. We've got a big bunch to feed."

"Well, I'd say your best bet would be to drive up the road from your place and meet your neighbors. There are several small farms down that way. Nobody's gonna have that many chickens to get rid of all at once. But, you might get a few from this farmer and a few from another. See what I mean?"

Benjamin nodded. "Okay, I see what you mean."

Avery then said, "Come to think of it, you might try Noah Gentry's place. They raise a lot of chickens. They're a little farther up the road from you, but might have just what you're looking for."

"What about a milk cow?"

Avery replied, "Ah! Now that's an easy one. We've got a man here in town that owns a dairy. He delivers milk and butter and such all over town. Name's Bradley. Cecil Bradley. His farm is on the north side of St. Joe, but he's got a place here in town where he sells from. It's over on Jules Street. You might be able to buy a cow from him."

Benjamin said, "That sounds good. I appreciate your advice."

Avery replied, "No problem. If you're ever in need of horse shoeing or anything horse like, just come on back."

"I'll do that," said Benjamin. "Oh, by the way, if you hear of anyone needing a pair of oxen, I've got a pair for sale."

"Good pair are they?"

Benjamin replied, "They got us all the way from Albany without any problem. They're both strong and healthy."

Avery said, "I'll ask around. Could be some folks traveling west might need em. How much you asking?"

Benjamin said, "Well, I bought them for twenty dollars. I'd like to get that out of them."

Avery said, "Well, I hear tell people are gettin thirty dollars a pair for oxen around here. That's more than twenty isn't it?"

Benjamin wasn't sure if Avery was kidding or not. "Yeah, thirty's a bit more than twenty. Tell you what, Avery. Anything over twenty dollars that you can get for the oxen, I'll give to you for a finders fee."

Avery's eyes lit up. "Well, now. That's mighty kind of ya. I'll see what I can do."

Benjamin and Avery shook hands, then Avery reached over to shake Stevie's hand. "Nice to meet you, Stevie."

Stevie replied, "Nice to meet you, Mr. Johnson."

Benjamin and Stevie climbed back onto the wagon and began driving up the street, searching for the dairy. They continued on Edmond Street for two blocks before finding the intersection of Fourth Street which traveled north off Edmond and ran parallel to the river. They drove three blocks crossing Felix Street and Francis Street before finding Jules Street. Benjamin pulled up and looked both directions down Jules trying to figure out which direction he should turn. A well- dressed gentleman happened by as Benjamin and Stevie sat pondering at the intersection. Benjamin called to him, "Excuse me, sir. Can you tell me which way to Bradley's Dairy?"

"Certainly," replied the man. "Take a left. The dairy will be down on the right near the docks."

Benjamin thanked the man, then continued to drive toward the docks. Finally, Benjamin found a building on the right with a sign that read, "Bradley Dairy." Benjamin pulled up in front of the building, and he and Stevie walked into the building. A young man who couldn't have been more than twenty met him at the front counter and asked, "May I help you?"

Benjamin said, "Yes, I'm looking for Cecil Bradley."

"I'm Cecil Bradley."

Benjamin was a little shocked that such a young man would be the owner of such an industrious business.

"You're Mr. Bradley?"

Cecil replied, "Please, call me Cecil. May I ask your name?"

"I'm Benjamin Watson and this is my son, Stevie."

Cecil said, "It's a pleasure to meet you both. What can I do for you?"

Benjamin answered, "We just moved here from Albany,

New York. We live on the old Parish Place and we are in need of a few things to help us get started. Avery Johnson over at the livery stable told me you might have a milk cow for sale."

Cecil was a little surprised at Benjamin's request. "Benjamin, I make my living from my cows. I don't typically sell them. My business grows continually as the population of St. Joseph grows."

Benjamin, disappointed, replied, "I understand. We have a fairly large family; there's eight of us, and it just makes more sense for us to buy a cow rather than buy milk and butter from a dairy. I'm sorry to have bothered you."

As Benjamin started to leave, Cecil said, "Wait a minute. I do have an older cow that doesn't produce much for me anymore. She only gives about a gallon a day. She really isn't worth the feed we put into her. Would you be interested in her?"

Benjamin replied, "Sure! We could get by on a gallon of milk a day. How much do you want for her?"

Cecil offered, "How does twenty dollars sound?"

Benjamin then asked, "How old is she?"

"She's about nine years old. We've been milking her for seven years." Benjamin then asked, "Holstein? Brown Swiss?"

Cecil replied, "Jersey!"

Benjamin was pleased with Cecil's answer. Jersey cows were known for the butterfat content of their milk. A higher butterfat content meant more butter and cream. "I'll take her!"

Cecil called to another young man in the back of the office, "Jacob?" Jacob came to the front and waited for instructions.

"Jacob, this is Benjamin Watson and Stevie. Take them out to the farm and give them Jezabel. They've just purchased her."

Jacob looked puzzled when he heard what Cecil wanted him to do.

Benjamin asked, "Jezabel? Something tells me you're trying to pull a fast one on me."

Cecil chuckled and replied, "She's just a little temperamental. Don't let the name scare you. Just be careful when you're milking her. You might want to hobble her to keep her from kicking over the bucket."

Benjamin smirked at Cecil's answer, then handed over the

twenty dollars.

CHAPTER 17

Benjamin and Stevie followed Jacob down the road and out of town, riding north. They traveled for thirty minutes before reaching Bradley Dairy Farm. Benjamin was impressed with how extravagant the farm was. There was a large white framed house on the property, not unlike the Watson's home. Behind the house stood a large barn that had been painted red. "Bradley" was painted on the side of the barn in large black letters. The Barn was three times the size of Benjamin's barn.

As they drove closer to the barn, Benjamin and Stevie saw a large pen on the left that must have been at least an acre in size. The pen held four Jersey bulls. In a pasture behind the bullpen were at least twenty yearling calves grazing. Jacob pointed to the calves and said, "Those heifers were born last year. They will be our replacement heifers for cows that no longer produce enough."

Benjamin asked, "How many cows do you milk?"

Jacob replied, "Right now we milk fifty cows a day."

Benjamin asked, "You sell that much milk everyday?"

"No. We sell a lot of milk but we also produce butter and cheese. Cheese is a big part of our business. We ship it to other parts of the country."

Benjamin asked, "How many acres do you farm?"

Jacob replied, "We farm about six hundred acres. It takes a lot of acreage to raise enough feed for all these dairy cows."

Benjamin replied, "I've never heard of anything like this. It's very impressive."

Jacob took them back to an area behind the barn where several cows were housed. Jacob called a young man over and said, "Put a rope on Jezebel and bring her out. These folks just bought her."

The young man did as Jacob instructed, and moments later, he walked out of the lot, leading a large Jersey cow. He handed the end of the rope to Benjamin and said, "Here you go, Mister."

Benjamin tied the rope to the back of the wagon and shook Jacob's hand. "Thanks, Jacob!"

Jacob replied, "Don't mention it. Good luck! She can be a handful."

Benjamin drove the wagon back down the road heading for St. Joseph.

Thirty minutes later, they pulled back onto Jules Street and turned right. Benjamin noticed a blacksmith shop on the right and pulled up to the door of the shop.

Benjamin got down from the wagon and walked into the shop, leaving Stevie behind to watch the wagon and the cow. A burly man with a red beard was inside the shop hammering a piece of metal against an anvil. A red-hot fire was burning behind him. Periodically, the man would stick his piece of metal into the fire to heat it up, then take it back out and hammer it some more.

Benjamin walked over to the smith and said, "Excuse me!"

The man looked up and finally noticed Benjamin. "Hmm? Oh, hello there. Good day to you, sir. How may I help you."

The smithy spoke with a strong Irish brogue.

Benjamin said, "My name is Benjamin Watson. I'm new to the area."

"My name is Sean Flynn. Nice to meet you, Mr. Watson."

Benjamin asked, "Do you know where I can get a turning plow?"

Sean said, "Aye, that I do. I has a few already to go in the back. Would you care to take a peek?"

Benjamin replied, "Yes, thank you."

Sean led Benjamin to the back of the shop. He pointed out three plows, each a little different in size. "What are you planning to pull with?"

Benjamin replied, "Two mules."

"Aye, that'll do her. I recommend this little lady. She's a wee bit heavy. Wouldn't recommend you try to pull it with one horse, but two mules will do the job. That little lady will last you two life times. She's sturdy and well built."

Benjamin asked, "How much?"

Sean replied, "Five dollars."

Benjamin said, "I'll take it."

"Would you be having a wagon for us to load her onto?"

Benjamin replied, "Yes, it's out front."

"Just pull her around back here and we'll load up your plow. I have a hoist that will do the trick. Getting her unloaded will be your own problem."

Sean raised the plow into the air with the hoist while Benjamin drove the wagon to the back of the shop and moved it as close to the back door as he could. Sean then lowered the plow into the back of the wagon and unhooked it from the hoist. Next, he and Benjamin lay the plow onto its side to help it ride better.

"There you go, now. She's all ready for you."

Benjamin handed Sean five dollars and thanked him. Then, he and Stevie got back onto the wagon and were on their way again. Thirty minutes later, they pulled into Parish Place and drove to the barn to unload the plow. Stevie untied Jezebel from the wagon and led her into the pen with the oxen and horses. Benjamin backed the wagon into the wide doorway of the barn. He tied a heavy rope around the plow and ran it through a pulley. Then he raised the plow enough to get it out of the wagon bed. Stevie drove the mules forward from under the plow so Benjamin could lower the plow to the ground.

Once the plow was secured in the barn and out of the way, Benjamin and Stevie unhitched the mules from the wagon and walked back to the house to check on lunch.

Ma and Maria had prepared a light lunch of sliced bread, cheese, and apple slices. By the time Benjamin and Stevie made it to the dining room, the rest of the family had already finished. Benjamin and Stevie made a cheese sandwich and grabbed apple slices to nibble on later. Stevie wrapped his apple slices in his kerchief and shoved it into his trouser pocket.

They ate the cheese sandwiches as they walked together back to the barn. Then, Stevie asked, "What are we going to do now, Pa?"

Pa said, "Let's saddle the horses again and take a ride down the road and see if our neighbors have any chickens for sale."

When Benjamin and Stevie got to the pen to retrieve their horses, they found Jezebel harassing and bullying the other livestock. She seemed especially aggressive with the oxen even though they were much larger than she. As Stevie and Benjamin entered the pen, Jezebel stopped and lifted her head as if she were smelling the air. A most desirable scent had caught her attention. She walked toward Stevie, still smelling the air. Jezebel lowed a deep gravelly "*moo*" as she moved closer.

Stevie grew nervous as the Jersey moved closer to him. He wasn't sure if she intended to harm him or just wanted to get to know him. Jezebel continued her lowing as she got even closer. Finally, she stopped in front of Stevie and began sniffing his trousers.

Stevie looked at Pa and said, "She smells my apples! Can I give her some?"

Pa jestingly replied, "I think you'd better. You might not make it out of here if you don't."

Stevie pulled his kerchief out of his pocket and opened it up. He took one of the apple slices and offered it to Jezebel. She quickly accepted the morsel and began to chew with satisfaction in her eyes. Stevie handed her another slice and then another until they were all gone. He rubbed the cow's face as she contentedly chewed the apple pieces. Drool dripped from her mouth, as she chewed the sweet bits of fruit.

Benjamin commented, "Looks like you've made a friend."

Stevie smiled as he continued to rub the cow's face.

Once the apple slices were gone, Stevie and Benjamin saddled their horses and began the ride southward from Parish Place. They came across several tiny farms along their way and met some of the families who tended them. But, unfortunately, none of them had enough chickens; they couldn't spare any to sell.

Benjamin and Stevie finally found the farm Avery had mentioned. The Gentry Farm was about a mile away from Parish Place. Noah Gentry and his wife Beverly owned twenty acres on the east side of the road that led to Kansas City. They raised chickens, guineas, and turkeys on their farm. They shipped the eggs to St. Joseph to be sold at the various dry goods shops, restaurants, and hotels.

Noah and Beverly had come to the St. Joseph area ten years earlier from Virginia. They were in their thirties back then, young and full of hope and drive. They built their business slowly over time as they saw a need and decided to fulfill it.

When Benjamin and Stevie rode up to the Gentry's house, they were amazed at how many birds were scattered around the place. Guineas announced their arrival as the father and son rode forward. Beverly came out of the house to see what the commotion was all about.

"Good afternoon, ma'am." said Benjamin.

"Good afternoon." she replied.

"I'm Benjamin Watson and this is my son Stevie. We just moved into the old Parish Place."

Beverly replied, "Oh, well nice to meet you. Won't you step down?" Benjamin and Stevie dismounted and walked toward the house to meet Beverly.

"We're trying to get set up on our place. There's eight of us in all. We were hoping you and your husband might be willing to sell us some laying hens." Beverly said, "Oh, sure! How many do you want?"

Benjamin replied, "Well, could you spare maybe twenty, and a rooster too?"

"I get twenty-five cents each for pullets, fifty cents for layers, and fifty cents for roosters. All my chickens are Leghorns."

Benjamin said, "Oh, that's fine. I'll take twenty layers and a rooster then."

Beverly then offered, "If you like, Noah can deliver them tomorrow morning, say around eight?"

Benjamin said, "That would be perfect, ma'am."

Benjamin paid Beverly five dollars and fifty cents, then he and Stevie got back on their horses and waved goodbye.

When they got back to the house, Benjamin told Stevie, "We need to get a place ready for the chickens. We'll want them to roost in the same spot every night. We'll fix up one of the stalls so the chickens will want to roost in there."

The first thing they did was build a row of nesting boxes in the stall. They lined three walls with the boxes and attached them to the wall about four feet high from the floor. Then Benjamin and Stevie searched the wooded area of the farm for suitable tree limbs they could set up inside the stall for the birds to roost on during the night. Benjamin wanted green limbs so they would last a while. He was afraid dried limbs might break under the weight of so many birds. They found four suitable limbs, cut them from their trees, and then dragged them back to the barn. They bucked the smaller unwanted branches from the limbs, then raised them into the corners of the stall and attached them with rope. Some roosts were hung up high, about six feet from the ground, while others were hung about five feet up.

By the time they finished the coop, it was time for Jezebel to be milked. Benjamin grabbed the milk bucket that had been left by the previous tenants, as well as a milking stool. He set them aside in the main entrance of the barn, then proceeded to catch up Jezebel to bring her inside. He and Stevie walked out together into the pen. Jezebel looked at them and lowed, "*Moo!*"

Jezebel walked up to Stevie, expecting more of the bits of apple. But, instead, Stevie reached up, rubbed her face, and spoke softly to her. "Hey, Jezebel! Good girl! I don't have any apples for you. How bout some corn, though."

Stevie wrapped a rope around the cow's neck and led her into the barn. He tied her up in the middle of the entry and opened the top of the grain bin where the corn was stored. Stevie scooped some of the corn out and placed it into a flat wooden box on the floor where Jezebel could reach it. Jezebel began gobbling up the corn as quickly as she could. Even though she had no other cows to compete against for the corn, old habits are hard to break.

Benjamin took the milking stool, set it next to her hind quarters, and sat down. He placed the milking bucket under her but not too far back; he didn't want her to step into the bucket while he milked her. He then showed Stevie how to milk her.

"Always warm you hands before you grab her teats. You don't want to surprise her."

Benjamin cupped his hands together and blew into them, then rubbed his hands together to warm them.

"Now, grab the teat at the top and roll your fingers down the teat to work the milk down and out of the teat. Like this."

Benjamin demonstrated his technique to Stevie, showing him how the milk should flow out of the teat. He then used his other hand as he grabbed a different teat. Finally, he rolled his fingers down the teats and drummed out a beat into the bucket. *Shick! Shick! Shick! Shick!*

"Now, you try it."

Stevie bent down next to his father and warmed his hands before grabbing the first teat. He squeezed it, but nothing happened. He tried again, but still, nothing happened.

Benjamin grabbed Stevie's hand and said, "Like this. Push your hand up against the bag and lift up. That helps the milk drop down into the teat. Then squeeze your forefinger, middle finger, ring finger and your pinky."

Milk squirted out of the teat but missed the bucket.

"That's right! Now you just have to aim for the bucket. Give it a try!"

Stevie gave it another try by himself. Success! Milk came out of the teat and landed in the bucket. *Shick!* "I did it, Pa! I did it!"

"Good work, son! Now keep going and get into a rhythm. Once you empty those teats, then milk the other two."

Stevie continued honing his milking skills until he had emptied her bag. Then, suddenly, Jezebel kicked over the bucket with her rear leg and spilled the milk.

Stevie disappointedly yelled, "Aw, Jezebel! Look what you did!"

Benjamin shook his head in disgust. "Sorry, son. I forgot what the Bradleys told us about hobbling her. We'll try again in the morning."

Chapter 18

The next morning, Pa woke Stevie at daybreak.

"Come on, son. We've got work to do."

Stevie got out of bed and dressed, then met Pa downstairs. They left the house together and made their way to the barn.

"Go catch up Jezebel and bring her in here for milking. I'll get some rope so we can hobble her this time."

Stevie walked into the pen and called Jezebel. She lowed to Stevie as she walked toward him. Stevie looped a rope around her head, then looped it over the bridge of her nose and tied it to make a halter. Then he led her into the barn where Pa was waiting.

Benjamin had already scooped corn into the feeder for her. Jezebel greedily began eating the corn as Pa tied a rope around the hocks of her back legs to keep her from kicking. Stevie sat down on the stool and began milking the Jersey as if he had been doing it all his life. While Stevie did the milking, Benjamin climbed the ladder to the loft and began tossing hay down to the other livestock.

Stevie found the rhythm Pa had told him about. *Shick! Shick! Shick!* The milk sprayed from Jezebel's udders into the bucket. The sound of the milking was relaxing. Stevie allowed his head to rest against the cow's flanks as he milked her. He heard the rumbles within her belly as she swallowed her corn. When Stevie had emptied the front teats of their contents, he moved to the back pair and continued. *Shick! Shick! Shick!*

When Pa finished feeding the stock, he climbed down the ladder and met up with Stevie, who was finishing the milking. Pa watched his son as he worked. He was proud of how quickly Stevie learned things. Stevie was smart and rarely made mistakes. But, when he did, he learned from his mistakes.

Once he was done, Stevie moved the milk bucket out of the way before untying Jezebel's back legs. He led her back to the stock pen to be with the other animals, then picked up the bucket to carry back home. Stevie struggled a bit as he carried the bucket; milk began to slosh. Benjamin reached down and took one side of the pail to help Stevie.

When they walked in the back door, Abigail was pleased to see they were delivering fresh milk. She took the milk bucket from Stevie, strained it through a cheesecloth into a clean pitcher, and placed it on the kitchen table. Maria brought in biscuits and bacon and set them on the table as the other children came in for breakfast.

Benjamin spoke up as they all sat around the table, enjoying their meal.

"William, you and Angelo are going to start helping around here. You're both old enough to do chores now. So after breakfast, you two will come out, and Stevie and I will show you what to do."

Abigail asked, "What about school? Stevie and the younger boys need their schooling."

"They can do their learning after supper. There's too much to do around here to waste the daylight hours doing something that can be done at night. We've got to get ready for winter and we're going to need everyone to pitch in some to get it all done."

Abigail asked, "Well, what needs to be done?"

"We need to cut hay and get it stored in the loft before winter sets in and we need to cut and split enough firewood to last us through the winter."

William asked, "What will be my job?"

Pa replied, "I need you and Angelo to work together everyday. You will be responsible for gathering eggs every morning. You'll also need to make sure that enough firewood is brought in to last each day. That means for the fireplace in the parlor and the stove in the kitchen."

William asked, "What's Stevie doing? Why can't he do the firewood?"

"Stevie has his own jobs to do. He does the milking everyday and he'll be helping me cut and split firewood as well as cutting and storing the hay."

Suddenly, a wagon could be heard pulling up outside. Benjamin said, "That will be Mr. Gentry with our chickens."

Pa got up from the table and went outside to meet Noah Gentry. Stevie was close on his heels. A wagon pulled up near the house's back door, and a man with black curly hair raised his hand and said, "Howdy! You must be Mr. Watson."

Benjamin replied, "Benjamin! Are you Mr. Gentry?"

"Just call me Noah!"

Benjamin said, "You want to pull up to the barn and we'll unload the chickens?"

Noah drove the wagon up to the barn entrance and waited for Benjamin and Stevie to catch up to him. Benjamin looked into the back of the wagon and saw a canvas tarp. Noah pulled the tarp back to reveal twenty hens and a rooster with their feet tied together.

"Here you go!" said Noah.

Benjamin started grabbing chickens by the feet and handed two to Stevie. "Take them into the coop, Stevie and start untying their feet. I'll keep bringing them in to you until we get them all in."

Stevie carried his two hens into the barn and placed them into the stall they had chosen to be their coop. He untied the hens' feet and let them loose. They ran from him and scattered to the far corners of the stall. Pa brought in two more and shut the door as he left to get more hens. They continued the process until Noah's wagon was empty.

Benjamin shook hands with Noah, then Noah drove back to his farm. When Benjamin returned to the coop, he said, "Why don't we toss down some of the hay and put it into the coop? It will give the chickens something to scratch around in til they get used to their new home."

Benjamin climbed the loft ladder and tossed a few forks full of hay to Stevie. Stevie carefully opened the coop door to throw the hay in. Benjamin found an empty bucket in the barn, walked down to the creek, filled the pail, and then placed it in the coop so the chickens would have fresh water to drink.

Stevie asked, "Now what, Pa?"

"Well, I think I need to start cutting some hay. Do you think you could work with the younger boys and get started on the firewood? I need you to move all the wood that's in the woodshed to one side so we can make room to bring in more wood. I need you to take a hatchet and split some of the wood that's in the shed so it will fit in the stove. Maybe you can split and let the little boys stack it."

"Sure, Pa. We can do that."

"Just be careful, son. That hatchet is mighty sharp. When I

was your age I tried to cut down a tree with my pa's ax. I didn't have a good grip on it though and when the ax head hit the tree, the ax head twisted in my hand and bounced off. It hit me in the ankle and I bled something awful. Ma had to put a few stitches in my ankle to make it quit bleeding."

Stevie felt a little sick to his stomach but replied, "I'll be careful, Pa."

Stevie grabbed the hatchet while Benjamin found the scythe in the barn. They began to walk toward the house when Abigail, Maria, and all the children walked up to meet them. Abigail said, "We wanted to get a look at the chickens and the cow."

The ladies and the children peeked through the spaces between the boards that made up the stall walls. They smiled as they watched the birds scratching around in the hay bedding on the coop floor. A few of the hens were perched on the branches that hung in the corners of the stall. Others were sitting in the nesting boxes attached to the walls.

Abigail looked at Benjamin and said, "I can't wait until we have fresh eggs again!"

Benjamin replied, "You shouldn't have to wait long. Looks like some of them are already setting up their nest."

He then looked at William and said, "Now William, you and Angelo need to come out every morning and collect the eggs for your ma."

"Yes, Pa."

Abigail then asked, "Where's the cow?" Benjamin replied, "This way."

Benjamin led the way through the barn and showed them the livestock pen at the back of the structure. There, Abigail, Maria, and the children got their first sight of their prized possession.

Abigail exclaimed, "Oh, she's beautiful!"

Stevie offered, "Her name's Jezebel!"

"Jezebel? Why did you name her Jezebel?"

Benjamin replied, "We didn't. The Bradley's named her. Turns out she can be a handful. The first time we tried to milk her she knocked over the bucket full of milk, out of spite."

"My word!" replied Abigail. "How did you manage to get

milk this morning?"

Stevie said, "We hobbled her back legs."

"Stevie, did you milk her any?"

"Yessum. I milked all of her this morning." Ma asked, "Do you like milking?"

"Sure do, Ma. I find it kinda relaxing."

Ma smiled at her oldest son and rustled his hair.

Abigail then said, "Well, we came to help. What do you want us to do?"

Benjamin replied, "Stevie and the boys are going to work on the wood pile. I was just getting ready to start cutting some hay. Do you want to help with that?"

Abigail said, "Sure! Do you have another scythe?"

Benjamin pointed to the corner of the barn and said, "There's two or three over there. Are you sure you feel like doing this? What about the baby?" Abigail replied, "I'm fine! The exercise will do me good. I'll take it easy, don't worry."

Abigail picked up one of the scythes, and Maria followed by taking one herself. They followed Benjamin to the front of the property, where they began cutting the tall grass. First, the women watched Benjamin as he swung the scythe backward, then swung it down toward the ground. The blade easily sliced through the tall sprigs of vegetation as he swung through. Next, he slowly walked along the edge of the uncut grass and continued cutting it down. Abigail picked a spot close by and began swinging her scythe too. It took her a little while to get the hang of it, but the cutting was easy once she did. Then Maria began cutting. She wasn't comfortable using the long implement. She struggled at first. A couple of times, she snagged the end of the blade into the dirt. However, eventually, she got the hang of it and was cutting right alongside Abigail and Benjamin. Lisa and Lillian played in the tall grass nearby. The parents heard the girls as they giggled together, chasing butterflies and picking wildflowers.

Periodically, Benjamin would pull a file out of the back pocket of his trousers and run it down the length of his scythe blade to sharpen it. Then he would return to cutting. Sometimes he would trade tools with one of the women so he could sharpen their blades too.

Meanwhile, the boys worked together, moving the stacks of wood in the shed. Finally, Stevie instructed the younger boys, "Why don't you two go ahead and load the wood boxes in the house while I start splitting some of this to go in the stove."

William was somewhat disappointed that he couldn't go and play today like he and Angelo had done the previous days.

"Alright. Come on, Angelo."

Some of the logs were quite heavy for the small young seven-year-olds. So they had to carry some of them together. The logs were nearly three feet long, but they finally managed to fill the wood box next to the parlor fireplace.

Then, Stevie said, "Come on. I need you to help me cut some of these logs in half so I can split them for the kitchen stove."

The boys lifted the longer logs onto a set of crossed boards that were set up like a saw horse. Then, Angelo and William held the log steady as Stevie pulled the bow saw across the middle of the log until he sawed it into two smaller lengths. They did this several times until Stevie was tired from the sawing. After he rested, he picked up the hatchet and began splitting slabs away from the smaller logs to make them small enough to go into the wood stove. William and Angelo stacked the sticks in the woodshed as Stevie cut them. By the end of the day, the boys had managed to split and stack all the available wood in the shed.

As the sun began to fade into the western horizon, Stevie said, "Come on. It's time to milk ole Jezebel."

William asked, "Can we help?"

Stevie said, "How bout you just watch this time? I'll show you how it's done. Maybe you can help next time. Only, don't get in the way. Ole Jezebel might kick you."

"We won't," said William.

The boys all walked to the barn together and walked through to catch up Jezebel. Stevie called to her, and she lowed as she saw him. "*Moo!*"

Jezebel walked forward and met Stevie as he put the rope halter on her, then led her into the barn. Stevie poured corn into her feeder box, then set up the milk pail and stool. Angelo and William stood next to Stevie as he crouched on the stool and began pulling on the cow's teats. As milk sprayed into the bucket, the two boys giggled. Jezebel seemed to respond to their giggles as she switched her tail, slapping Angelo across the face.

Angelo screamed out, "Ah!" as mud from her tail swiped across his face. Angelo backed away from the cow and was silent as he tried to decide how he felt about his situation.

William turned and began to laugh when he saw the mud painted across Angelo's face. Then, Jezebel swiped William's face too. Mud crossed his face and found its way into his mouth because it was opened as he laughed at Angelo. William began to spit, trying to free his mouth of the mud that had invaded his palette.

Stevie snickered to himself at the boys as he continued his milking.

CHAPTER 19

For the next few weeks, the Watsons and Maria's family worked together cutting, raking, and storing hay, then cutting and splitting firewood. Benjamin felt assured they would be well-supplied for the winter. However, he wasn't really sure what to expect in the way of winter weather in Missouri. He knew Albany presented unbearable winters; snow at times was as deep as three feet with blistering winds. Shops and businesses were shut down most of the time.

If it happened to get that bad in Missouri, Benjamin wanted to be prepared. The family gathered food and stored it in the spring house cellar. Benjamin hunted game and did some trapping along the Missouri River. Stevie helped by tending to the cow and providing the family with milk. William and Angelo had learned to do their part by gathering eggs every morning and keeping the wood box full inside the house.

Gathering eggs sometimes proved to be challenging for the younger boys. The hens weren't always willing to give up their eggs very easily. So when William or Angelo tried to reach under the hens while they sat on the eggs, the boys often received a quick peck on the hand. It startled the boys more than it hurt; although sometimes the hens would draw blood. They also had to deal with the rooster. The old cock seemed determined to torment the young boys every time they entered the coop. Eventually, the boys learned to open the door to the coop and allow the chickens to run free during the day, then close them up at night. That allowed them to collect the eggs unmolested.

A month after arriving at their new home, Benjamin decided they would take the day off one Sunday morning. Of course, they still had daily chores, but the two families drove into town to attend church once they finished.

The ladies loaded up in one of the wagons with the four youngest children sitting in the back. Benjamin and Stevie rode ahead of them, riding on horseback. As they entered the town, Benjamin pulled up at Johnson's Livery and walked inside to find Avery

Johnson.

"Hello!" cried out Benjamin.

Avery poked his head out of one of the stalls and said, "I'm over here."

"Avery, it's me, Benjamin Watson."

"Oh, howdy, Benjamin! What can I do for you?"

Benjamin asked, "Can you tell me where we can find a church here in town?"

Avery said, "Oh, that's an easy one. Go up here a ways til you see Francis Street. Follow Francis til you get to Ninth Street, then take a left. Then, go down a ways til you see Church Street. Guess why they call it Church Street?"

Benjamin smiled as he replied, "I'm guessing that's where all the churches are located?"

Avery said, "You got it, son! Oh, by the way. I think I may have a buyer for those oxen. Why don't you bring them by this week and I'll pay you for them."

Benjamin said, "That sounds good. I'll bring them by tomorrow."

Avery said, "See you then. Happy Sunday to you!"

Benjamin climbed back onto Jack and led the way to Church Street. They turned right onto Church Street and almost immediately saw a large stone structure on the left. A sign outside the building read, "Cathedral of St. Joseph." Several families were walking into the front door of the cathedral.

Benjamin stopped just outside and said to Maria, "Would you like us to let you out here? We can pick you up later."

Maria smiled as she responded, "Oh si, Signore Benjamin!"

Maria, Lisa, and Angelo climbed down from the wagon and proceeded into the large church.

Benjamin said, "Well, let's see what else they have down the street."

There were several churches along the street, and they all seemed to be the first of their kind; First Presbyterian Church was across from the Catholic church. Then they found the First United Methodist Church next to it. Across from that church was the First Christian Church. Finally, they saw what they had hoped for; The

First Baptist Church of St. Joseph.

Although it wasn't as grand as the cathedral up the street, it was larger than any other church the Watsons had ever attended. Benjamin found a place where others were parking their wagons and pulled in next to them.

The Watsons walked together with other families as they eyed the large white building with a bell in the tower announcing that it was time to come to worship. They walked along a stone walkway that led to the front of the church. Two men stood outside the doorway, greeting people as they entered the sanctuary.

Abigail walked arm in arm with Benjamin as they walked through the doorway. As they entered the sanctuary, they were amazed at how large it was. The ceiling stretched upward at least twenty feet. Large beams encased the room, framing the arched stained glass windows lining the north and south walls. Each window displayed a story from the Bible. On the eastern wall behind the pulpit was an even larger window showing an image of Jesus hanging on a cross. The Watsons, especially the children, were fascinated by the windows. They had never seen such extravagance in a church before.

Benjamin led his family to a bench that was only half filled with worshippers. He allowed Abigail to lead the family into position with the children following; Benjamin sat on the aisle.

As worship service began, the congregation stood to sing the selected hymns led by the pastor. The songs were all familiar to Abigail, and she sang along with the congregation. Chills ran down her spine as the songs echoed throughout the sanctuary. She had never experienced such worship as this in their little local church in Albany.

After worship was concluded, the Watsons returned to the wagon and drove up the street to meet Maria and her children. Once they picked up the Sangierris from the cathedral, they returned home to have lunch. They spent most of the day relaxing on the front porch. It was the first time they could sit and relax since arriving at their new home.

Just before dusk, Stevie walked to the barn to milk Jezebel. Benjamin walked along with him so he could feed the livestock.

Benjamin said, "Stevie, Avery Johnson found a buyer for our oxen. He said we could bring them by this week and he'd pay us for them."

Stevie said, "That's great, Pa! How much?"

"Twenty dollars, at least that's what we agreed he'd pay us. He's probably selling them for more than that."

Stevie then asked, "Can I go with you?"

Benjamin replied, "No, I don't think so."

Stevie was a little disappointed at his pa's answer.

Then Benjamin said, "I was thinking I'd let you take the oxen by yourself so I can continue working here."

Stevie's face lit up. "You mean it, Pa?"

"Sure! I think you're old enough and responsible enough to handle it on your own. You can leave after you do the milking in the morning."

Stevie replied, "Thanks, Pa. I won't let you down."

The next morning, Stevie awoke early in anticipation of the day. It would be the first time Stevie had traveled anywhere alone. Of course, he knew it was a great responsibility his pa had placed upon him, but he was excited to prove he could be trusted with such a task.

Stevie finished the milking and delivered the milk to Ma. As he stepped out the door, Ma called to him, "Stevie, where are you going in such a rush?"

Stevie replied, "Pa wants me to take the oxen to town for him."

"Not yet, you don't. Come in here and have your breakfast, then you can leave."

Stevie's shoulders slumped as he returned to the dining room to join his family for breakfast. Although he hated to admit it, Stevie enjoyed every bite of the fried eggs and bacon Ma had cooked. He washed it down with a fresh glass of Jezebel's milk, then asked, "May I be excused?"

Pa said, "Hang on there, son. Let me finish my breakfast, then I'll help you catch up the oxen. There's no hurry. Enjoy the day!"

Stevie waited impatiently as everyone, but he, finished their breakfast. It seemed to Stevie to be the longest breakfast ever served at any time and any place on earth. He watched in anticipation as Pa slowly took each bite of his bacon and eggs, then sipped his coffee. Everyone except Stevie seemed at ease as they discussed what they had planned for the day. Ma and Maria planned on doing the laundry and baking bread. William and Angelo thought they might get in some fishing down at the bank of the Missouri. Ma thought otherwise. "You boys don't go near that river without Pa! You can fish in the creek instead."

Pa talked about cutting down some more trees so they could build a smokehouse. Stevie quietly sat while he waited, even though it took every ounce of his energy to do so. *"Will this breakfast never end?"* he thought to himself.

Finally, Pa finished his last sip of coffee and decided it was time to put Stevie out of his misery. Pa stood up from the table and said, "Okay, boy. Let's go."

Stevie dashed out of the dining room and out the back door as he ran to the barn. He saddled Dusty, led her out of the corral, and then tied her up at the barn door. Pa walked up and said, "Okay, let's round up those oxen."

Benjamin took two lengths of rope and handed one to Stevie. Pa walked into the stock pen and looped his rope over the head of the first ox. He passed the rope to Stevie, then roped the other ox. Stevie and Pa led the oxen out of the pen together and towed them to where Dusty was waiting.

Stevie mounted Dusty, and then Pa handed him the ends of the lead ropes so Stevie could escort them to town.

Benjamin instructed Stevie, "Be watchful and be smart."

"I will, Pa."

Stevie walked his painted pony down the path that led to the road to St. Joseph. He wore a huge smile when he left home on this critical mission. Stevie held tightly to the ropes leading the oxen as he walked his pony down the road.

As he came within sight of Avery's livery, he noticed a freight wagon pulled up next to Avery's barn. When he got closer, he saw the wagon was loaded with grain sacks, and men were unloading them into Avery's barn.

Stevie rode up to the barn and tied Dusty to a hitching rail. He then dragged the oxen with him as he searched for Avery. Stevie found Avery watching the men as they unloaded the wagon.

Stevie announced, "Mr. Johnson, I brought the oxen to you for my pa."

Avery glanced at Stevie and recognized him as Benjamin Watson's boy. "Okay, son. Put them in one of those empty stalls back there."

Stevie did as Avery requested and stood by until Avery finished his business with the freight men. Stevie watched as the men finished unloading the grain sacks from the wagon. He counted eighteen bags on the ground, with two more still in the wagon. Once they unloaded the last two sacks, one of the men said to Avery, "Okay Avery, that's twenty sacks of grain at a dollar twenty-five each. That comes to Thirty dollars."

Avery questioned the man, "Wasn't it twenty-seven last month?"

"Yeah, but it's gone up this month. Who knows, it might go up even more next month."

Avery shook his head as he pulled out his purse and searched for the money when Stevie said, "Excuse me, Mr. Johnson."

"Just a minute, boy. I'll be right with you."

"Yessir," replied Stevie. "It's just that, I think you're being charged too much."

Avery stopped what he was doing and looked at Stevie, "What do you mean?"

Stevie glanced at the two men and saw fire in their eyes as he told Avery, "They told you each sack cost a dollar twenty-five, right?"

Avery said, "Yeah, that's right."

"Well then, you owe them twenty-five dollars, not thirty. A dollar twenty-five times twenty is twenty-five."

Avery looked at the man and said, "Nate Henry, you've been cheating me all this time. Well you won't be doing it anymore. Here!"

Avery held out twenty-five dollars and waited for Henry to take it. But, instead, the man sneered at Stevie and said, "Kind of nosey, ain't you boy?"

Stevie remained silent but didn't move.

"I ought to tan your hide you little turd!"

Avery said, "I've got a better idea. Why don't you leave before I call the sheriff and tell him what you've been up to? Don't come back here again. I'll be buying my grain elsewhere."

Nate angrily snatched the money from Avery's grasp and left. As Nate and his son drove away, Avery looked at Stevie and asked, "What's your name again, son?"

"Stevie Watson. I'm Benjamin Watson's son."

Avery then asked, "Where'd you learn to cipher like that?"

"From my ma. She teaches me how to read, how to do arithmetic and lots of stuff."

Avery asked, "How old are you, Stevie?"

"I'll be nine next month."

"Hmm. How'd you like a job working for me." Stevie replied, "Really?"

"Sure, I could use some help. Especially when it comes to keeping up with money and such. I never got any schooling myself. But, it'd be hard work. You'd have to muck out stalls and brush down folks' horses and other things. What do ya say?"

Stevie said, "I'd love to but, I'd have to ask Pa first."

Avery said, "I'll pay you seventy-five cents a day. If you can't work everyday, that's okay. Just as long as you can work at least three days a week and one of those days has to be Monday. That's the day I get my deliveries."

Stevie replied, "I'll ask and let you know in a day or two. I need to get back home right now. Did you have some money for my pa?"

Avery said, "Oh, sure. I almost forgot."

Avery shelled out twenty dollars and handed it to Stevie. "Here you go. Let me know as quick as you can."

"I will! Thanks!"

CHAPTER 20

While Stevie delivered the oxen to Avery Johnson's livery, Benjamin took his ax and walked up the hill to find suitable trees to cut down for the smokehouse. First, he searched for young trees that wouldn't have to be split; he could simply stack them like a log cabin.

A cool breeze whisked its way through the trees as he searched for suitable trees to use. Most of the conifer were bare of leaves, but a few still fell from the sky as the wind freed them from their stems. As a result, the ground was covered with orange and brown leaves, and they rustled as Benjamin walked through them.

An acorn fell from high above and hit Benjamin on the top of his head. When he looked up to see from where it fell, Benjamin saw two squirrels playing together, running circles around and around the trunk of a large Oak.

After quite some time, Benjamin found what he was hoping for. A tall, straight Poplar with few branches. It was only about eight inches in diameter. It would be a perfect start for his smokehouse.

Benjamin took his ax and began swinging it at the tree's base. As he carved a notch into the tree, large chips started to fly through the air. Benjamin continued to chop until he had cut nearly through the tree trunk. Then, he heard the tree moan and creak as it started to lean and it slowly fell to the earth with a crash.

Benjamin searched for his next victim. He eyed another Poplar nearly identical in size to the first. He decided which way he wanted the tree to fall, then began chopping on the opposite side of the tree trunk. Again, large chips flew away from the tree as he swung his ax and struck the tree. It took very little time for him to chop halfway through. Suddenly, the wind gusted and caused the tree to lean in the wrong direction. Benjamin braced the tree with his hand, trying to keep it from falling toward him. He heard a loud "*crack*" as the tree broke free. The Poplar began to fall toward him. As it crashed into other trees surrounding it, the Poplar rolled and changed directions again. Benjamin turned to run, but as he did, he slipped on the leaves beneath his footing and fell. The Poplar landed on his legs and pinned him to the ground.

Benjamin couldn't move. Small branches had whipped his face as he fell to the ground leaving him bleeding. His head began to spin, and Benjamin became nauseous. His right leg was in tremendous pain, so much pain that he passed out.

Stevie was excited as he rode back down the road that led home. He cantered Dusty, looking forward to getting home quickly so he could talk to Ma and Pa about working for Avery. But instead, Stevie began to dream about everything he could do with the money he would earn by working at the livery.

It took Stevie less than half an hour to reach the entrance of Parish Place. He continued up the drive to his house and stopped outside the back door. He excitedly sprinted into the house, searching for his parents to tell them the good news.

"Ma! Ma!"

Ma was in the kitchen preparing bread dough to bake in the oven. "What is it, Stevie?"

"Where's Pa? I've gotta tell him!"

Ma asked, "Tell him what?"

"Mr. Johnson wants me to work for him! He offered me a job!"

Ma replied, "A job? I don't know, Stevie. You're only a boy. What about your chores and school work?"

Stevie replied, "I can do it! I can do it all! Please, Ma!"

Abigail said, "I don't know. We'll have to discuss it with your pa." Stevie asked, "Where is he?"

"He was going up on the slope to cut trees for the new smokehouse."

Stevie ran out the door and jumped on Dusty's back as he galloped up the slope in search of Pa. As he got closer to the tree line, he called, "Pa! Pa!"

No one answered. Stevie walked Dusty through the trees as

he searched for Benjamin. He continued to call out to Pa but never got an answer. Then, suddenly, he saw a freshly cut tree that had fallen away from the tree line. Stevie rode closer to inspect it. The tree had fallen fifty feet outside the tree line. Stevie rode toward the base of the fallen tree to see if he could find where Pa might have gone. As he reached the base of the tree, he looked up into the woods and saw another fallen tree in the distance. He dismounted Dusty and walked up the slope to get a closer look. When he reached the other tree, he found Pa. There he was, lying underneath the fallen tree. Both his legs were pinned underneath the tree, and he was unconscious.

"Pa!" Stevie cried out as he ran to Benjamin's side.

As he knelt next to Benjamin, he could see him breathing. His face was bloody, and his right leg was strangely twisted, but he was alive. Stevie tried to rouse Pa by shaking his shoulders.

"Pa! Pa! Wake up!"

Finally, Benjamin awoke. He was groggy and incoherent as he spoke. "Did I get him? Did I shoot that rabbit?"

"Pa! It's me, Stevie! Wake up!"

Benjamin continued to talk out of his head. His eyes were closed, and he breathed heavily. It was as if he were having a nightmare.

Stevie decided he needed to get help. He quickly returned to where Dusty was waiting, nibbling on the grass next to the fallen Poplar. Stevie quickly mounted Dusty and galloped her back to the house. However, he didn't wait to enter the house before calling, "Ma! Ma! Come quick! It's Pa! He's hurt!"

Abigail came running from the parlor as she heard Stevie's call.

"What happened?" she asked.

Stevie replied, "A tree fell on him and trapped his legs. I think one of them is broken. You've gotta come quick!"

Abigail followed Stevie outside, mounted herself on Dusty, and then pulled Stevie up to sit behind her. They rode together up the slope to find Benjamin. Stevie pointed the way she should travel and took her to the fallen Poplar. They dismounted, and Stevie led the way up the slope to where Benjamin lay.

When Abigail arrived at Benjamin's side, he was still talking nonsense. "I caught a red and black fish. He was eating a butterfly."

"Benjamin! It's me, Abigail. Wake up."

Benjamin still wouldn't wake. Abigail looked him over to assess the situation. She determined they might be able to dig underneath Benjamin's legs to free him.

"Stevie, run back to the barn and get a shovel. We'll try to dig him out. While you're down there, tell Maria to hitch up the mules to the wagon and bring it up here."

"Okay, Ma!"

Stevie slid back down the slope to where Dusty was waiting, quickly mounted her, and rode back down to the house. He burst through the door and called Maria.

"Maria! Maria!"

Maria ran into the kitchen while holding a dust rag.

"Maria, Ma wants you to hitch up the mules to the wagon and bring it up the slope so we can bring Pa down. He's hurt real bad!"

Maria exclaimed, "Aiutami Dio!" (Help me, God) as she crossed herself. Maria turned and called Lisa and Lillian to follow her. They all ran to the barn to hitch the mules to the wagon. Stevie was already there when Maria and the girls arrived. He was searching for the shovel. When he found it, he got back on Dusty and galloped back up the slope.

Maria watched the direction Stevie traveled as she harnessed the mules in front of the wagon. When she finished, she put the girls in the back of the wagon and then drove it in the direction Stevie had traveled. As she drove forward, she caught sight of Angelo and William playing in the creek nearby. She stopped the wagon and called out to Angelo, "Angelo! Vieni qui presto! Presto!"

William asked, "What did she say?"

Angelo replied, "She wants us to come, quickly."

The boys ran to the wagon to meet Maria.

William asked, "What's wrong, Miss Maria?"

"Signore Benjamin! He is hurt. Come! Come!"

The boys climbed into the back of the wagon as Maria began to drive to the spot she had seen Stevie go. As she traveled farther, she saw Dusty grazing next to a fallen tree. Maria pulled the wagon up next to the tree and looked to see where Abigail and Stevie might have gone. Finally, she saw Stevie waving and calling to her.

"Up here!"

Maria instructed the children to stay with the wagon as she proceeded up the slope. When she arrived, she found Benjamin lying unconscious with his legs pinned under the fallen tree. Abigail was digging underneath Benjamin's legs, trying to free him.

As Abigail dug, Benjamin began to groan as the position of his legs began to shift, causing him pain. Finally, Abigail said, "We need a few sturdy sticks to use as splints for his legs. Two for each leg."

Stevie and Maria began searching for suitable fallen branches that they could use for the splints. Once Abigail felt she had dug enough to free Benjamin, she used the ax blade to cut and rip her apron into strips. Stevie and Maria handed Abigail the sticks they found for the splints and then helped Abigail hold Benjamin's legs steady as she tied the splints in place with the apron strips.

"Maria, can you help me pull Benjamin out?"

Abigail took Benjamin's left arm as Maria took the right arm. They carefully pulled him away from the fallen tree. Benjamin groaned again as they did.

After they freed Benjamin from underneath the tree, they slowly made their way down the slope to the wagon. They started to carry him feet first but discovered it was too painful for Benjamin, and he was too heavy for them to carry. So, they dragged him down the slope with Maria and Abigail on each arm again. Stevie followed behind, carrying the shovel and ax.

They struggled mightily to load him into the back of the wagon. It took both women and all three boys to do so. Once Benjamin was loaded, they slowly drove the wagon back to the house.

When they arrived, Abigail asked, "How are we ever going to get him to the bedroom. He's too heavy for us."

Stevie stood in the back of the wagon and pondered the problem. Then, something caught his eye as he looked around for an answer.

"I've got an idea! I'll be right back!"

Stevie leaped from the wagon and ran to the barn. His solution was leaning against the wall of the barn. It was a wheelbarrow. The previous owners had used it to haul large sacks of grain from one area to another. Stevie grabbed both wheelbarrow handles and rolled it to the wagon where everyone was waiting.

Abigail smiled as she realized Stevie had solved their problem. "Good job, son!"

They placed Benjamin onto the wheelbarrow, and they all worked together to maneuver Benjamin through the doorway, the house, and the bedroom. When they finally reached the bed, they carefully picked Benjamin up and placed him in bed.

Abigail turned to Stevie and said, "I need you to get a fresh horse and ride to town. Find a doctor and bring him back."

Stevie replied, "I don't need a fresh horse. Dusty will make it. She's strong."

Stevie sprinted out the door and ran to his Pinto. Sensing that she would be traveling fast, Dusty began moving forward before Stevie could get mounted. Stevie held onto the saddle horn as the horse started to run. He then dropped his feet to the ground and bounced as hard as possible to propel himself into the air. He landed with his belly in the saddle. Finally, he managed to lift his right leg over the horse's back and found his proper place in the saddle.

Dusty ran even faster, sensing that Stevie was properly mounted; galloping like Stevie's buckskins were on fire. She scattered a stream of dust in the air behind her as she galloped toward St. Joseph. Several minutes later, Stevie pulled her up at the livery stable. Dusty's momentum carried them just inside the doorway of the barn.

"Mr. Johnson! Mr. Johnson!"

Avery came running out of the tack room and asked, "What's all the fuss about?"

Breathlessly, Stevie said, "I need to find a doctor. My pa is hurt!"

Avery instructed, "Head straight down the street for about three blocks. Doc Adams' office is on the left."

Without another word, Stevie turned Dusty and galloped down the street, searching for the doctor. He slowed Dusty to a canter as they rode down the street until, finally he found a sign that read, "*Dr. Trenton Adams, M.D.*" Stevie jumped down from his pony and ran inside. A bell tinkled as the door opened and then again as it closed. Stevie panted as he waited for someone to come out to meet him.

Finally, an older woman came out to see who had entered the office. "Hello, young man. May I help you?"

Stevie replied, "My pa is hurt, ma'am! A tree fell on him and I think his leg is broken. My ma sent me to fetch a doctor."

The lady replied, "Oh my! Just a moment please."

She stepped back into the next room and spoke to someone Stevie couldn't see. A moment later, a gentleman of about forty years walked out and introduced himself.

"I'm Dr. Adams. Who might you be?"

"My name is Stevie Watson. My pa's name is Benjamin. We live on the old Parish Place south of town."

"Yes, I know where it is."

Stevie continued, "Pa was pinned under a tree and we think his legs are broken. He wasn't awake either. My ma said come find a doctor. Can you come?"

The doctor replied, "Yes, of course. Ride down to the livery and ask Avery to ready my buggy. I'll be their shortly."

Stevie nodded, then ran out the door. He jumped back onto Dusty and turned her to ride back to the livery when Stevie spotted Avery driving a buggy in his direction. Stevie waited for Avery to pull up beside him.

Avery said, "I thought I'd save some time. I knew Doc would be needing his rig."

Dr. Adams walked out of his office carrying a black satchel. "How did you get here so quickly, Avery?"

Avery replied, "Stevie came to me looking for a doctor. I told him to come see you. I knew you'd be needing your buggy."

"Very good, Avery. You've saved me some time. Lead on, young man. I'll be right behind you."

Stevie kicked Dusty forward, and she sprinted like lightning down the street. Doc Adams whipped his horse forward. The big black horse was a trotter but did very well at trotting closely behind.

When they arrived at Parish Place, Stevie led the doctor to the house's front door. Stevie tied Dusty at a hitching rail and ran to open the door.

"Ma! The doctor is here!"

Abigail came from her bedroom and met Dr. Adams as he walked inside. "Thank you for coming so quickly, Doctor. I'm Abigail Watson."

"Dr. Trenton Adams at your service, Madame. Where is the patient?"

"Follow me."

Abigail led Doc Adams into the bedroom where Benjamin was resting. Adams looked at Benjamin's eyes and head first.

"Do you know if he hit his head?"

Abigail replied, "We don't know for sure. He was passed out when Stevie found him. He was talking nonsense at one point, but hasn't said anything since we got him into bed."

Doc Adams then checked Benjamin's legs. Benjamin's right leg was severely twisted. His left leg didn't seem to have any damage other than some scrapes.

Adams announced, "We'll need to cut these trousers off so I can set the leg. Would you mind while I wash up?"

Abigail retrieved a pair of large scissors from her dresser and cut away Benjamin's trousers from his bloody leg. Once the doctor finished washing, he instructed, "I'll need your help setting the bone. Is there anyone else in the house who might be of help?"

Abigail said, "Stevie, asked Maria to come in, please."

Stevie left the room to find Maria. A few moments later, Stevie and Maria walked back into the bedroom. Adams looked at Maria with an admirable glance. He recognized right away that she was a beautiful lady.

"Now ladies, I need each of you to hold him down at the top of each leg. I will pull against you, so try to keep him as still as possible."

Maria and Abigail each put pressure against Benjamin's legs and put as much weight against the expected pull as possible. Next, Doc Adams took hold of Benjamin's right foot with both hands. He pulled slightly at first, then increased the pressure. Then the doctor gave a great tug and a twist to Benjamin's leg, as everyone heard a great *"crunch"* as the leg moved back into place.

Doc then replaced the splints with special splints he had with him. He wrapped them in place with cotton strips and secured them.

"Mrs. Watson, your husband will need to remain immobile for at least a month. Don't let him get out of bed. Keep his right leg elevated on some pillows for the next few days. I'll come and check on him soon. If things get worse, send for me. I'll come straight-away."

Abigail replied, "Thank you, Doctor. How much do we owe you?"

"How about two dollars? If you don't have the money now, you can pay me later."

Abigail said, "Oh, no! I'll pay you now."

She went to her dresser, found the money, and paid Dr. Adams what was owed.

Doc Adams reminded Abigail, "Be sure and send for me should you need me. Day or night."

Adams excused himself and returned to his buggy for the drive back to town.

CHAPTER 21

Stevie awoke and dressed the following day before heading downstairs to do his chores. He knew Pa would not be able to work for a while, so he took it upon himself to see that the livestock were fed, and cared for.

Before leaving his bedroom, Stevie woke William and Angelo and told them to get up and start their chores.

William moaned, "Why do we have to get up so early?"

Stevie said, "Cause Pa needs our help. He won't be able to do anything for at least a month. We've got to do our chores and his."

Stevie made sure the other boys were up and dressed before he left the room. Stevie heard someone in the kitchen when he made his way through the house. It was Ma getting the fire restarted in the stove so she could cook breakfast.

"Morning, Ma!"

"Good morning, Stevie! Is your brother up?"

"Yes, ma'am. He should be down shortly."

Stevie slipped out the door and walked to the barn. He decided to do the milking first. So Stevie brought Jezebel into the barn and began the ritual he had become so accustomed to. After he finished, Stevie covered the milk pail with his kerchief while he continued his other chores.

William and Angelo finally walked into the barn to take care of the chickens. Angelo carried a woven reed basket that they used to gather the eggs. William opened the coop door and let out the chickens who wanted to scratch around in the barnyard. He shooed the rooster out so he wouldn't have to contend with him while they gathered the eggs.

Stevie climbed the ladder to the loft and began tossing down hay to the livestock below in the pen. When he finished feeding the livestock, he climbed down the ladder to join the other boys as they walked back to the house for breakfast.

While they were sitting at the table having their breakfast, Abigail came into the dining room. She had been delivering breakfast to Benjamin. She sat down to join everyone as they ate their morning meal. Everyone quietly ate, glancing from time to time at the empty chair at the far end of the table.

Finally, Abigail spoke, "Stevie, your pa wants to see you after breakfast."

Stevie looked up from his eggs and bacon and replied,

"Yes, ma'am." Stevie continued to chew on his bacon as he pondered what Pa had to say to him. What had he done wrong? Was he in trouble? Was he in for a switching? Stevie grew less and less interested in the food set before him. Finally, he set down his fork and asked, "May I be excused?"

Abigail noticed that he hadn't finished his breakfast.

"Are you feeling alright?" she asked.

"Yes, ma'am."

"You may be excused. Don't forget to go see Pa before you leave the house." Stevie nodded in agreement and slowly made his way to Pa's room.

Abigail smiled ever so slightly as Stevie walked away.

When Stevie arrived at his parent's bedroom door, he knocked quietly.

"Come in!" announced Pa.

Stevie slowly opened the door and peeked inside.

Pa saw him and said, "Come in, son!"

Stevie slowly walked inside as if he thought he might hurt Pa's leg if he walked too heavily on the bedroom floorboards. He saw a tray of food sitting on Pa's lap. Benjamin picked up the tray and set it next to him on the bed.

"Come over here, Stevie."

Stevie approached his pa until he was standing next to him at the side of the bed.

Benjamin said, "I understand you had quite a day yesterday."

"Sir?"

"Well, your ma tells me you made not one but two trips into town. She said you found me under that tree and you were the one responsible for getting me out of that mess."

Stevie protested, "I wasn't the only one. Ma and Maria

helped too."

"Yes, but your ma said you were the one who figured out how to use the wheelbarrow to get me into the house. You were the one who rode to town to find a doctor. You handled yourself like a man, yesterday, Stevie. I want to thank you."

"You're welcome, Pa."

Benjamin then said, "Ma says Avery offered you a job."

Stevie shrugged as he said, "Yes, sir, but I don't think I'll take it."

Pa asked, "Why not?"

"Well, there's too much to do around here. I need to be here to help."

Benjamin smiled at his son's sense of responsibility.

"It won't be that way for long. Why don't you speak to Avery. Ask him if you could just work on Mondays for him until I get back on my feet. Then, we can talk again about working three of four days a week for him. How does that sound?"

Stevie's face lit up with excitement. "Really, Pa!"

Benjamin replied, "Sure. As long as you don't shirk your responsibilities here and you get your school work done. I think it would be good for you."

"Can I go and talk to him, now?"

Benjamin replied, "Sure, son. But come right back. I need you to start raking the hay. You need to get it into stacks so we can move it to the barn."

Stevie exclaimed, "Thanks, Pa!" as he ran to the barn to saddle Dusty.

After saddling Dusty, Stevie led her to the barn door and held onto the saddle horn. He clicked his tongue to get her moving forward. Dusty started moving slowly, then Stevie clicked his tongue again. Dusty realized what Stevie wanted. She began to run with Stevie by her side. Stevie curled his legs up next to Dusty's side, then dropped down and bounced off the ground. He propelled himself into the air and landed in the saddle. Stevie kicked Dusty forward, and she galloped down the drive and onto the road that led to St. Joe.

Dusty seemed to love to gallop. Stevie loved it too. He loved the way the wind felt against his face. Dusty's gait was even, so Stevie barely moved in the saddle. People who lived along the road were beginning to get used to the small boy riding the Pinto up and down the road at such a high rate of speed. However, they weren't especially fond of the dust that was stirred when the boy rode past. He left an enormous cloud each time he rode by their homes.

Stevie arrived at the livery in less than thirty minutes. He pulled up Dusty just before reaching the barn. As Dusty stopped, Stevie swung down from the saddle and landed on his feet. He took a couple of steps next to the horse as she came to a complete stop.

Avery stood in front of them as they entered the barn.

"Well, now. What's your hurry there, Stevie?"

Stevie replied, panting, "Pa says I can work for you."

Avery replied, "That's good! I'm glad to have you."

"Only, I can only work on Mondays for now. Pa broke his leg and can't get out of bed. He needs me to work around the farm for now until he can get back on his feet. It'll be about a month, maybe more. But he said I can help out whenever you need me after that."

Avery smiled at Stevie and said, "Your pa depends on you, don't he?"

Stevie replied, "I'm the oldest. I have to take care of the family until Pa can get well."

"Well then, let's do it. You come work for me on Mondays until your pa gets better. Then, we'll see how it goes. I'll pay you seventy-five cents a day. You'll be cleaning out the stalls, feeding the horses, saddling up folk's horses for them, and anything else that I might need you to do. Fair enough?"

Stevie smiled and said, "Sounds good!"

Avery said, "Alright. I'll see you Monday morning at first light."

Stevie woke early before the sun rose. As he looked out his

window, he saw the sun peeking through the trees that grew along the slope. The sky was a hazy color of blueish grey. Stevie quickly donned his clothes and quietly walked downstairs and through the kitchen. No one else was awake yet. He went to the barn, fed the livestock, and milked Jezebel before walking back to the house.

By the time he walked back into the back door, Ma had risen and started breakfast. Stevie handed her the milk pail, then said, "See you tonight, Ma."

"Wait a minute!"

Abigail handed him a poke.

"Take this with you. I made you some breakfast and there's enough for lunch as well. Will you be back before dark?"

Stevie replied, "I'm not sure. Avery didn't tell me what time I would get off from work."

"Well, you be careful. Stevie, we're mighty proud of you, son." Stevie smiled at his mother and said, "Thanks, Ma!"

Stevie ran to the barn and saddled Dusty. He put his food poke into his saddlebags and mounted the pony for the ride into town.

He arrived at the livery as the sun was rising above the horizon. Avery walked out of his quarters just as Stevie walked into the barn.

"Mornin'!" Avery announced.

"Good morning, Avery."

Avery instructed, "You can put your Pinto in that first stall, there. Give her a scoop of grain to make her feel at home. Then, you can feed the rest of the horses. They all get a scoop of grain in the morning and one in the evening. After that, you can start cleaning out the stalls. There's a wheelbarrow out back. There's also a dung hill out there. That's where you'll dump the wheelbarrow. That should keep you busy until our load of grain arrives."

Stevie looked around as Avery gave his instructions and replied, "Yessir!"

Stevie got busy feeding and cleaning around the livery while Avery busied himself with other matters. Stevie wasn't sure what those matters were. Avery seemed to be gone most of the time.

Around noon, Avery walked back into the livery and announced to Stevie, "Lets take a break. Are you hungry?"

Stevie replied, "Yessir, but Ma fixed me a lunch."

Avery said, "Well, I usually go down to the cafe and have my lunch. You care to join me?"

Stevie replied, "No thanks! I'll sit here and eat my lunch. Besides, someone should be here if a customer shows up needing a place to leave their horse."

"Your a smart boy, Stevie. I'm glad to have you."

Avery walked out of the barn and left Stevie to his lunch.

Stevie sat on a wooden crate and leaned against a post to relax while he ate his lunch. Inside his poke, he found two boiled eggs, a hunk of cheese, a slice of bread, and an apple. Stevie took his time munching on his lunch. He felt no need to hurry. Instead, he relaxed and thought about his life here in Missouri. Missouri had so much more to offer than Albany. He couldn't imagine himself working in Albany at such an early age. People in Albany only saw Stevie as a little boy, not someone who could be of value.

Then he wondered what he could do with the money he earned. What would he buy? The first thing he thought of was the pistol. Pa had said Stevie could have the gun once he had a job and earned the money to buy ammunition for the pistol. He wondered how much the bullets for the gun would cost.

Then he realized his family needed new clothes. Most of them wore rags around the farm. They saved their one set of nice clothes for special occasions like church. What they needed were some new work clothes. Stevie decided that would be his priority. Christmas was coming in about a month. He would save up his money to buy work clothes for everyone.

Stevie's mind turned to Avery. He wondered about the livery business. He knew Avery struggled with numbers. He might not be making any money at his trade. Stevie had already seen how others took advantage of Avery's lack of education.

When Avery walked back into the barn, Stevie asked, "Avery? How much do you charge for folks to keep their horses here?"

"Well, I usually get two bits per horse."

Stevie asked, "A day?"

"Yeah. Why?"

Then Stevie asked, "How much does it cost you to feed each horse for a day?"

"I don't rightly know. I give em a scoop of grain twiced a day. So, however much that comes to."

Stevie then asked, "How many scoops of grain can you get out of a sack?"

"I ain't never counted."

Stevie said, "Let's find out."

Stevie led Avery over to where the grain was stored. He handed Avery an empty grain sack and began scooping grain from a full bag into the empty one. Stevie counted aloud as he moved each scoop into the new sack. When they finished, Stevie counted eighteen scoops.

Stevie then said, "You paid a dollar and twenty-five cents for each sack of grain, right?"

Avery nodded and said, "That's right."

Stevie found a stick and scratched in the dirt. He wrote 1.25 divided by 18, then scribbled some numbers as Avery watched.

"Avery, it cost you six cents per scoop of grain. If you feed a horse two scoops a day it cost you twelve cents a day just to feed them. That leaves you thirteen cents a day to pay for everything else."

Avery asked, "What other things?"

Stevie replied, "Well, me for one thing. You said you'd pay me seventy-five cents a day to work for you. You also need to pay yourself. You're not making much money are you?"

Avery replied, "Well, not really. Money seems to be getting harder for me to keep seems like."

Stevie asked, "What do other liveries in town charge their customers?"

"I don't rightly know. I wouldn't feel right going to one of them and asking them. I'd feel too nosey."

Stevie replied, "Well I can go ask. They don't know me. I'll go ask some of the other livery owners how much they charge and then we can decide what you should charge."

Avery said, "Okay, boy! Let's give it a try!"

Stevie saddled up Dusty and began his ride through town to

meet the other livery owners. First, he rode north to the Livingston Livery, which sat on the northwest side of St. Joe. It was owned by Harper Livingston, a young man of about thirty. He was a rugged individual with a burly beard and pale blue eyes. Harper was an intimidating figure who spoke with a gravely voice.

As Stevie approached the livery, he noticed a large corral in the rear of the barn with several horses. Unfortunately, many of the horses were in poor condition, what Stevie's pa would have called "nags."

Livingston saw Stevie riding up and asked, "Can I help you, young man?"

Stevie gathered as much fortitude as possible before asking, "Yes sir. My Pa is home sick. He's got some friends that are planning to come for a visit and they need a place to board their horses. So Pa told me to come and see how much you charge."

Livingston replied, "Well, they'll get the best care in town if they board their horses with me. Plenty of grain and hay. They'll get groomed daily, and I'll treat them like they're my own. The price is seventy-five cents a day."

Stevie then asked, "How many stalls do you have? Pa wouldn't want them turned loose in a pen with other horses."

"I've got ten stalls. Best get here early, though. They fill up pretty quick." Stevie replied,

"Thanks, Mr. Livingston. I'll let him know."

Stevie rode away and turned east. He remembered seeing a livery as they rode into town from Albany. It had a much larger barn and corral than Avery's or Livingston's livery. When Stevie walked inside the barn, he counted twenty stalls. Black's Livery was owned by Owen Black, an elderly gentleman with white hair. It was run by his son, Jacob, and Jacob's two sons, Henry and Gus. Jacob Black was a slender man with a long pointed nose. His eyes were set narrow on his face, and he almost seemed to be cross-eyed. Jacob spoke to Stevie as he entered the barn.

"Howdy, son! What can I do for you?"

Stevie gave his speech about Pa needing a place to board horses for his visiting friends.

"Well tell you Pa we've got the largest and finest facility in town. Plenty of hands to take care of all the stock. His horses will get good quality grain and hay, fresh water, and daily grooming for seventy-five cents a day."

Stevie replied, "Thanks Mr. Black. I'll let him know."

Stevie then rode Dusty to the southeastern part of town where Hyde Livery was located. Homer Hyde was a little older than Jacob Black. He was much like Avery in that he worked primarily alone. His barn was older and a little run down. Homer had a crooked back from years of being kicked and stomped by unruly equine.

Stevie found through discovery that Homer charged fifty cents a day, but he didn't groom horses without an extra charge. He was a one-man operation and didn't have time to brush down horses. So they were lucky if he got their stalls cleaned out every day.

When Stevie arrived at Avery's, he saw that a freight wagon had arrived and was unloading into the barn. Stevie approached and kept a close eye on the grain sacks as they were unloaded. Stevie checked the grain inside each bag to ensure it wasn't moldy. He counted the sacks as they were placed in the barn and then stood next to Avery as the bill was presented.

Two individuals that Stevie had never seen before delivered the grain . One was about the same age as his pa, maybe a little older. The other was a boy just a few years older than Stevie.

John Grady and his son, Tom, were of Irish descent. They had moved to Missouri five years ago and were farming two hundred acres of wheat, oats, and barley on the east side of St. Joe.

John Grady spoke with a strong Irish brogue as he asked Avery, "Is this your grandson, Avery?"

"Hmm? Oh no. This is my new hand, Stevie."

Grady said, "Nice to meet you, Stevie. This is my son, Tom."

Tom nodded his head without saying a word. Stevie returned the nod.

Avery turned to Stevie and asked, "Well, Stevie, how does it look?"

"The grain's all good, Avery. We've got twenty- two sacks."

Avery looked at Grady and asked, "How much for the grain?"

John replied, "A dollar twenty-five a sack. That comes to. . ."

"Twenty-seven dollars and fifty cents," replied Stevie.

John Grady raised his eyebrows as he looked at Stevie and asked, "Did you just figure that all up in your head?"

Avery said, "He's a smart one, now. That's why I hired him. He saved me from getting cheated last week. Feller tried to charge me thirty dollars for a load that cost twenty-five."

Grady said, "Well I had to write it all out on paper this morning so I would know how much to charge. That's impressive, young man."

Avery reached into his pocket and pulled out his purse. He opened the purse and told Stevie, "Help me find the right money, Stevie."

Stevie rummaged through the little poke, found the correct change for Mr. Grady, and handed it to him. Grady accepted the money, then reached out to shake Stevie's hand. "Nice to meet you, Stevie."

He then shook Avery's hand and said, "I hope we can do more business."

Avery replied, "Yessir! I'll see you next week."

After the Gradys pulled away, Avery asked, "What'd ya find out?"

Stevie replied, "Avery, you're not charging nearly enough for boarding. The other liveries are charging either fifty cents or seventy-five cents a day. From what I've seen, you should be charging at least fifty cents a day. If you raise your prices too much, it might scare some of your customer away. But, once they see how much everyone else is charging, they'll come back to you."

Avery replied, "Really now? You think that's what I should do?"

"Yes sir, I do."

"Alrighty then. I'll start charging fifty cents from now on. Thanks, Stevie! Now, you run on home. I won't need you anymore today. You did a good job." Avery reached into his pocket and fished out seventy-five cents, then handed it to Stevie.

Stevie replied, "Thanks! See you next week, Avery!"

Chapter 22

December 3, 1853

The day began like any other day on Parish Place. Stevie rose early to start his chores. It had been nearly a month since Pa had broken his leg. Stevie was ready for Pa to get back on his feet.

With the help of Ma, Maria, and the boys, Stevie was able to store the hay that had been cut before Pa's accident. Stevie worked every waking hour raking the hay into piles that could be loaded onto the wagons, then transferred to the barn loft.

Stevie had changed in the past four weeks. Not only had he accepted more responsibility and duties as the man of the family, but he had also begun to change physically. His arms and legs were thicker. He had grown two inches in height. He no longer looked like an eight-year-old little boy but a nine-year-old young man.

After Stevie finished the feeding and milking, he walked back to the house to deliver the pail of milk to Ma. William and Angelo followed closely behind, carrying a basket of eggs collected from the chicken coop.

As they reached the house, Stevie saw a horse and buggy turn onto their drive from the St. Joseph-Kansas City Rd. Stevie recognized it immediately. Dr. Adams came to check on Pa. Stevie met the doctor at the front door and let him in. Doc Adams was carrying his medical bag and a set of crutches he had made for Benjamin.

"Good morning, Stevie!"

"Morning, Dr. Adams."

"How's your pa?"

Stevie replied, "He's going nuts laying up in that bed all the time."

Doc said, "Well, maybe these will cheer him up."

They all walked in the front door and parted ways. Doc Adams proceeded to Benjamin's bedroom while Stevie and the other boys walked into the kitchen.

Stevie announced, "Doc Adams is here, Ma."

Abigail quickly turned and walked through the parlor and into her bedroom, where she found the doctor examining Benjamin's leg.

"Hello, Abigail!" the doctor said.

"Good morning, Doctor. How is he?"

"He seems to be healing very nicely. I think he's well enough to start walking around as long as he uses the crutches I brought."

Benjamin slid his legs over the side of the bed as the doctor handed him the crutches. Benjamin slowly stood, putting most of his weight on his left leg. He positioned the crutches under his arms and gingerly took his first steps. Benjamin was careful to keep his weight on his left leg as he moved about, but he finally found it liberating to be out of bed.

Benjamin crutched his way into the dining room to join the rest of his family for breakfast. The doctor followed along to ensure Benjamin made it safely on his first voyage.

Abigail asked, "Won't you join us for breakfast, Doctor?"

Dr. Adams replied, "Oh, no, thank you. I have to get moving. Mrs. Wilson is having a baby this morning, and I'm already late. It's her eighth baby, though. So I figure she knows how to do it without me."

After the doctor left, the family began breakfast. Maria had made a special addition to their usual breakfast of bacon and eggs. She prepared flapjacks. The Watsons hadn't eaten flapjacks in a long time. It was indeed a special treat. There wasn't any syrup for the flapjacks, but they had molasses or blackberry jam from which to choose. Stevie chose to have his with jam. The hotcakes were delicious as they nearly melted in Stevie's mouth. He couldn't help himself; he had to eat two large cakes.

After breakfast, Stevie began to excuse himself so he could start his work day. "May I be excused?"

Ma replied, "Not just yet."

Stevie was already standing when he realized his mother had denied his request to leave the table. He slowly sat down to see what was wrong.

Benjamin announced, "Today is a special day for our family. I'm thankful to be back here eating with all of you at this table.

I'm proud of how all of you have pitched in to keep this farm going while I've been stuck in bed. But I'm especially pleased with how Stevie has worked so hard in my place. He has proven himself to be a man capable of manly things. Stevie, you don't even realize what today is, do you?'

Stevie suddenly realized the date, December third. It was his birthday. "It's my birthday! I completely forgot about it!"

Benjamin continued his speech, "You're nine years old and already a man. You've always been mature for your age and you've always been a big help to me and your ma, but this past month you've proven to be more than just a nine year old boy. You're a fine young man and we're very proud of you. We want you to have something."

Pa looked at Ma and gave her a nod. Abigail got up from the table and retrieved a parcel wrapped in brown paper and tied up with a length of cotton string. She lay the package in front of Stevie and said, "Happy birthday, Stevie!"

Stevie was astonished to see a package sitting before him. Typically, a birthday gift would be a homemade cake or pie or, on a rare occasion, a gift like the small pocket knife he received when he turned seven.

Stevie couldn't imagine what was inside the brown paper.

Ma said, "Go ahead! Open it!"

Stevie took out his jackknife and cut the string that held the package together. Then, he unwrapped the paper and found to his amazement, the .36 caliber Navy Colt revolver and gun belt they had taken from "Bug-eyed" Bill just a few months ago. Stevie sat looking at the gun with his mouth open. He couldn't believe his fortune.

Benjamin said, "Stevie, your ma and I feel like you've proven yourself as being responsible enough to own this gun. We hope you will prove to us that we haven't made an error in judgment. I want you to wait until I'm able to take you out and show you how to fire it before you take it out of this house. Its unloaded now and I want it to stay that way anytime it is in this house."

"I promise, Pa! I won't let you down."

Benjamin then said, "One more thing."

His demeanor changed as he looked at William and Angelo.

"You two boys aren't to go anywhere near that gun. I don't care if its loaded or not. You don't touch that gun or any gun unless I say its okay. You hear me? If I find out either of you has done otherwise, I'll tan both your hides. Do you understand?"

"Yes, Pa."

"Yes, Mr. Benjamin."

Benjamin continued, "Stevie, after breakfast I'll show you how to clean and care for you Colt. Then we'll store it someplace safe so the younger ones won't be tempted to touch it."

"Thanks, Pa!"

After everyone else left the table, Stevie and Benjamin remained. Abigail brought in a small can of gun oil and a rag and handed them to Benjamin before she left the room.

Pa showed Stevie how to take the revolver apart and clean each part. First, he used a small wire brush to remove dirt or rust from each piece. Next, he ran the brush through each cylinder chamber that held the cartridges. Then, Pa showed him how to load the cylinder and replace it into the pistol. Then, he let Stevie take it all apart and do it himself. They worked together for over an hour, taking the gun apart, oiling it, cleaning it, and putting it back together until Benjamin was sure Stevie understood the process.

After a while, Pa said, "Okay son, lets put it away."

Stevie collected the revolver and holster and carried them as he followed Pa to the downstairs bedroom. When they entered the bedroom, Pa said, "Close the door."

Stevie closed the door and followed Pa to the chifforobe at the far end of the room. Benjamin stood bearing weight on his left foot and handed Stevie one of his crutches.

"Here. Let me have it."

Stevie handed the gun and holster to Pa and watched as he reached high above the chifforobe and hid the weapon out of sight.

"You, Ma, and me will be the only ones who know where its hidden."

"Yessir!"

Three weeks later, Stevie awoke to snow falling outside his bedroom window. He had seen heavy snowstorms while living in Albany. However, this was nothing like that. The snowflakes were tiny and icy, more like sleet than snow. It had accumulated into little mounds throughout the grounds of the farm. Ice-cycles hung from tree branches and eaves of the house and barn.

Then it dawned on Stevie that today was Christmas Day. So Stevie went to the bed and shoved William as he said, "William, get up! It's Christmas!"

The boys leaped from the bed and dressed quickly before darting out of the bedroom and down the stairs yelling, "It's Christmas! It's Christmas!"

Maria heard them bound down the stairs from her room, so she dressed and collected Lisa and Lillian to join everyone downstairs. The boys were impatiently waiting in the parlor, continuing to announce that Christmas had arrived.

Benjamin and Abigail joined the gang as they entered the parlor from their room. Packages wrapped in brown paper with a ribbon tied around them sat underneath the Fir evergreen that stood in the corner of the room. Everyone had worked together the night before decorating it with tiny handmade ornaments and bows made of ribbon.

The adults sat in chairs near the fireplace while the children sat on the floor around the tree. Abigail stood momentarily and handed out five stockings that were hung on the mantle above the fireplace. One for each of the children. Inside the stockings was an orange from Abigail and Benjamin. Oranges were a rare sweet treat, especially in Missouri. The children were excited to see the orange-colored citrus rolling out of their stockings as they upended them. Maria had made gingerbread cookies and placed them in the stockings. The children were just as excited to see the delicious-smelling cookies as the cookies tumbled from the stockings.

Abigail then passed out packages to everyone. She had knitted socks and mittens for everyone in the family, including Benjamin and Maria. Then, Maria handed out her gifts to everyone. She had knitted wool hats for everyone.

They all celebrated their new gifts. They felt so blessed with everything they had been gifted. Then, Stevie stood up suddenly and announced, "Wait! I'll be right back!"

Stevie ran upstairs to his room and briefly disappeared. Moments later, he came back down carrying his saddlebags. When he walked back into the parlor, Stevie reached into the first saddlebag and took out a handful of stick candies. He passed them out to the children giving them two each. The kids were excited to receive yet another gift. It wasn't expected.

Then Stevie walked over to Maria and handed her a package from the same saddlebag. Maria was stunned that Stevie would give her a gift. She opened the bundle and found a small bolt of cotton fabric colored light blue. Maria looked at the cloth with her mouth hanging open. Then she finally managed to say, "For me? It is beautiful, Stevie. Graci! Thank you!"

"You're welcome, Maria!"

Stevie then handed Ma a bundle from the other saddlebag. Abigail was also pleased to see the bolt of fabric in her package. Hers was a light green color. Abigail was so excited. "Stevie, you shouldn't have! That was your hard-earned money!"

"I wanted to, Ma! I noticed how ragged some of your clothes were looking. I wanted you to have a new dress."

Stevie then handed the last bundle to Pa.

Benjamin accepted the package and opened it, finding a brand new pair of dungarees.

Stevie said, "These are to replace the pair of trousers Doc Adams had to cut off of you."

Pa replied, "Thanks, son! Thanks so much!"

The family celebrated together all day, eating a special meal and enjoying their gifts and each other. Then, in the evening, just before bedtime, they gathered once more around the fire as Abigail read from the Bible about the birth of baby Jesus.

It was the perfect ending to the perfect day!

CHAPTER 23

April 15, 1854

Stevie awoke to the rumble of thunder as he lay in his bed next to William. Flashes of lightning lit up his room under the dark cloudy sky. The rain fell hard against the wooden shingles of the roof. Stevie hoped the storm would move past sooner rather than later. He had an appointment with a gun today, and he didn't want to delay it.

Stevie had been saving his money for months. His days of labor at the livery had increased since Pa could work again. He now worked for Avery four days a week. Avery spent much of his time wandering the streets of St. Joseph whenever Stevie was around to look after the livery.

Today was one of his days off, and he made a purchase yesterday in anticipation of the day. He bought a crate of .36 shells for his Colt revolver. It cost Stevie eighteen dollars for a thousand rounds of ammunition for the pistol. He planned to set up targets on the far side of the property so he could practice shooting the gun.

Pa had shown him back in January how to shoot the pistol, but a limited number of bullets were stored in the gun belt, and they were spent very quickly.

Suddenly, Stevie heard the wails of a baby disrupting the momentary silence after the rain and thunder had subsided. He knew he might as well get out of bed. The whole household would be up now that baby Heather was awake.

Heather Watson was born on April 1st, the newest addition to the Watson clan. At two weeks old, she had the lungs of an elephant. No one would be able to sleep if she got herself worked up.

Stevie rose and dressed before making his way into the kitchen. No one was there yet, so Stevie started the fire in the stove so breakfast could be made. By the time he had the fire going, Maria had walked in and said, "Good morning, Stevie."

"Morning, Maria. I got the fire started for you."

"Buona! I will start the breakfast."

Stevie picked up the milk pail and walked to the barn. Stevie now did the milking and fed the horses every morning as his regular chores. Pa could have gone back to feeding the stock, but he found it difficult to climb the ladder up to the loft after his accident. However, Stevie didn't mind; it took very little effort for him to toss down hay for the horses and mules.

The rain picked back up as Stevie sat next to Jezebel and extracted the milk from her four large udders. As usual, Stevie rested his head against Jezebel's flank as he tugged on her teats. He found it relaxing to hear the rumbles of her belly beneath her thick hide. Jezebel seemed to enjoy it too. She never swatted Stevie with her tail as she had with the younger boys.

Just before Stevie had finished with the milking, William and Angelo arrived. They both proceeded to the chicken coop to gather the eggs.

Stevie reminded the boys, "Remember not to collect all the eggs. Ma wants some of them to hatch so she can have some pullets."

William was in a bit of a mood when he replied, "I know!"

Angelo looked at Stevie and said, "He knows because you just told him."

Stevie replied to Angelo, "I know!"

Angelo shrugged and walked away to help collect the eggs.

Stevie was finding it hard to get along with his little brother. He and William used to do everything together, but things seemed to change when Maria's family joined theirs. It was like Stevie had two little brothers, and neither wanted to be told what to do. At least, not from Stevie.

Stevie walked away without saying another word. He had better and bigger things to be concerned about. He walked back to the house, carrying the bucket of milk, striding quickly to dodge the rain as it fell. Stevie found Ma and Maria working together to prepare breakfast when he walked through the door. Pa was sitting at the table in the dining room holding little Heather, who, for the moment, was content.

Pa asked Stevie, "How's everything?"

"It's okay, Pa."

"Are you looking forward to having a day off today?"

Stevie replied, "If this rain ever lets up. I was hoping to go out and do some shooting today."

"What are you planning on shooting?"

"Oh, I've been saving up some old tin cans that Ma's been throwing out. So I figured I'd shoot some of 'em."

Abigail walked into the room carrying a plate of fried eggs and corrected Stevie, "Some of them! Don't you go wild on me, Stevie. Remember to use proper grammar."

Stevie replied, "Yessum! Uh, yes ma'am."

About mid-morning, the rain finally made its way east and left Parish Place. Just what Stevie had been longing for. He asked Pa if he could go out and practice his shooting. Pa went into his bedroom and retrieved the six-shooter from its hiding place. He walked out and handed it to Stevie. "Mind if I tag along?"

"Sure, Pa!"

The two saddled their horses and mounted up for the ride to the south side of the property. Stevie stored the gun belt in his saddlebags and carried an old flour sack that contained several old tin cans.

Benjamin and Stevie rode together in search of a good place to set up targets. The sun was starting to peek out of the clouds, and as they rode along, they could hear the quail calling to one another. *"Bobwhite! Bobwhite!"*

As they neared the end of their property to the south, Benjamin spotted an outcropping of limestone against the tree line. The large boulder spread out for about twelve feet across. This was just what he had hoped to find.

Benjamin walked out to the rock and set cans across the top of it. Stevie waited for Pa to return before pulling the revolver out of the saddlebags. Benjamin watched Stevie as he loaded the cylinder in the revolver. Four other cylinders were stored in the gun belt, so he loaded them too. After loading the weapon, Stevie stood next to Pa and aimed at one of the cans. The Colt was lighter than he remembered it being the last time he held it. Stevie hadn't realized how much stronger he had gotten while working at the livery. His hand had grown a little, too; he could cock the pistol with one hand. Stevie pulled the hammer back, aimed, then squeezed the trigger just as Pa had taught him. The gun kicked back on him, and he missed his first shot. It went high of his mark.

"That's okay, son. Just take a breath and let it out before you pull the trigger."

Stevie tried again. He aimed, took a breath, let it out, then squeezed. *Bang!* The tin can flew backward off the ledge of the rock.

"I hit it! I hit it, Pa!"

"Good job, son!"

Stevie continued taking shot after shot. He missed often, but just barely.

Benjamin took a few tries at hitting the targets, too. Unfortunately, his aim wasn't much better. Shooting a handgun was much different from shooting his muzzle- loaded rifle.

They spent about two hundred shots of Stevie's ammo before Pa decided it was enough.

"We should get back and check on the others."

Stevie unloaded all the cylinders and put the gun and belt back into his saddlebags before they rode back home.

The next day, Stevie awoke to a sunny morning sky. It was Sunday, and the family planned to ride into town for church. Stevie and the other boys quickly finished their chores before breakfast. After breakfast, they changed into their "Sunday-go-to-meeting" clothes. As the boys came down to meet the rest of the family, there was a knock on the front door. It was Dr. Adams. Dr. Adams had recently begun to call upon Maria. He was attracted to her the first time he saw her the day Benjamin was injured. Today, he had asked to drive Maria and her children to Sunday Mass. Dr. Adams was also Catholic and a long-time parish member that met at St. Joseph's Cathedral.

Since Dr. Adams showed up to drive Maria and her children to town, Abigail decided to wait until baby Heather was a little older before she took her to town and church. So, the family sat outside on the front porch and read from the Bible together.

Sundays were very relaxing on the farm. The Watsons could put away their work for one day and just enjoy each other. Abigail and Benjamin sat together on the porch swing and talked as the wind blew against their faces. William sat on the porch steps and whittled on a piece of wood with his jack-knife. Lillian walked around the front yard picking Dandelions and blowing off their seed heads. Often, the wind blew the seeds back into her face and tickled her nose.

Stevie leaned against one of the porch posts and listened. He listened to Ma and Pa's conversations. He listened to William's knife blade as it cut against the length of wood he was whittling. He listened to Lilian's chirps of laughter as she played in the yard. He listened to the birds that sang in the treetops in front of the house. He listened and listened until he fell asleep.

Chapter 24

February 25, 1860

Fifteen-year-old Stevie Watson rode his horse into town and dismounted at Avery's livery. Stevie no longer rode Dusty. Instead, he rode a Bay gelding he had named Buster. Buster was the second of Dusty's foals she had produced in the past six years. Stevie now owned four horses. He traded Dusty's first foal, a filly, to a neighbor for a young stallion. He then bred Dusty to the stallion that produced Buster. Dusty's last foal was a Chestnut colt she was still nursing.

Stevie now stood 5' 8" tall, an inch taller than Pa. He had a slender build but was very strong for his size. Years of working for Avery and the farm suited him very well.

Stevie was a handsome Scottish American lad who now dressed like a cow hand with his boots, hat, and dungarees. He didn't wear his gun belt but carried it in his saddlebags.

Stevie put Buster in a stall and began his work, feeding and cleaning the horses that had been boarded overnight. Avery was nowhere to be found, as usual. He probably drank too much last night and was still in bed.

As Stevie began cleaning out the stalls, a gentleman wearing a three-piece suit walked into the barn.

Stevie asked, "May I help you, sir?"

"My name is William Russell."

"Yes, Mr. Russell. I've heard of you. My name is Stevie Watson. What can I do for you?"

Russell said, "My associates and I are starting a new delivery venture. We're calling it the Pony Express. President Buchanan has agreed to help subsidize us as we develop a way to transport mail from St. Joseph to Sacramento, California. We're going to be hiring young men to carry the mail on horseback and it should take only ten days for a letter to travel across country."

"Wow!" replied Stevie. "I can't imagine making it from here to Sacramento in just ten day."

"Mr. Watson, I'd like to post a few of these bills around your establishment to announce our hiring of young men like yourself to work for us in this endeavor. Would you mind?"

Stevie replied, "Well, I don't own this place. Avery Johnson is the owner, but I don't think he would mind. He pretty much looks to me in matters such as this. So, sure! Go ahead and post your bills."

"Thank you, Mr. Watson."

"Oh, just call me Stevie. Everyone does."

Mr. Russell began tacking up copies of the notices on posts inside and outside the barn. Stevie took the time to read one of them. It sounded exciting to him as he read the description posted on the bill. Finally, he approached Mr. Russell and asked, "Mr. Russell, how much will you pay your riders?"

"$125.00 a month!"

"What?"

"You'll earn every penny of it. You'll ride through some of the most rugged and dangerous country around. You'll work long days and sleep little. You'll have to outride bandits, thieves, and Indians. How does that sound?"

Stevie said, "That sounds intriguing."

Russell narrowed his brow and said, "Intriguing you say. Stevie, you seem to me to be a well educated young man. How old are you?"

"I'm fifteen."

"Well, you're just the right age, but why would someone such as yourself be interested in such a dangerous endeavor?"

Stevie replied, "Well the money for one thing. That's more money than I could earn in nine months working here. But, it sounds exciting, too."

Russell asked, "Do you know how to use a gun?"

"Yes sir. I keep a Colt revolver in my saddlebags."

"Hmm, have you ever had to kill a man?"

Stevie's head dropped as his face turned red. He thought about telling a lie but said, "Mr. Russell, I won't lie to you. I've never told anybody before other than my family. I killed a man when I was eight years old. He was an outlaw named Billy Hayes."

"Bug-eyed Bill?"

"Yes sir. He was trying to rob my folks while we were camped outside of Columbus, Ohio. In fact, the Colt in my saddlebags was his."

"My, my! Stevie, it sounds to me that you are exactly the type of young man we are looking for. We'll be conducting interviews in two weeks at my farm. Do you know where it is?"

"I've never been there, but I know where it's located. When should I be there?"

"Saturday, March 10th at eight o'clock. I look forward to seeing you. Tell all of your friends who you think might qualify to come as well. We need about eighty good men."

Stevie asked, "How old do you have to be?"

Russell replied, "No younger than fifteen." "I'll see you then, Mr. Russell."

Stevie made it home just in time for supper. Ma had prepared fried chicken, creamed potatoes, pinto beans, and biscuits, Stevie's favorites. Stevie sat down at the table at his usual spot opposite Pa. William sat to his right with Lillian on his right. Ma sat to Pa's right, with Heather on her right. Maria and her family no longer lived at Parish Place. Maria married Doc Adams four years ago, and she and her children moved to his home in St. Joseph. The Watsons very rarely saw them anymore. When Maria moved out, she left her mules behind as a gift to Benjamin for his help when she lost her first husband, Antonio.

As they began to eat, Benjamin asked Stevie, "Any news in town?"

Excitedly, Stevie declared, "As a matter of fact, yes. I spoke to Mr. William Russell today."

Pa asked, "Who is he?"

"He is a businessman. He owns several businesses around St. Joe. He and some of his associates are starting a new venture, called the Pony Express."

Ma asked, "What kind of business?"

"A delivery business. They will carry the post from St. Joe to Sacramento, California by horseback. It'll only take ten days for a letter to get all the way out there."

Pa replied, "Really! That sounds interesting. I don't see how they can make a trip like that in only ten days though."

"He's setting up relay stations along the trail. He plans to have eighty riders. I'm not sure how it all works, but he said It would be long hours with little sleep."

Ma asked, "You're not thinking of working for him, are you?"

"Yes ma'am. He said I'd be a perfect candidate for the job."

Benjamin asked, "What about Avery? What's he going to do if you leave him?"

Stevie thought for a moment, then replied, "Maybe William could work for him."

William said, "Wait a minute! Why can't I ride for the Pony Express like you?"

"Because you have to be at least fifteen. That's why!"

Pa asked, "Stevie, what makes you think this would be a better job than you already have? You make pretty good money working for Avery."

Stevie said, "I love working for Avery, but this job pays $125.00 a month."

Benjamin nearly choked on the biscuit he had just taken a bite from.

"How much?"

Stevie repeated, "$125.00 a month!"

For a moment, no one said a word. Instead, everyone sat in disbelief at the mention of so much money.

Finally, Abigail asked, "Why would they pay someone so much money to ride a horse?"

Sheepishly, Stevie replied, "Well, there's a catch. The country I'd be riding in is dangerous. It's rugged territory. There's a danger of bandits and Indians."

Ma said, "Oh Stevie! How could you think of doing something as dangerous as that? I would be worried the whole time you were away. I think we should talk some more about this. When would you start?"

Stevie replied, "I'm supposed to be at Mr. Russell's farm on March 10th. That's when they'll select the riders."

After supper, Stevie stepped out onto the front porch to clear his head. However, he couldn't stop thinking about the job offer. It all sounded so exciting to him. Riding into the west, where wild animals roamed. Having to dodge wild Indians and fight off bandits, would be dangerous, but for some reason, he wasn't even nervous about it.

Pa stepped out onto the porch and stood next to Stevie. "You've already made up your mind, haven't you?"

"Yes sir. I know I can do it, Pa! I feel like my whole life has led up to this. All the things I've experienced have prepared me for it. I want to do this more than anything I've ever had the opportunity to do."

Benjamin and Stevie silently stared into the darkness of the night. A billion stars shone brightly in the night sky. The new moon was barely visible. A pack of coyotes cackled and yelped in the distance.

"I'll speak to your Ma. She'll come around after while."
"Thanks, Pa!"

CHAPTER 25

MARCH 10, 1860

Stevie awoke early. He barely slept during the night. Thankfully, he didn't have to bother with feeding the livestock or milking the cow. Jezebel was long gone. The Watsons owned a new cow that was less temperamental, so ten-year-old Lillian was in charge of the daily milking.

Stevie sliced a piece of cheese and some bread to eat as he rode to St. Joe. Then, he saddled up his Bay, Buster, and began his ride to the Russell farm. As Stevie rode past the house, Pa stepped out the back door and waved to him.

"Good luck, son!"

"Thanks, Pa!"

Stevie cantered his Bay down the road heading north. A strong wind blew from the north, which bit Stevie like a slap in the face. Stevie wore a canvas slicker, trying to stave off the bitterness of the wind.

As Stevie entered St. Joe, the town seemed busier than any other Saturday morning. Young men had arrived the day before in anticipation of the event at William Russell's farm. Some were older men who appeared to have come from the western plains. They were weathered, weary, and broken. Others were dudes wearing dress clothing who seemed to look uncomfortable astride a horse. Then there were those like Stevie, well-mounted, experienced riders who looked like they could handle themselves in nearly any situation.

Stevie rode confidently along with the others. Then, a familiar face suddenly rode up next to him. It was Tom Grady, the grain farmer's son. Tom and Stevie had gotten to know each other well over the past few years. Stevie liked Tom, especially his Irish accent. Many boys and young men in town had begun calling him *"Irish Tom."*

Tom asked Stevie, "Are you lookin' for a new job, now?"

Stevie replied, "Aye, and what about you?"

"Aye. I'm lookin' forward to getting away from that wheat

field. My Da is not so keen, though. Had to sneak out this mornin'. How 'bout you?"

Stevie said, "Nah! Ma wasn't fond of the idea, but Pa smoothed it over with her."

Tom asked, "How many of these men do you think will make it?"

"Not many I'd guess. Mr. Russell said they plan to hire about eighty men."

"You talked to Mr. Russell?"

Stevie replied, "Yep. He came into Avery's livery looking to post his bills about the Pony Express. He told me all about it. He gave me a personal invitation."

Irish Tom said, "Well I'm stickin' to you, lad. Maybe whatever you've got will rub off on me."

They both chuckled as they rode together down the street. The mob eventually turned off the road and onto the drive leading to Russell's farm. The farm was expansive and well-kept. A large frame mansion was nestled on a small hill a quarter of a mile from the main road. Cattle were scattered throughout the pastures that surrounded the mansion.

Everyone was directed to park their horses in a large pen outside a massive barn of which Stevie had never seen the like. When Stevie dropped Buster off, he took his gun belt with him. He didn't expect trouble; Stevie just didn't want his gun to be snatched by some thieving cowboy.

As he walked away from Buster, Stevie noticed that some men were already walking back to collect their horses to leave. They wore disappointment on their faces as they walked past Stevie. Stevie later found out that they were denied because of their weight. The Pony Express wouldn't take anyone who weighed more than 135 pounds. Stevie wasn't sure how much he weighed. His stomach started to roll as he grew nervous.

A small group of well-dressed men was gathered underneath a canopy nearby. The riders were directed to register with one of the men. Stevie and Tom stood in line for at least thirty minutes until they finally made their way to the front of the line. The gentleman that addressed Stevie was all business. There was no time for small talk.

"Step on the scales."

Stevie nervously approached the scales and waited as the man moved the counterweight back and forth until it balanced.

"125 pounds. Name?"

"Stevie Watson."

"Where you from?"

"I live here, in St. Joe."

"How old are you?"

"Fifteen."

"What kind of experience do you have?"

"Well, I manage Avery Johnson's livery stable for him. I'm good with horses and cattle. I help out on my Pa's farm."

The man then noticed Stevie was wearing a gun. "You know how to use that thing?"

"Yes, sir. I'm a pretty good shot."

"How did you hear about the Pony Express?"

"I met Mr. Russell at the livery. He invited me to come."

The man then looked more closely at Stevie.

"Wait here." he instructed.

He walked to the back of the canopy and then returned with another gentleman. It was William Russell. Russell approached Stevie and held out his hand.

"Mr. Watson, so glad you decided to come out. I'm looking forward to seeing you in action today."

Stevie replied, "Thank you, sir."

Then Stevie grabbed Tom by the arm and pulled him forward.

"Mr. Russell, I'd like you to meet my friend, Tom Grady."

Tom said, "Nice you meet ya, sir. Most folks call me Irish Tom."

"Very nice to meet you, Tom. I wish both of you success in todays events."

Stevie then asked, "What kind of events?"

"Well, once you make it through the interview process, which I'm sure you won't have a problem with, you will be put through some skill tests to find out how you will do in certain situations on the prairie. Your riding skills and shooting skills mainly."

Stevie smiled, "Sounds good. Thanks for inviting me, Mr. Russell."

"My pleasure, my boy."

Mr. Russell then turned and walked back to the rear of the canopy to join his compatriots.

The gentleman interviewing Stevie said, "He thinks very highly of you, young man. He asked us to be on the lookout for you this morning. Welcome!"

"Thank you, sir!"

Stevie stepped aside and waited while the gentleman interviewed Tom. "Step on the scales."

Tom stood on the scales and waited.

"Alright young man, you weight 130 pounds. What's your name?"

"Tom Grady."

"Where are you from?"

"St. Joe."

"How old are you?"

"I just turned seventeen."

"What kind of experience do you have?"

"I work for my Da on the farm. Good with horses."

"Can you shoot?"

"I can shoot a rifle. I don't own a pistol."

"And, how did you hear about the Pony Express?"

"I saw one of the bills posted around town."

"So, you can read?"

"Yes, sir."

"Good! You pass. You two can proceed to the barn for further evaluation."

Tom and Stevie said, "Thank you!" as they left the canopy and headed to the barn.

Inside the barn was a huge arena. Fifty men were allowed to enter at a time.

The applicants were instructed to take a seat around the arena. Once seated, three gentlemen stood together at the center of the arena and called for silence. One of the men was Russell, who spoke, "Gentlemen, my name is William Russell, and these gentlemen next to me are Alexander Majors and William Waddell. We have come together as businessmen to create a new service for our great nation that will expedite communication from the eastern part of our country to the Pacific coast. The Pony Express!"

Everyone cheered!

"This endeavor will begin next month, so we have no time to waste. You will be tested here today to see if you have the skills to participate in this great endeavor. We are looking for strong, brave young men, who can handle themselves in precarious situations should they arise. And let me add, they will arise. If you are selected, you will endure hunger, thirst, a lack of sleep, attacks by Indians and bandits. Some of you will die. Let me say that we don't want you to die. At least not until you have made it to your final delivery point. That gentleman is all that counts. The mail must go through at all cost. We want to be completely honest with you when we say, our concern is not whether you live or die, it is only if you get the mail delivered. So, if you are not willing to put your life on the line for this company, I invite you to leave, now!"

Russell paused to allow anyone to leave who wanted. Stevie and Tom watched as men slowly trickled out of the arena area. Stevie counted twenty-one who finally left.

Russell said, "Alright, those of you who remain may follow these men to my left, and they will lead you to the firing range where you can demonstrate your shooting skills. If you don't prove proficient, you will be asked to leave."

Stevie and Tom moved with the rest of the crowd to an area outside the barn into a pasture where targets had been set up at a distance of twenty yards. Everyone gathered around the two men conducting the test, and one of them said, "Alright, gentlemen, each of you will be allowed one opportunity to show his skill with a firearm. If you don't have one with you today, one will be provided for you during this demonstration. You may use a rifle or a handgun, whichever you prefer. However, a handgun would be preferred.

Stevie and Tom lingered near the rear, waiting to see how proficient the others might be. Then, one at a time, each man walked to the firing line and selected their weapon. Twenty yards away stood six vertical posts. Each post had a large target painted on it. In the middle of each target, a small bell hung. The object was to hit each target, preferably ringing the bell, in the shortest amount of time. Scoring was based on accuracy as well as speed.

The first candidate chose to use a rifle. He stood at the line and waited for a signal from the judges to begin firing. He began shooting, one shot for each target. He hit every target but only rang one of the bells. His time was seven seconds. He took his time on the last target to ensure he hit the bell.

The next contestant chose a handgun. He stood at the line and waited for the signal. He then fired his first shot. He took his time, selecting accuracy over speed. He hit every bell, but it took him thirty-one seconds.

The third young man to approach the line seemed very young. Stevie thought he must have lied about his age. He was dressed like a cow hand, his clothing tattered, and his hat had seen better days. A six-shooter rested on his hip, and he wore it in such a manner that said he knew how to use it. Stevie stood closely behind the boy as he stepped to the line. When the judge gave him the signal, the boy fired six shots, hitting every target in succession and ringing every bell. His time was three seconds.

Stevie was amazed, along with everyone else who stood behind the line. Stevie looked at the young man and said, "That's very nice shooting!"

"Thanks! The name's Charlie Miller. They call me Bronco Charlie."

"Stevie Watson, nice to meet you. This is Irish Tom."

Charlie shook hands with both of them, then said, "Let's see what you've got."

Stevie approached the line and checked his Colt, ensuring it was fully loaded. He put the revolver back in its holster and waited for his signal. Then he drew and fired. Stevie's left hand rolled over the hammer as he squeezed the trigger with his right forefinger. *Bang, bang, bang, bang, bang, bang.* Six shots hit six targets, ringing six bells.

The judge announced, "Time! Five seconds!"

Stevie smiled, knowing his time practicing through the years was paying off.

Tom congratulated him, saying, "I didn't know you could shoot like that, lad!"

Charlie also congratulated Stevie, "Not bad!"

At the shooting session's end, only nine contestants were deemed worthy of going on to the next competition. Irish Tom was the last man to make it through. He hit six bells in ten seconds with a rifle.

Stevie and the other eight contestants were directed to an area on the west side of the big barn. As they walked away from the target area, Stevie noticed Russell, Majors, and Waddell sitting on a raised platform, watching the boys as they walked away. William Russell smiled and nodded to Stevie as they made eye contact. He hadn't realized that Russell and the others were watching him and the others as they competed. Stevie nodded back.

They waited again. It was two hours before the shooting competition was completed. In the end, only seventy-four men made it to the next stage of the selection competition. Stevie heard rumors that one poor guy shot his finger off while trying to load his handgun during the shooting match.

Once all the remaining candidates arrived at the next area, one of the judges announced, "Alright! This is the riding part of our skills test. Here you will mount a horse and gallop to the next station, where you will dismount and move to the next horse. Each time you leave a horse to go to the next, you will carry your mochila with you. A mochila weighs about 20 pounds. It is what your mail is carried in along the trail. You will make a total of three transfers in this test. By the way, these horses are trained to begin running as soon as they feel you tug on the saddle horn. Sometimes sooner. So be ready."

Stevie turned to Charlie and Tom and asked in a low voice, "Have either of you ever done anything like this?"

Charlie said, "Yeah, it's easy. I've been breaking broncs since I was eleven."

Stevie then asked, "How old are you now? I know you aren't fifteen."

Charlie remained silent.

"Don't worry! I'm not gonna tell. Besides, you wouldn't have made it this far if they really cared how old you are."

Charlie quietly said, "I'll be twelve in a couple of months."

Stevie smiled and shook his head in amazement.

"How about you, Tom?"

"No, I'm really sixteen!"

Stevie laughed, "No! I mean have you ever mounted a horse at a gallop?"

Tom shook his head.

"As soon as you grab the saddle horn, lift up your feet, then bounce off the ground and jump into the saddle. Don't bother with the stirrups, they'll just tangle you up. When you get to the next horse, just slide off and do it again."

Tom nodded to Stevie, but Stevie noticed the nervous look on Tom's face.

The three of them watched as man after man attempted to mount the horses. Most who tried didn't understand the concept. Finally, after ten failures in a row, Stevie stepped up to take his turn. Confidently, he walked up to the first pony while holding a mochila in his right hand. Then, Stevie ran to the horse, tossed the mochila over the saddle, and grabbed the saddle horn. The horse began galloping immediately, with Stevie hanging off the left side of the saddle. Stevie dropped his feet, bounced into the air, and landed in the saddle. He rode to the next station, where another pony was waiting. Stevie grabbed the mochila and pulled against the reins to slow his horse, then slid off the side, ran to the next pony, and did it all over again. Stevie made three perfect dismounts and remounts as he circled the course. Everyone cheered as he arrived unscathed.

Charlie and Tom congratulated Stevie as he walked back, panting. Stevie glanced up to the platform where William Russell sat and saw Russell applauding as well.

Stevie turned to Tom and said, "Alright. It's your turn."

Tom gathered as much fortitude as he could manage as he walked toward the first pony. He threw his mochila onto the saddle and began his run. He hung from the left side of the saddle and dropped his feet to the ground. He stumbled but held onto the saddle horn. He tried again and managed to bounce high enough to get one leg over the saddle. Finally, he pulled the rest of his body into the saddle just in time to make it to the next station. Tom made his dismount and moved to the next horse. He was ready this time. He made the running mount with relative ease. Tom was able to finish his run without falling. He arrived at the finish line with cheers from the crowd of men still waiting their turn.

When Charlie's turn came, his style was a little different. He wasn't nearly as tall as Stevie or Tom. As the horse began running, Charlie held onto the saddle horn, then dropped to the ground. But his legs weren't strong enough to bounce him all the way into the saddle. However, he was able to slide his left foot into the stirrup as he bounced up, allowing him to swing himself into the saddle. It wasn't as pretty as Stevie's mount, but impressive nonetheless.

Rider after rider attempted the feat; some were successful, but many failed. Several men had to be carried off the field after being run over by the horse—some with broken legs or arms. One poor soul had his head stepped on and was killed.

After over two hundred applicants went through the process, only forty were selected. Stevie, Charlie, and Tom were among them.

The finalists were brought back into the big barn to complete the application process. As they stood again in line, William Russell announced, "Gentlemen, thank you for coming today and proving your worth and skill as the first Pony Express riders. We will now have you sign an oath to complete the process. All of you will meet back here on March 31st to begin your duties as Pony Express riders. Let me stress the importance of your commission here. Your sole existence with this company is to protect the mail you are entrusted with. We expect you to defend your mochila at every cost—even the cost of the life of your horse and even your life. If you are still ready to make that commitment, then step forward and sign your oath.

As each man stepped forward, Alexander Majors, a very religious man, handed him a special edition Bible. Then each man signed their oath.

Stevie stepped to the table and read and signed his oath.

"I, Stevie Watson, do hereby swear, before the Great and

Living God, that during my engagement, and while I am an employee of Russell, Majors, and Waddell, I will, under no circumstances, use profane language, that I will drink no intoxicating liquors, that I will not quarrel or fight with any other employee of the firm, and that in every respect I will conduct myself honestly, be faithful to my duties, and so direct all my acts as to win the confidence of my employers, so help me God."

Stevie, Charlie, and Tom all shook hands and prepared to part ways. Then, Stevie asked Charlie, "Are you going to stay in town for the next two weeks?"

"I'll probably find a place to camp until we come back."

Stevie invited, "Come home with me. There's plenty of room at our house and Ma's a real good cook."

Charlie replied, "Thanks! I will!"

CHAPTER 26

Tom Grady waived to Charlie and Stevie as they parted ways riding through town. Stevie decided to stop a Greenwald's Mercantile before heading home. Stevie and Charlie tied their horses outside the store and walked in. Stevie could see Charlie was a little uncomfortable walking into the store. Everyone inside was well dressed; even Stevie wore relatively new clothes compared to Charlie's.

Charlie asked, "What are we doing in here?"

Stevie smiled and said, "I thought you could use some new duds."

"But I ain't got no money, Stevie."

"It's alright. I'll spot you some until payday."

Charlie bristled up and said, "I don't need no charity, Stevie. I'm just fine on my own."

"It isn't charity, Charlie. It's a loan. You can pay me back come first payday."

Charlie thought about it for a minute, then said, "Alright. I'm gonna pay you back, though."

Stevie replied, "Absolutely!"

Mrs. Greenwald came over to help the boys pick out something.

"Hello, Stevie!"

"Hello, Mrs Greenwald! This is Charlie! He and I will be working together for the new Pony Express service that William Russell is starting. Charlie here is looking for some new clothes."

"Alright!"

Mrs. Greenwald rummaged through trousers and dungarees, looking for what she thought might be the right fit for Charlie. She held a pair in front of him to check the size.

"These might fit. They'll be a little long, but you can roll up the legs a little. Here, try this shirt. Do you need socks and underwear?"

Stevie said, "Yes ma'am. Fix him up with everything. He'll need some new boots and a hat, too."

Mrs. Greenwald found everything Charlie needed in the correct sizes and handed them to him. She pointed to a small cubby hole at the back with a curtain.

"You can try them on in there if you like."

Charlie carried the bundle of clothes into the dressing closet and tried them on. Everything seemed to be just about right. Charlie walked out feeling like a new man, even more grown than he made himself believe he was already.

Stevie said, "Look out ladies! Here comes Charlie Miller!"

Mrs. Greenwald smiled at Stevie's jest while Charlie blushed.

"Thanks, Mrs. Greenwald. We'll take it all."

Stevie and Charlie followed Mrs. Greenwald to the front counter and waited while she totaled up the purchase.

"Looks like that will be $47.50, Stevie."

Stevie reached into his pocket and pulled out a wad of cash to pay her. Charlie had never seen so much money before.

Mrs. Greenwald asked, "Would you like to take your old clothes with you?"

Charlie replied, "Nah. I won't be need'em."

Stevie and Charlie walked out together and got back on their horses.

Charlie asked, "Are your folks rich or something?"

"No, I earned that money myself working at Avery Johnson's livery. I've been working for him for six years."

Charlie said, "He must pay you real good!"

"Just a dollar a day. I started out when I was eight years old getting seventy-five cents a day. I pretty much run the place for him, now, so he pays me more now."

"Who's gonna run it when you're gone?"

Stevie replied, "My brother William is going to take over. He's itching to get away from the farm. So Avery said he'd take him on since I'm leaving."

The boys kicked their horses to a canter and rode south to Parish Place. When they arrived at the entrance, Charlie asked, "Is that your name up there?"

Stevie replied, "No. That says Parish Place. The Parish family owned it before us. They died and we acquired it."

Then Stevie remarked, "I'm guessing you can't read?"

Charlie said, "Nah. I never went to school. I do alright though."

"I can teach you if you want. It's not that hard."

Charlie replied, "Maybe. We'll see."

The boys rode up to the barn, unsaddled their horses, and then walked to the house. As Stevie opened the back door, the aroma of freshly baked pie filled his senses.

Charlie commented, "Wow! Something sure smells good!"

As the boys entered the kitchen, Abigail pulled an apple pie from the oven. Then, without looking, she said, "Hi, Stevie! How did it go?"

She then glanced up and saw Stevie wasn't alone.

"Oh! Hello!"

"Ma, this is Charlie Miller. I met him today at the Russell farm. He and I both got hired. Tom Grady got hired, too. Anyway, I invited Charlie to stay with us until we start work next month."

Abigail said, "Well, that's fine! It's nice to meet you, Charlie. Where do you live?"

"Nowhere in particular, ma'am. I been on my own since I was nine. Ma and Pa died in a Indian raid. I'd be dead too, 'cept I was off playin' with a boy that lived up the road from us. I been workin' breaking broncs for the past year. When I heard about the Pony Express, I figured it was worth a look see."

"I see," said Abigail. "Stevie, supper will be ready in about a half hour. Why don't you boys get washed up before then."

"Sure, Ma. We'll go down to the creek."

Ma said, "Here's a couple of fresh towels and a bar of soap for you."

Stevie took Charlie upstairs to his room first. He wanted to change into some clean clothes for supper. Stevie gathered what he needed, then led Charlie downstairs and out the door. They walked past the barn to the creek. Stevie set his clean clothes and towel on a large rock next to the stream. Then, he stripped off his clothes, walked into the water, and sat down. Charlie followed Stevie and sat in the water nearby. The water was only two feet deep and had a slippery rocky bottom.

Not long after Charlie and Stevie entered the water, Lillian walked up carrying a fresh pail of milk. When Charlie spotted her, he panicked and covered his bare chest with his arms crossed.

"Hey, Stevie!"

"Hi, Lillian! This is my friend Charlie. He's going to be staying with us a couple of weeks."

Lillian said, "Hello, Charlie!"

Charlie remained silent.

"Stevie, can I come in?"

"No, Lillian. You need to get that milk up to the house."

"I know. I mean after?"

Stevie said, "Not this time, Lilian. I think Ma needs you to help with supper."

"Alright," Lillian said as she walked away, pouting.

After Lillian entered the house, Charlie exclaimed, "Quick! Let's get out before she comes back!"

"Relax." said Stevie. "She won't be back. Ma will keep her busy."

Charlie quickly finished bathing, then got out and dried off, keeping his eye on the house's back door. He was sure Lillian or Stevie's ma might come out at any minute. Stevie, on the other hand, took his time. He walked around in the nude, allowing himself to air dry for the most part. He then dressed and led Charlie back to the house.

As they walked, Charlie asked, "Would she really have gotten in the creek with us?"

"Sure! If I had let her."

"Necked?"

Stevie smiled and said, "Charlie, that little girl has been swimming in that creek with me since she was three years old. There's nothing wrong with it."

"Well, I don't want no girl seeing me necked as a jaybird."

Stevie chuckled as they continued their stroll to the house.

When Stevie and Charlie walked into the kitchen, Ma said, "Okay boys. Supper is on the table."

Charlie followed Stevie into the dining room, where they found the rest of the family seated and waiting.

Lillian said, "Can I sit next to Charlie?"

Ma pursed her lips, then asked, "William, would you mind switching places with Lillian?"

Ma then said, "Charlie, I hope you don't mind. We don't get company very often."

Charlie replied, "No ma'am. I don't mind."

The family began passing dishes of fried chicken, potatoes, baked apples, and biscuits around the table. Charlie hadn't eaten like this since his parents died almost two years ago. After everyone finished serving themselves, Stevie said, "Charlie this is the rest of my family. That's my Pa, next to him is William, you've met Lillian and Ma, and this is Heather."

Charlie replied, "Nice to meet you all."

Benjamin asked, "How old are you, Charlie?"

"I'll be twelve next month."

William nearly choked on his food when he heard. "Stevie, I thought you said you had to be fifteen to ride for the Pony Express."

Stevie replied, "That's what Mr. Russell told me. I guess they made an exception for Charlie."

"How come?" asked William.

"William, Charlie has been working as a buckaroo since his folks died. He breaks wild horses. He can ride and shoot better than I can. Evidently, they didn't pay much attention to his age when they saw how well he performed out there."

William grudgingly said, "I could have done it!"

Stevie replied, "No, William, you couldn't. Do you know how I've been mounting my horses since I was nine? That's exactly what you had to do in the tryouts. You've never been able to do it. We had to mount and dismount at three stations without failing once. And shooting? You had to ring a bell at six different targets as fast as possible. You've seen me shoot. It took me five seconds, and I didn't miss. It only took Charlie three seconds."

William replied, "I still should have gotten a chance!"

"William, men got hurt out there today. One guy shot his finger off. Others broke their arms or their legs trying to mount the ponies. One man was killed when a horse stepped on his head."

"Stevie!" Ma cautioned Stevie. "Don't talk of such things in front of the girls." "Sorry, Ma!"

Angrily, William threw his napkin into his plate of uneaten food and said, "I still should have been given a chance!"

William then stormed out of the dining room and went to his bedroom.

The family ate silently until Stevie said, "Sorry Ma, Pa. I didn't mean to make him mad. He just needed to know there's no way he could have made it out there."

Benjamin replied, "It's not your fault, Stevie. William's just frustrated. He's always wanted to be his big brother, but he just doesn't have what it takes. You have always found it easy to succeed at everything you try. I have to show William over and over how to do things, while you could just watch me do something, then do it yourself. Don't be embarrassed because things seem to come naturally to you. Be grateful. Just, give him some room. He'll come around."

CHAPTER 27

MARCH 31, 1860

Stevie awoke to the sound of thunder rumbling in the distance. He lay in bed and watched the raindrops hitting the window panes next to his bed. Charlie still slept in the bed next to him, unaware of the weather that would travel with them as they made their way into St. Joseph.

Stevie heard footsteps outside his door and surmised them to be Lillian's as she made her way to the barn for the morning milking. So Stevie rose and dressed quickly to join her. He wanted to spend as much time with her as possible before he and Charlie left. Stevie wouldn't be seeing his family again for at least a month.

Stevie caught up with Lillian as she exited the back door.

"Lillian," he called out in a whisper. "Wait up."

Lillian turned and waited as her brother ran to catch up with her. Stevie grabbed Lillian's free hand and walked next to his younger sister.

"Stevie, when will you be coming back?"

"I'm not sure. Not for at least a month. Maybe longer."

They walked quietly together and entered the barn. Stevie climbed the ladder up to the loft and pitched hay into the corral for the horses while Lillian rounded up the cow to be milked.

While Lillian milked, Stevie climbed down, entered the coop, and collected the eggs. Helping Lillian with her chores would allow Stevie to spend more time with her before he and Charlie left.

When they returned to the house, they discovered Ma in the kitchen cooking breakfast. Stevie helped Lillian filter the milk before pouring it into a pitcher and placing it on the table. Ma was cooking bacon, eggs, and pancakes; a special breakfast to send the boys off in style.

William and Charlie made their way downstairs and joined the others in the dining room as breakfast was placed on the table. As they began eating, six-year- old Heather started to ask questions. She was a curious little child, much like William was at her age.

"Stevie, are you going to St. Joe today?"

"Yes, Heather."

"Why?"

"Because I have a new job."

"What kind of job?"

"Working for the Pony Express."

"What's the Pony Sus-sex?"

"Pony Express! We deliver the mail to far away places."

"Oh! When will you come back?"

"Not for a long time."

"Oh!"

William finished his breakfast quickly, then excused himself from the table. "I've got to get going. Avery wants to show me everything before I get started." Stevie said, "I'll walk you out."

As the two of them walked together to the barn, Stevie said, "I really am sorry you're not going with me, William. I'm going to miss you."

"You won't have time to think about any of us."

Stevie replied, "That's not true. I could never forget my family. Look, I know you're upset that you couldn't go too, but somebody needs to stay and help Pa with the farm. Keep practicing your riding and shooting, and maybe you can get hired next year."

William saddled his horse without speaking, then mounted and rode away without saying goodbye.

The rain started letting up, so Stevie decided to saddle his and Charlie's horses. He led them both to the house and tied them to the hitching rail near the back door. Stevie and Charlie packed their saddlebags with their gear, then walked downstairs to say goodbye to everyone.

Stevie picked Heather up and held her as he kissed her and said, "Goodbye." Then he knelt on one knee, pulled Lillian to him, and kissed her.

"Goodbye, Lil Sis!"

"Bye, Stevie! I'll miss you!"

Stevie shook hands with Pa as Benjamin said, "You be careful out there, son. Watch your back."

"Yes sir, Pa!"

When Stevie moved over to Ma, her eyes were tear-filled. Her cheeks were soaked, and she sniffed as she reached for him. Abigail hugged Stevie tightly and said, "I love you, son!"

"I love you too, Ma!"

Stevie and Charlie walked out the back door, mounted their horses, and rode away. Stevie felt no need to ride away quickly. He took his time riding all the way to St. Joseph. Sensing Stevie was not in the mood for talk. Charlie remained silent.

When they reached St. Joseph, Stevie and Charlie dropped their horses off at Avery's livery so William could take them back home when he left work later that afternoon. The boys would not need their horses because the Pony Express would furnish their mounts.

Stevie retrieved his gun belt from his saddlebags and strapped it on. Charlie already wore his gun most of the time; it was a part of his usual attire. They walked together through town, making their way to William Russell's home. As they made their way up the long driveway that led to Russell's mansion, Charlie and Stevie met a group of young cowboys riding toward them. The cowboys tipped their hats to Stevie and Charlie as one of them said, "See you on the trail."

When Stevie and Charlie arrived at the mansion, they found Russell, Majors, and Waddell sitting under a canopy, observing the arrival of each rider. Stevie waved to Mr. Russell as he and Charlie walked to a tent where a line of cowboys had formed. As Stevie stood in line, Russell walked over to speak to him.

"Stevie, I'm glad to see you."

"Thanks, Mr. Russell. Do you remember Charlie Miller?"

"Why yes. How are you Charlie?"

"Fine, sir."

Russell then said, "It's very exciting isn't it?"

Stevie replied, "Yes, sir. I couldn't sleep last night thinking about it."

"Well, that's alright. You better get used to riding without sleep, eh? You boys will get your assignment from Mr. Griggs, there. Then pick a horse from the herd and be on your way."

"Thank you, Mr. Russell." Stevie said.

"God speed to you, Stevie."

Russell walked away and joined Majors and Waddell under the canopy. Stevie and Charlie remained in line, slowly moving forward as each rider was given his assignment. They listened as the assignments were given.

Griggs, an older man with the looks of someone who had spent many years on the trail, was apparently a man of few words.

"Name?"

"John Anson."

"Proceed to Ft. Kearny. See a man named Dobson. He'll give you your next assignment. Pick one of the horses and go. Here's a ticket to the ferry. Once you cross the river you'll find the first stop at Elwood. From there, follow the trail all the way to Kearny. The trail should be pretty well cut by the time you get there. If you need to switch horses along the way, just check with one of the station masters. You've got four days to get to Kearny. The quicker you get there, the better off you'll be."

The line moved forward as Anson left and found his mount.

"Next! Name?"

"Ed Bush."

Griggs said, "Alright, same thing. Go to Ft. Kearny and talk to Dobson. Pick out a horse and go."

"Yes, sir."

Stevie stepped up to Griggs as Griggs asked, "Name?"

"Stevie Watson."

Griggs looked up at Stevie for a closer look, then glanced over to William Russell and saw Russell nod his head.

"Alright, Watson. You're going farther down the trail. I need you to get to Ft. Laramie in five days. I want you to ride like the wind the whole way. Understand? Stop at each station and switch your mount. Don't take a break until you get to Rock Creek. That should take you about ten hours. Take a five hour rest, then get back on the trail. Continue switching horses along the way until you get to Ft. Kearny. Take another five hour break. Your next break station will be Freemont Springs. After another break proceed to Mud Springs. Your next break will be Ft. Laramie. Do you think you can handle that?"

"Yes, sir!"

Stevie's adrenaline began to rush as he realized he would be cast into the wild frontier alone with only a horse and a pistol. Then he heard Griggs ask, "Are you, Miller?"

Charlie replied, "Yes, sir."

"Miller, you'll be riding with Watson. Same assignment until You get to Ft. Laramie."

"Yes, sir!"

The boys smiled as they looked at each other, then made their way to the corral to pick out their mounts. Stevie picked a brown and white Pinto that reminded him of Dusty, while Charlie selected a Buckskin. They quickly mounted and cantered down the driveway until they reached the road. Then, they turned their horses right and headed to the river.

By the time Charlie and Stevie reached the river, the ferry was on the western bank, dropping off a group of Express riders. Stevie and Charlie waited thirty minutes for the ferry to return to the eastern bank to dock. By that time, six more riders had joined them at the dock. One of them was Irish Tom Grady.

Tom approached the two familiar faces and said, "Well, top of the morning, fellas! Where might you be heading?"

Stevie smiled and shook Tom's hand as he replied, "We're on our way to Ft. Laramie. How about you?"

"Me? Oh, I'm only going to Ft. Kearny. Looks like they're feeling sorry for this young Irish buck."

Stevie teased Tom as he asked, "What's that animal you're riding, there? It looks like a mule."

Tom pretended to take offense as he replied, "I'll have you know there's not a better judge of horse flesh in this entire world than Irish Tom Grady and don't you be forgetting it."

Stevie said, "Look at the ears on that animal. Are you sure that's not a jack rabbit?"

Tom replied, "Har, har, har, my friend. But I'll be laughing when this little lass and I leave you two mongrels and your nags behind choking on a cloud of dust."

All the cowboys who had gathered together to wait on the ferry laughed as the banter between Stevie and Tom continued.

The ferry finally arrived and disembarked the few who rode it. Then Stevie and the other riders led their ponies onto the boat and settled in for the short ride across the Missouri. Charlie seemed a little uneasy as he looked over the boat's rail.

Stevie asked him, "Have you ever been on a boat?"

"No. I've never even seen one. Have you?"

"Sure. We crossed the Mississippi on a steamboat when I was little. It was much bigger than this one."

"I be durned!" Charlie exclaimed. "Is there anything you haven't done?"

"I've never been this far west. I've never left home before. I've never been out on my own. I never ridden a wild bronc. You've done lots of things I've never done and you're a lot younger than I am."

Charlie felt proud that Stevie would admire some of his accomplishments. Charlie had never felt like anyone even cared for him. Not since he lost his ma and pa. Most people just gave him orders or yelled at him. He felt he had found a true friend in Stevie.

As the boat docked on the western bank of the river, the riders disembarked and led their horses off the ferry. Just off to their right, they spotted a small house with a corral behind it. They mounted their horses and rode ahead. Just outside the shack was a newly painted sign that read, "Elwood."

An old man with a long white beard walked out of the shack. He wore a slouched hat that looked like it was full of holes. He wore trousers held up by suspenders, and his trouser legs were tucked inside the tops of his worn-out boots.

"Howdy, boys! Name's Homer Elwood. This here is the first stop on the Express trail. Do you all have your assignments?"

The riders all answered, "Yes, sir."

"Well then, head on down the trail. The next stop is Troy. He'll have horses if you need to trade out. Any of you going to Ft. Laramie?"

Stevie and Charlie both called out, "Yes, sir!"

"Alright, you boys better get a move on. Times a wastin'. The rest of you can take a little more time, but be sure you make it to Ft. Kearny before the fourth."

Stevie looked at Charlie and asked, "You ready?"

Charlie replied, "Let's go!"

They both kicked their horses forward and galloped down the trail westward toward Troy.

CHAPTER 28

Stevie and Charlie took off like a shot. Irish Tom decided he would ride with his pals as far as he could, so he too kicked his horse into a gallop. The other riders rode down the trail at a canter taking their time.

The trio left Elwood in a cloud of dust as they rode down a path leading to their first stop, Troy. The rain began falling harder as they rode west. Dark thunderclouds hovered over them as they traveled. Stevie noticed lightning strikes in the distance, but they were too far away to hear thunder.

Ten miles down the trail lay Troy. It wasn't much different from Elwood. Maybe a little newer, but a shack nonetheless. As they rode up to the cabin, Stevie saw several saddled horses tied up outside. Nathan Troy had seen the riders coming, untied three ponies, and led them out into the open so the switch could be made.

Stevie and the others came into the clearing at a full gallop, then slid their horses to a stop just in front of Troy's position. The riders dismounted quickly and then used their running mount to get into the new ponies' saddles.

An hour later, they rode into Kennekuk to make the next exchange. The rain had let up, but the boys were all soaked to their skins. Stevie didn't care. He was doing what he had dreamed of doing. He had never felt freer than he did now.

The boys rode fast through the open prairies, shallow gulleys, and small hills of Kansas. The stations were placed nine or ten miles apart from each other. Sometimes as many as twelve miles. From Kennekuk, they rode to Kickapo', Grenada, Log Chain, and Seneca. They switched their horses at every stop.

When they reached Seneca, light began to fade. The sun had moved directly into the line of sight, making it difficult to read the terrain as they rode. Still, they never slowed. The light was completely gone when they reached Guittard's Station. The cloud cover made it extremely difficult to see. As Stevie led the way, he had to depend on his horse to decide the path taken. Their gaits slowed, but they still galloped. Even though the ride between Guittard's and

Marysville was only nine miles, it took an extra twenty minutes to reach the exchange at Marysville.

The ride to Hollenberg took even longer. It was twelve and a half miles away, and the ride took even longer since they traveled in total darkness. Stevie grew anxious as they rode down the trail. He began to feel as if they would never find the station at Hollenberg. Finally, Stevie and the others started to tire. They had been riding for twelve hours without a break. Stevie began questioning his decision to take this job. What had he gotten himself into? He tried to shake away the thought. He told himself if anyone could do it, he could.

Shortly after nine o'clock, the boys rode into Hollenberg Station. Weary and tired, they slowed their horses and stopped in front of the house. A lamp was burning in the glass window of the house. John Hollenberg stepped out of the house to greet the boys.

"I was starting to think you boys weren't gonna make it."

Stevie replied, "We were thinking that, too."

"Well, come on in. I've got some supper for you and then you can get a little sleep. I'll wake you at one o'clock so you can get back on schedule. I know it's only four hours, but we've gotta schedule to keep and you're behind."

They all replied, "Thanks, Mr. Hollenberg."

They sat at a table where plates of rabbit stew were waiting. Each boy quickly ate the stew and swallowed a cup of coffee before retiring to one of the cots in the corner of the cabin.

It seemed like only ten minutes when Mr. Hollenberg woke the boys.

"Here! Drink this down real quick. It will wake you up."

Hollenberg handed each boy a cup of black coffee and a pouch containing two biscuits and some jerky to eat along their way.

Stevie was bleary-eyed as he took the coffee from Hollenberg and began to drink. The hot coffee felt good as it ran down his throat. Finally, Stevie accepted the pouch and walked out the door to find his next ride. Charlie and Tom followed closely behind as they started their ponies into a gallop and mounted them.

As they rode away, Hollenberg yelled, "When you get to Rock Creek you'll be in Nebraska!"

The clouds had cleared somewhat while the boys slept. The

moon was waning but provided enough light to see the trail as they traveled northwesterly.

The trail to Rock Creek was like a dry river bed. All sizes of rocks lay along the route, making it a difficult path to travel. The nine-mile trek took the boys better than an hour to traverse. After switching horses at Rock Creek, the rocky terrain continued for another mile before changing to an almost desert-like and sandy trail. Vegetation was a rare sight. The land was barren as the boys continued the journey that led them to their next station, Big Sandy.

They reached Big Sandy around three o'clock in the morning. It was still dark, but the darkness was fading slightly. Again, they exchanged horses and continued their journey. An hour later, they found themselves arriving at Thompson's relay. The landscape was ever-changing from station to station. This land was fertile with prairie grass, and evergreen trees scattered throughout the terrain.

After leaving Thompson's, Stevie nearly lost his place in the saddle as a prairie hen flew from her nest next to the trail causing Stevie's horse to jump from fright. Stevie managed to regained his balance in the saddle as they galloped down the path to Kiowa.

The trail between Kiowa and Liberty Farm was most worrisome for Stevie and the others. A band of ten Kiowa scouts paralleled the riders as they rode down the trail. The Indians never came any closer or farther away. They matched the speed of the Express riders all along the path. Their presence was unnerving to the trio.

Stevie was relieved when they arrived at Liberty Farm and saw that the Kiowa were no longer trailing him and his partners.

The riders arrived at 32 Mile Creek around six o'clock. The sun fully rose at their backs as they continued west. They crossed the creek without incident. The stream was only three feet deep at its deepest point. Deep enough, however, to get Stevie's feet wet. Once they reached the west bank, Stevie momentarily stopped to pull his boots off and empty the water. Tom and Charlie imitated Stevie, ridding their boots of water too.

An hour later found them at a place called Lone Tree. A small cabin was built on an empty prairie with only one tree to give it shade. A large Shagbark Hickory towered over the house. A few sage-grouses strutted around the yard surrounding the cabin with their white breast expanded. They had two yellow sacks on their breasts that looked like they were wearing two eggs fried sunny side up on their chest. Lone Tree Station was different from most other stations in that a woman ran it. Mamie Prosser was a forty-year-old widow who inherited her farm from her late husband, Mark, who had been killed by Kiowa ten years earlier. Miss Mamie had run the farm and survived on her own ever since. She was outspoken and not to be trifled with. She could ride and shoot as well as any man. The Kiowa named her "Deadly Woman" because she had killed any Indians who dared trespass.

As Stevie and the others stopped to change their horses, they saw the woman come out of her house to meet them.

"Howdy! My name's Mamie Prosser. I run this place. Are you boys hungry?"

Charlie announced, "And Howdy, Ma'am!"

"Well ya'll come on in. I'll fix you some eggs. There's bacon and biscuits already cooked. While you eat, I'll switch out your horses."

Stevie tied his horse to a hitching post and said, "Thanks, Miss Mamie. We haven't eaten in about seven hours. Eggs and bacon sound good. By the way, I'm Stevie Watson. This is Bronco Charlie Miller and That's Irish Tom Grady."

"Nice to meet you boys. You're the first I've had through here. Wasn't sure when to expect you for sure."

As they followed Mamie into the house, Stevie explained, "Well, they should be coming through pretty regular, now. Tom is going to Ft. Kearny and Charlie and I are headed to Ft. Laramie."

The boys sat down at Mamie's table while she scrambled a dozen eggs in the iron skillet. She brought the eggs to the table along with the bacon and biscuits, then poured the boys a cup of coffee each.

"Dig in and help yourself. I'll get your fresh horses ready for you."

"Thanks, Ma'am," said Stevie.

The boys ate like wild animals, ravaging the bacon, eggs, and biscuits. Finally, they each divided the remaining biscuits and put them in their pockets to eat along the trail. Stevie swallowed his last gulp of coffee as Mamie returned to the house.

"My! You made quick work of that!" she said as she looked at the cleanly, scraped plates.

"You're ready to ride. See you boys next time."

Stevie said, "Thanks, Miss Mamie!" as he ran to mount his new pony.

As the boys rode away, Mamie called out to them, "You boys keep an eye out for Injuns!"

The ride from Mamie's was a little more challenging. Stevie and his partners found themselves riding uphill. It was a steady upward incline all the way from Lone Tree to a place called the Summit. Another station waited for them atop the hill where they exchanged mounts once again.

The terrain leveled out from Summit, and the ride was much more manageable. By nine-thirty, they arrived at Hooks Station. Old man Hooks had their new ponies ready to go as soon as they arrived. He was a bow-legged old man whose back was nearly as crooked as his legs.

As Stevie approached his new horse he noticed a river running behind Hooks' cabin.

"What river is that?"

"That's the Platte. You'll be following that for the next few hours. If you're going to Ft. Laramie, you'll have to cross it twiced."

Stevie asked, "Is it deep?"

"Yep! Sho is! You won't be wading it though. Hope you can swim. Hey! Ft. Kearney's your next stop!"

Stevie smiled and waved to the old man as he led the way down the trail.

Stevie was relieved to hear the news. He was ready for a break. But, unfortunately, his lack of sleep was starting to catch up with him. He found himself shaking his head, trying to keep himself awake. Stevie tried to busy himself with looking at the country to his north. The area around the Platte was impressive. Tall Pines and Cedars lined the north side of the river. Stevie spotted an eagle as it glided over the river, swooped down into the water, caught a large trout, and then flew away from sight.

After an hour of riding, Stevie caught sight of a large wooden structure in the distance. Stevie had never witnessed a fort before. As he and the others rode closer, they were in awe of how tall the walls were and how strong a fortress it must be. Indeed, no one would try to attack such a fort as this.

As they rode to the fort's entrance, they were stopped by two sentries. "Halt! What's your business here?"

Stevie announced, "We're riders for the Pony Express. We were told to check in here."

The sentry said, "The Express office is on the west side of the fort, just ahead on your right."

"Thank you, sir."

Stevie was disappointed he wouldn't be entering the fort. He had hoped to see if it was just as impressive on the inside as it was outside. He led the others a few yards farther until they found another cabin with a corral on the backside. This cabin had been newly built and was much larger than the others. It looked more like a hotel than a wait station.

A man met them when they rode to the cabin and dismounted their horses. "Walk on in. Mr. Willy will help you get settled."

The boys entered the house and were immediately greeted by a tall, slender man with a handlebar mustache.

"Gentlemen! Welcome to Ft. Kearny! I am Joseph Willy, station manager." Each boy introduced themself to him, then he instructed, "There are empty rooms upstairs for each of you. Make yourselves at home. Will any of you be going on to Ft. Laramie?"

Stevie replied, "Charlie and I will be."

Mr. Willy said, "Well, you've made good time so far. Get plenty of rest for the second leg of your journey. You won't need to leave until early tomorrow, say around six."

Stevie replied, "Sounds good. Are we allowed to go into the fort?"

"You may, however, they close the gates at dusk. You won't be able to go in or out after that."

"Thanks!" said Stevie.

The boys went upstairs and chose a room. Stevie immediately went to sleep while Charlie and Tom decided to check out the fort. Stevie slept for three hours before the rumbling of his stomach awoke him. Finally, he decided to go down and find a bite to eat. He sat down to a plate of chicken stew that had been kept warm for him in the kitchen, when Charlie and Tom walked in. Tom was excited as he sat next to Stevie and proclaimed, "Look at this, lad!"

Tom rolled up his left shirt sleeve and revealed a newly placed tattoo on his forearm.

"What is it?"

"It's called a tattoo. One of the soldiers did it for me. He was doing them for all the soldiers and I asked him to do one for me."

Stevie asked, "What's that symbol?"

"It's a four leaf clover, son. It will bring me luck."

Stevie suggested, "More likely infection than luck."

"Oh, don't be jealous lad. He'll do one for you, too."

"No thanks."

Stevie looked at Charlie and asked, "How about you?"

"Nah! He said my arm was too small. I wasn't crazy about getting one anyway."

"I knew you were smart!" said Stevie.

CHAPTER 29

tevie and Charlie left early the next morning. They ate a quick breakfast along with Tom and said goodbye to him. Then, the two of them mounted new ponies and began the long ride to Ft. Laramie.

Stevie rode side by side with Charlie most of the way, allowing for conversation from time to time. Each would point out some exciting site along the way; a rock formation shaped like a hand, a flock of geese flying overhead, or a herd of antelope grazing next to the river. They followed the Platte River most of the way. The stations were situated along the Platte, which made sense. If a person were going to set up a homestead in the middle of nowhere, they would need plenty of fresh water.

Platte Station was their first relay. They arrived within the allotted hour and made the transfer without a hitch. Thirty seconds later, they were back on the trail.

Halfway to Craigs, Stevie pointed north, across the Platte, to show Charlie what he had spotted. A mother Grizzly bear with two cubs was on the opposite side of the river. The cubs were playing and wrestling together while the sow was busy fishing. Stevie was tempted to stop so they could observe the family longer, but he knew he didn't have time.

Everything Stevie saw along the trail made him excited to be alive. Being out in the frontier where few people lived, experiencing nature like very few would ever see in their lifetime, and the exhilaration of riding with the wind in his face was more than he could have ever hoped for. Yet, he wondered how much he had missed while riding in the dark. What strange creatures had seen him ride past that he might never have the opportunity to see in daylight? Trees, vegetation, and rock formations were in abundance. Yet he had missed them while traveling in the night. He wanted to see it all, experience it all.

Today was the perfect day for a pleasure ride; for Stevie, a ten-mile-an-hour gallop was a pleasure. He had always enjoyed the thrill of galloping from home to St. Joe and back in the afternoon.

Again, the weather was perfect today. Stevie had the sun on his back to warm him; the skies were clear, and no rain was in sight.

They made good time as they rode into Craigs by eight o'clock. Luther Craigs had their new ponies ready when they arrived. Stevie and Charlie quickly dismounted and mounted the new horses with only time for a quick "Howdy!"

Their next stop was Plum Creek, where a grove of yellow plums grew next to a small stream that ran into the Platte. Then Willow Springs, a pretty little cabin nestled between two giant Willow trees that grew along the bank of a pond that was fed by a natural spring and flowed into the Platte. Every station seemed to offer something different. Stevie wished he had more time to experience every little detail.

Around eleven o'clock, the boys rode into a station called Midway. Stevie wondered why it was called Midway. It didn't seem to be named because of its location. It wasn't midway between Ft. Kearny and Ft. Laramie. He could only surmise that the cabin was midway between falling in on itself and standing. It was a wreck. The door only hung by one hinge, the roof was full of holes, and the steps that led to the front door were caving. As the attendant came running out of the house to help the boys switch horses, he was followed by two chickens that flew out the door behind him. Stevie didn't know whether to laugh or feel sorry for the man.

An hour later, they rode into Gilmun's Station, where a boy of about thirteen was waiting with their new mounts. As they switched ponies, Stevie asked, "What's your name?"

"Toby! What's yours?"

"Stevie! This is Charlie!"

As Stevie started to mount the new pony, a tiny voice came from the house.

It was Toby's younger sister. "Wait, Mister!"

Stevie looked to the house and saw the young girl running toward him carrying a small sack. She ran up to Stevie, handed him the bag, and said, "Here! Ma said you might be hungry."

"Thanks! We are!"

Stevie and Charlie mounted the horses, and they rode away. Stevie let out a

"Yeehaw!"

Toby answered with his own, "Yeehaw!"

When Stevie opened the sack, he found four warm biscuits with bacon. He handed two to Charlie, and they ate them as they galloped along the trail. The biscuits were a welcomed treat for the boys. Their spirits seemed to pick up after eating. The next few legs of the ride came much easier.

Stevie and Charlie soon found themselves at Sam Mettache's, where they once again changed mounts. Then, an hour later, they rode into the Cottonwood Station where Cottonwood trees surrounded the little cabin. Stevie thought it was snowing for a moment, although he knew the temperature was too warm for snow.

The winds were scattering the seed pods of the Cottonwoods. The feathery seeds floated through the air giving the illusion of snow falling.

Around three o'clock that afternoon, Stevie and Charlie rode into Cold Springs Station. The station was operated by Millard Garner, an elderly gent who wore a long white beard stained with tobacco juice from his nasty habit of chewing. Unfortunately, Garner was unable to spit far enough to clear his beard, so the juice ran down his furry chin.

Stevie noticed the Platte River split into two rivers behind Garner's corral. "Which fork do we take?"

Garner replied, "Take the south one. That's the south Platte. Follow it til you get to Julesburg. That's when you have to cross the river."

Stevie said, "Thanks!"

They mounted their new horses and continued riding west. Stevie was anxious to arrive at Fremont Springs, so he pushed his pony as hard as possible. He looked forward to taking a break for a few hours, then going on to Ft. Laramie.

When they arrived at Fremont Springs, they found a younger man who ran the station, not much older than they were. Henry Fremont had been homesteading the place with his father since Henry was six years old. Unfortunately, his pa died four years ago, and Henry had all but given up trying to survive in the frontier alone. So when the Pony Express showed up wanting to use his place as an exchange station, he jumped at the chance. It would bring him the much-needed money to help him survive on his own.

"Welcome! I'm Henry Fremont."

Stevie dismounted and replied, "I'm Stevie Watson. This is Charlie Miller."

"Miller?"

Charlie replied, "Yes, sir! Charlie Miller. They call me Bronco Charlie."

"Well, Bronco Charlie, I've been waiting for you. You'll be staying here. This will be your home station until the Express arrives in a couple of days."

Charlie was a little disappointed. He had hoped to continue to Ft. Laramie with Stevie. He had come to depend on Stevie over the past two weeks. Stevie treated him like a little brother, and Charlie enjoyed it. Stevie was a little disappointed too. He enjoyed Charlie's company along the trail. They rode well together. It was as if they knew what each other was thinking.

Henry prepared an early supper for the boys, then Stevie retired to a corner cot to get some rest before continuing his ride. Stevie asked Henry, "Would you wake me around ten? I want to get started on the next leg."

"Sure. I'll have your horse ready for you."

Stevie lay on the cot and eventually drifted off to sleep. It seemed like only minutes had passed when Henry woke Stevie.

"It's ten o'clock. I've got your horse ready for you."

Stevie rose from the cot, still half asleep. His body rocked as he tried to gain his balance. Henry handed Stevie a poke sack and said, "Here's some food for the trail."

"Thanks!"

Stevie slowly walked to the door and paused to find Charlie asleep on another cot. Stevie started to wake him, then decided against it. Instead, he told Henry, "Tell him I'll see him on the trail."

Stevie wasn't thrilled about the night ride, but he at least had clear skies to ride under. He made good time considering the conditions, but at several of the stops he made, no one was awake. Stevie had to change horses out himself. He felt a little strange going into another man's corral and saddling a strange horse, but he told himself, "*These horses belong to the Pony Express and I am the Pony Express.*"

Stevie made his way through O' Fallon's, Alkali, Beauvais, Diamond Spring, and South Platte before finally arriving at Julesburg Station. He had left Nebraska while at South Platte and crossed into Colorado. The trail ended at the South Platte River just north of Julesburg. When Stevie arrived at the river's edge, he thought about what he should do next.

Stevie knelt down and dipped his hand into the river. The water was icy cold. Stevie wasn't looking forward to swimming in frigid waters, then riding down the trail with wet clothes. He decided the smartest thing to do would be to strip off all his clothes. So he did. He undressed and then rolled his clothes, wrapping them around his boots. He then wrapped his gun belt around the clothes and fastened the buckle to hold the clothes together. He looped the bundle onto his saddle horn and secured it with a leather thong customarily used to tie a lariat to the saddle. Stevie mounted the pony and moved him into the water. The horse slowly walked through the river until he could walk no more. Finally, the water became so deep the horse could no longer reach the bottom. The pony had no choice but to swim. He lunged forward and moved as close to the top of the water as he could manage. Stevie allowed himself to drift off the end of the pony, then grasped the horse's tail and let the horse pull him through the water.

When they reached the north bank of the Platte, Stevie crawled forward back into the saddle until his pony was back on dry ground. Stevie slid off the horse and unrolled the bundle of clothes. He used his shirt to dry off before dressing. He put the shirt back on even though it was damp. He barely noticed the dampness through the thickness of his long johns. Stevie mounted again and continued his ride.

Stevie rode without incident and made his exchanges at Lodge Pole, 30 Mile Ridge, and then arrived at Midway Station at seven o'clock. This was the second station named Midway that Stevie had traveled to. However, he soon discovered that many of the stations repeated names as he traveled farther west.

Midway was the mark of the route's end. Stevie had ridden

for ten hours, give or take since he left Charlie. Stevie wasn't ready to stop, but he thought he should at least get some food in his belly before moving on.

Samuel and Elizabeth Harper, a middle-aged couple with no children, ran Midway Station. Stevie was delighted when Mrs. Harper offered to cook him breakfast.

"Thanks, Mrs. Harper. That sounds nice."

Samuel asked, "Will you be staying for a while before moving on to Ft. Laramie?"

"No, Sir. Just long enough to stretch my legs a bit and fill my belly. Then I'll be moving on. I want to get to Ft. Laramie before dark."

Samuel replied, "Well, you be careful. I've heard the Kiowa are causing trouble between here and Laramie. Keep your eyes and ears open."

"Thanks, I will."

Stevie ate slowly. He decided to enjoy what might be his last full meal in quite a while. Stevie wasn't sure what to expect the rest of the way to Ft. Laramie.

When he had finished his last bite, Stevie stood and thanked Mrs. Harper for the delicious breakfast. He then got on his fresh horse and galloped to the next station.

Stevie rode to Mud Springs, Court House Rock, Junction Station, and Chimney Rock, making his relays without incident. However, five miles outside Chimney Rock, Stevie noticed black smoke rising above the trees to his west. Stevie continued to ride toward the smoke as his stomach began churning. He feared what he might find up ahead. Half an hour later, he discovered the next station, Ficklin's, had burned to the ground. Stevie stopped his pony and then moved forward cautiously, searching for any survivors. Unfortunately, nothing was left of the cabin except smoke and smoldering embers.

Stevie searched through the charred remains of the cabin and found what must have been Mr. Ficklin. The body was too burned to even know if it was human or animal. Stevie contemplated what to do. Should he bury the black mass of burnt flesh, or should he continue on and try to find help. Stevie looked for a shovel or pick or anything he could use to dig. There was none. Everything had been burned. He decided the ground would be too firm to dig without proper tools, so Stevie decided to move on and let the army take care of Ficklin.

Stevie checked the corral for a new mount but discovered the corral was empty. Several tracks led from the corral northward toward the North Platte River. An arrow had been shot into one of the posts of the corral. Stevie removed the arrow and carried it with him. Stevie had no choice but to continue down the trail on the same horse. Rather than running the horse at full gallop, he allowed the pony to canter most of the way. After a while, the pony's breathing became labored. He snorted, trying to catch his breath. Stevie slowed the horse to a walk allowing him to rest a bit. The horse was sweating so badly that white foam had formed around the saddle's edge and where the reins rubbed against his neck. Stevie finally dismounted and walked alongside the horse for the last two miles before reaching Scott's Bluff.

Jake Scott met Stevie as he walked into the front of the station.

"Howdy! Can I help you?"

Stevie replied, "I'm Stevie Watson. I ride for the Pony Express."

Jake was shocked to see Stevie arrive in such poor condition with his horse. "What happened to your horse?"

"He just made twenty miles without rest. The last station was attacked by Indians and burned to the ground. All the horses were gone."

Jake asked, "How about Old Man Ficklin?"

"I didn't find any bodies. He must have been burned up in the house or taken captive. I did find this."

Stevie showed Jake the arrow he had found in one of the corral posts.

"Looks like Kiowa!" Jake exclaimed.

Stevie said, "I need to get moving. You be careful, Mr. Scott. They might be headed this way next. I'll get to Laramie as quick as I can and let then know."

"Good luck, son!"

Stevie mounted a fresh horse and took off at a gallop. An hour later, he rode into Spring Ranch and switched horses before moving on again. On his way to Bedeau's Station, he crossed into Wyoming. Stevie's head was forever on a swivel as he rode along. He was more intent on looking for trouble along the path now.

From Bedeau to Ft. Laramie, the elevation began to rise. Stevie's horse found it more challenging to climb the steep hill at a full gallop, but Stevie pushed him onward. Then, finally, the sun started to lower itself behind the distant mountains to the west.

Stevie finally arrived at his ultimate destination around seven in the evening. Unfortunately, two sentries stopped Stevie as he rode toward the gates that entered the fort.

One of them asked, "What's your business here?"

Stevie replied, "I'm Stevie Watson, rider for the Pony Express. Ficklin's Station was attacked by Kiowa a few hours ago and burned to the ground. They stole all the horses."

The sentry said, "Ride on in and ask for Sergeant Lang. He'll want to hear about this."

Stevie proceeded into the fort and was immediately directed to Sergeant Lang. Sergeant Lang was a fairly young man, clean-shaven and buttoned up. Stevie was impressed with how clean the sergeant looked, considering he lived on the frontier.

"What can I do for you?" the sergeant asked.

"I'm Stevie Watson and I ride for the Pony Express. When I came through Ficklin's Station I found it burned out and all the horses were missing. I didn't see any survivors."

Then Stevie handed Lang the arrow.

"I found this had been shot into a post of the corral."

Lang commented, "Kiowa. Thank you, Mr. Watson. I'll report this to the Colonel. Your quarters are located outside the fort next to the river."

"Thank you, Sergeant."

Stevie left the fort and walked his pony to the Express station. A man walked out of the newly built cabin to meet Stevie. Russell and his associates hired Arnold Reese to run the Ft. Laramie Station. Ft. Laramie wasn't halfway to the Pony Express terminal at Sacramento. However, it was an essential part of the Express.

"Are you Watson?" asked Reese.

"Yes, sir. Stevie Watson."

"Glad to meet you. This will be your home station. You'll be dispatched from here on your route. Some days you'll travel west and other days you'll go back east. You made good time?"

Stevie replied, "I think so. However, I ran into one snag. Ficklin's was burned out so I had to ride my horse an extra leg until I could switch out."

"What happened?"

"Kiowa. I reported it to Sergeant Lang when I rode in. He said he'd report it to the Colonel."

"Good man." said Reese. "I'll need to post a letter to Mr. Russell to let him know. We'll have to see about setting up a temporary station until Ficklin can be rebuilt. Are you hungry?"

"Yes, sir."

"Come inside. Mrs. Reese probably has supper ready by now. Then, I'm sure you're ready for some sack time."

"Yes, sir I am."

CHAPTER 30

June 6, 1860

Henry Butterfield was like most Pony Express riders, only a little older than most. Henry was twenty years old and had worked herding cattle along the plains of Oklahoma for the past four years. When he heard about the Express and how much money was being paid to young men who could ride and shoot, Henry jumped at the opportunity. He signed on as a rider a month after the initial crew was hired.

Henry was not a good-looking young man. He had been kicked and stomped on by cattle and horses until his face was scarred and disfigured. Another reason the Pony Express was appealing to Henry was he wouldn't have to put up with the glares and snares people gave him when he walked down the streets of town. Instead, he would spend all his time on the trail coming in contact only with the station managers, the horses, and other riders.

Henry was on the last stretch of his route from Rock Creek to Ft. Kearny. He had just left Hooks Station and had an hour left on his ride. Henry looked forward to his soon-to-be rest period as he had been riding most of the night. Like most riders, Henry didn't particularly care for night riding. Too much could go wrong at night. Your horse could step in a gopher hole, or you might run into a pack of wolves out on the hunt. Also, you could easily get lost in the darkness if the moon wasn't shining. However, Henry had ridden through the night without incident.

As he rode into the station at Ft. Kearny, Henry slid his pony to a halt, snagged his mochila from the back of the horse as he slid off the pony's back, then handed the mochila to the next rider.

Irish Tom took the mochila from Henry and mounted his fresh pony as the animal galloped away. Tom had gotten a full five hours of sleep while resting at Ft. Kearny Station. He felt fresh and alive as he sped down the trail leading to Platte Station. Tom had been one of the designated riders concentrating on the route between Rock Creek and Ft. Kearny and between Ft. Kearny and Fremont

Springs. Today he would ride to Fremont Springs, heading west.

Tom received his mochila from Henry at seven o'clock. The air was heavy with humidity already. It promised to be a terribly warm day out on the trail. No matter, Tom was feeling spry and in his mind, he sang a delightful Irish tune. The song's rhythm matched well with the beating of his horse's hoof beats.

In Dublin's fair city,
Where the Girls are so pretty,
I first set my eyes,
On sweet Molly Malone,
As she wheeled her wheelbarrow,
Through the streets, broad and narrow,
Crying cockles and mussels,
Alive, alive o!
Alive, alive o!
Alive, alive o!
Crying cockles and mussels,
Alive, alive o!

The words to Molly Malone kept Tom's spirits up as he rode the many hours along the trail past Platte Station and beyond.

Alive, alive o!
Alive, alive o!
Crying cockles and mussels,
Alive, alive o!

Tom rode on through Craigs, Plum Creek, and Willow Springs, singing his tune in his head all along the way. He rode to Midway, Gilmun's Station, and Sam Mettache's without incident, switching his ponies along the way.

Alive, alive o!
Alive, alive o!
Crying cockles and mussels,
Alive, alive o!

Two miles past Sam Mettache's, Tom noticed a group of riders to his north. The singing in his head ended. Instead, it was replaced with suspicion and worry. *"Who are these lads riding stride for stride with me?"* he thought.

Tom kept his pony galloping along, ever mindful of the ones who seemed to be following him. Finally, with eight miles to go before he reached Cottonwood, Tom began to panic as he witnessed the riders veering toward him. He counted six riders, and as they moved closer to him, he saw they were not white men. *"Kiowa!"*

Tom reached for the rifle that was slung around his shoulder. Tom had never opted for the handy six-shooter. He had never gotten the knack of firing one. He checked his load to make sure it was ready to fire. However, he was in an awkward position to fire against his would-be attackers. They were moving in on his right side, and he was right-handed, but he wouldn't be able to aim correctly or use his left hand to steady the weapon.

Six braves moved in closer to Tom, yelling out war cries as they came closer and closer. One of the braves shot an arrow at Tom and just missed his head. Tom heard the projectile whiz by his ear.

Tom pointed his rifle at the Indians with his right hand, holding the gun as he would have a pistol. He squeezed the trigger and hit one of his attackers in the leg. However, the shot seemed not to phase the brave as he continued to ride closer and closer to Tom.

More arrows flew at Tom as he gathered his rifle in his left hand to cock another round into the firing chamber. This time, when he fired at the Indians, he hit one in the chest, causing the man to flip off his horse backward. When the brave hit the ground, one of the following horses ran over him. Tom watched momentarily as the brave lay motionless in a cloud of dust.

Arrows were fired at him again, and one struck Tom in his right flank. "Ugh!" He moaned and contorted, trying to remain in the saddle.

Blood trickled from Tom's side, and he felt the arrow bounce up and down inside of him as his pony galloped along. Another arrow struck Tom in the right thigh as he cried out again. Still, he managed to remain in the saddle.

Suddenly, the Indians were upon him, riding side by side with him. One of the braves raised a war club into the air and swung it down into Tom's face knocking him off the pony. Tom hit the ground with a thud.

Tom tried to raise himself from the ground, but his head hurt too much. He rolled his head and noticed his rifle lying next to him. He reached over and picked up the gun, cocked it, and fired at one of the braves who was now on foot coming at Tom. *"Bang!"*

The shot hit the man in the face, and the brave fell dead to the ground. Before Tom could cock his rifle again, three of the braves were upon him, beating him with clubs about the face and torso. The other brave chased and caught Tom's pony and returned to the others with the newly stolen horse in tow. One of the three braves that stood over Tom took out a long knife from its sheath, knelt down on one knee next to Tom, and grasped Tom's hair with his free hand. The brave sliced through Tom's forehead removing his scalp with one full slice of his knife.

Tom screamed out in terror and pain as the brave raised Tom's scalp in victory to show the other braves. They all celebrated with "whoops" and screams. Then, the braves worked together, stripping Tom of all his belongings, including his clothes. One of them took Tom's boots and immediately put them on his own feet. Another took his hat and rifle. The other removed his shirt and pants. Finally, they all gathered up their spoils and left, celebrating their great victory. The fourth rider followed behind, towing the pony with Tom's saddle and mochila.

Tom lay in the dirt, the tune of Molly Malone still playing in his head. He tried to sing out loud, but his voice failed. Blood flowed from his leg, his side, and his scalp. His face was unrecognizable from being beaten with the Indian clubs. Flies began to collect around his wounds to feed and lay their eggs. Tom's death was brutal and painful, but die he did.

Chapter 31

June 7, 1860

Charlie awoke just before daybreak. He had ridden into Fremont just after midnight, running the eastern route. He would now be heading farther east toward Cold Springs, where the Platte River splits, as soon as his mochila arrived.

The mochila was a bag that fits over the rider's saddle. It had four pockets, one on each corner, that held mail and small parcels. The rider sat on the mochila as he traveled and transferred it from horse to horse. The mochila was also transferred from rider to rider once it reached the layover stations, which marked the end of a rider's shift. Ft. Laramie, Midway, Fremont Springs, and Ft. Kearny were just a few of those layover stations.

Charlie ate breakfast while he awaited the rider coming in from Midway to hand off his mochila. Michael Casey sat across the table from Charlie. Michael was waiting for the next mochila coming from the east. It was overdue. It should have arrived late last night, but the rider never showed.

Michael didn't seem to mind much. He got paid the same whether he rode or sat still. Casey was sixteen and hailed from Iowa. His pa was a crop farmer who mostly raised corn and wheat. Michael had ever longed to get away from the farm, so when the Pony Express posted bills in his nearby town of Council Bluffs, Michael jumped at the chance. He packed what few belongings he had, saddled one of his pa's horses, and left immediately. He never looked back nor told his family where he was going.

Charlie asked Michael, "What are you still doing here? Weren't you supposed to leave last night?"

Michael replied, "My exchange never showed up."

"Who was the rider?"

"I don't know for sure. Last time it was that Irish feller."

Charlie asked, "You mean, Irish Tom?"

"Yeah. That's him. Don't know if he was coming last night or if it was somebody else."

Charlie contemplated over his bacon and eggs. A feeling deep down in his gut told him something was wrong. Before Charlie could finish his breakfast, he heard a horse ride into the station. Charlie and Michael scrambled to their feet to see which direction the rider was coming from.

They saw a pony coming in from the west as they walked out the door. It was Charlie's exchange. Michael, somewhat relieved, walked back to the table to finish his breakfast. Charlie strapped on his gun belt and walked out to the corral to receive the mochila and a fresh pony.

"Any problems?" Charlie asked the incoming rider.

"No. All's clear."

Charlie said, "See ya in a day or two."

Then, Charlie mounted his horse and galloped away. Charlie felt refreshed after the long rest at Fremont. It felt good to be back out on the trail. The Sorrel Charlie rode seemed to enjoy running because he galloped very evenly. His gait was level, and Charlie had no problems staying in the saddle as the Sorrel ran.

Charlie seemed to arrive at Cold Springs in record time. He saw old man Garner leading a fresh pony from the corral as Charlie approached. Tobacco juice was dripping down the old man's chin.

Charlie asked as he dismounted, "Any news?"

Millard Garner hastily spit before saying, "Naup! Nerry a word."

Charlie made the running mount onto the new horse and left without saying another word. He glanced to his left and noticed the North Platte and South Platte where they merged. The prairie lay beyond the river as he rode along the southern bank. Charlie's ride was smooth and quick. The sun was burning brightly already, and the temperature was steadily rising. The wind that blew against his face as he rode was warm.

Charlie reached Cottonwood around nine o'clock. When he arrived, he found Ike Slater wasn't ready for him. Ike was still saddling Charlie's pony.

"What's the word, Ike?" Charlie asked.

"Don't know it! Say, have you heard anything about the westward route coming from Ft. Kearny?"

"No, sir! Why?"

Ike said, "Well, no one ever showed yesterday. I haven't seen a rider come through since day before yesterday."

Charlie began to worry.

"Have you seen any Injuns?"

Ike replied, "No. But they're around. I wouldn't be surprised if they ain't watchin' us right now."

Charlie looked around, searching for any sign of the red devils. He took his mochila from the previous pony and placed it on the freshly saddled horse before he performed his running mount heading toward Sam Mettache's. Charlie kept his eyes roaming the areas around him as he rode. His eyes shifted north, then south. He peeked over his shoulders to make sure no one was following him. The hair on the back of his neck stood up as he rode. A chill ran down his backbone. He began to sweat even more than the bright sun would have warranted.

Seven miles down the trail, just as he settled down, Charlie saw movement from the corner of his left eye. His body tensed again as he searched for what had caught his attention. There they were. To the north rode four riders who paralleled Charlie. Then, he saw the riders change direction and ride at an angle that would eventually intercept Charlie. He wasn't sure whether to push his pony harder or find a place to make a stand. A quarter of a mile later, he decided to take cover. A fallen tree among some large boulders would make a perfect place to pick them off as they approached.

Charlie pulled against the reins to stop the pony behind the fallen tree. Then, he dismounted and checked his six-shooter to make sure it was loaded. He then checked the four additional cylinders that hung on his belt to ensure they were all loaded. Then, he waited.

The Indians seemed confused as they rode to where they had expected the lone rider to be. They slowed their ponies to a stop just a hundred feet from where Charlie hid. Suddenly, a shot rang out, and one of the braves fell to the ground dead. Charlie shot him between the eyes. The Indian ponies reared up and spun as they searched for an escape. Charlie took careful aim and pulled the trigger again. *"Bang!"*

Another brave hit the ground. One of the other braves spotted where the shot had come from. He raised a rifle and shot, but because he was unskilled with the new firearm and because his horse was nervously spinning around, the shot went wide and missed Charlie.

Charlie then stood and quickly squeezed off four quick shots. *"Bang! Bang! Bang! Bang!"*

Two shots entered into the brave holding the rifle and two into his partner. Both men fell dead. Charlie hesitated before leaving his spot of safety. He waited and listened to make sure no one else came near.

Charlie slowly left his hiding place, leading his pony behind him. He checked each of the Indians he had shot to make sure they were dead. He was surprised to see that their ponies had not fled. Instead, they were all roaming nearby as if they had been trained not to run away during a battle.

One by one, Charlie checked the braves.

"Kiowa!" Charlie said aloud to himself.

He removed anything from their bodies that might be useful to him. He found the rifle with which one of the braves had tried to kill him. Charlie also found knives and war clubs. Then, he spotted something he had not expected. One of the ponies had a mochila on its back. Charlie checked the pouches of the mochila, but they were all empty. Undoubtedly, whatever had been in the mochila at one time was useless to the Kiowa. He attached anything he thought he might want to keep to the ponies; then, he tied them in a line so he could lead them behind his own horse.

Charlie mounted his horse and moved forward, managing to get the ponies up to a canter. He knew taking the Indian ponies with him would slow him down, but it would be worth it.

Half a mile down the trail, Charlie noticed buzzards flying in a circular motion up ahead. Some of the birds flew in a ring in a clockwise motion, while others flew counterclockwise. The motions made it seem as if they were all flying in a figure eight.

Charlie continued east until he found a lifeless body ravaged by another group of black death birds. Charlie fired his gun into the air several times to scare away the vultures. Finally, he dismounted and walked over to see what the birds had been feeding on. There it was. A human body stripped naked. The body had numerous wounds, some by birds and some by other means. Charlie walked closer to examine the body. It turned his stomach to see the raw flesh and dried blood that covered what was once a man. The man's scalp was gone and his face was unrecognizable because it had been badly beaten and because of the birds.

Charlie decided whoever it once was didn't deserve to stay here and be eaten by these vultures or any other scavenger. So he returned to the ponies and took a blanket off one of the Indian horses. Charlie took the blanket to the corpse and began to roll it up inside the blanket. As he wrapped the body, he noticed a marking on the man's right forearm.

Charlie walked back to his pony and grabbed his water bag. He used the water to wash away the blood on the man's arm. Charlie's heart sank when he realized what he was seeing. A tattoo of a four-leaf clover.

Tears filled Charlie's eyes as he recognized whose body he had found. "Irish Tom." Charlie whispered.

CHAPTER 32

JUNE 14, 1860

Stevie awoke around six o'clock on Thursday morning. He arrived at Ft. Laramie at one o'clock, having traveled the eastward run from Sweetwater, Wyoming. Stevie awaited the next mochila coming from Sweetwater, which should be arriving any minute.

Four riders stationed at Ft. Laramie traveled between Sweetwater, Wyoming, and Midway, Nebraska. Two riders were always traveling westward while the other two went eastward.

Stevie was waiting on Johnny Sinclair to arrive with Stevie's next mochila. He sat at the table eating a big breakfast of ham, eggs, and biscuits. Arnold Reese, the station master, sat at the opposite side of the table from Stevie. His wife, Elise, sat next to Arnold. Bill Trotter sat next to Stevie.

Bill was one of the four riders assigned to Ft. Laramie. He was from Lincoln, Nebraska. Bill came from meager circumstances like many of the Pony Express riders. His pa worked at a dry goods store in Lincoln, and his ma took in laundry to bring in extra income. Bill had worked at a livery stable, much like Stevie, only he didn't manage it. Instead, he only did menial labor. However, working at the stables allowed him to learn how to ride the roughest of stock imaginable. The livery owner not only boarded animals in his stable, but he also bred and trained horses.

While the four of them sat around the table, they talked about their families and where each of them was from. Stevie learned that Elise was a Baptist preacher's daughter back in Ohio before she met Arnold. Arnold had worked for William Waddell in the freight business before moving to Ft. Laramie to work for the Pony Express. He was an assistant manager in St. Joseph at one of Waddell's warehouses. Arnold jumped at the opportunity when Waddell offered him a position managing a Pony Express station. He and Elise had always talked about moving farther west, and this was just the chance they had hoped for.

Suddenly, everyone heard horse hooves beating quickly outside. The three men rose from the table and sprinted toward the door to see who was coming. Arnold had already saddled two ponies waiting for the next two relays that were both due. When Arnold opened the door, he saw the rider coming from the east.

"It's Whipsaw! Bill, you're up!"

Bill ran to retrieve one of the ponies tied to the corral. He led the pony into the open to meet Whipsaw. Whipsaw rode in at full speed and slid his horse to a stop next to Bill. Whipsaw then dismounted, removed his mochila, and handed it to Bill, who threw the mochila over his saddle and began his mount as the pony galloped west.

After Bill rode away, Whipsaw asked, "Did I miss breakfast?"

Arnold replied, "I'm sure Elise will have something for you. Come on in." As Stevie turned to follow Whipsaw and Arnold into the house, he heard a faint "Yeehaw!" in the distance.

It came from the west, where Bill had just rode toward. Stevie realized that Bill must have met Johnny Sinclair on the trail not far away and given him the customized greeting Express riders had been known to give each other when they met on the trail.

Stevie ran inside to retrieve his gun belt, then ran back to the corral to untie the other pony that had been readied. He led the horse into the open and waited for Johnny to arrive. Johnny Sinclair rode in hot and slid his pony to a halt, dismounting all in one motion. He snatched his mochila and handed it off to Stevie, who threw it over his saddle and began his running mount.

Two and a half hours later and two relays into his ride, Stevie was halfway between Spring Ranch and Scotts Bluff. Stevie rode through a canyon about fifty yards wide where the river flowed westward. Scotts Bluff rested at the east end of the long narrow canyon.

Suddenly, Stevie felt something sting his right shoulder. Then immediately, he heard a gunshot from above him on the right. Steve looked and saw a puff of gun smoke rise from the southern bluffs of the canyon.

Stevie quickly swung his right leg over to the left side of his pony while putting all of his weight into the left stirrup. Then, he crouched next to the horse to hide from the shooter.

Then suddenly, another gunshot came from behind the pony. Stevie saw two men on horseback following him and shooting. Stevie took out his Colt with his right hand and aimed at the attackers. He fired his first shot but missed. Stevie took more care on the next shot to account for the horse's rhythmic bounce as she galloped. This time when he fired, he hit his target in the chest. Stevie watched as the man fell from his horse and landed in the river. Another shot came from above but missed Stevie again.

The canyon began to wind slightly to the south and created a bend that matched the direction of the river. Stevie no longer had to worry about his attacker from above. He hoped, however, that another gunman wasn't hiding around the bend. His concern now was the single rider who followed him through the canyon. The bandit was gaining on Stevie, who realized his pony was slowing while Stevie rode from the side of the saddle.

Stevie took a chance and swung back into the saddle, then turned to shoot at the rider following. Stevie fired his gun more as a deterrent rather than trying to kill the man. He shot four times and emptied his revolver. Stevie reached into his gun belt and switched his cylinder out for a fully loaded cylinder. Stevie fired twice more and somehow managed to hit his target. The second bandit fell to the ground with a thud. Stevie didn't know if he had killed the two men or just wounded them, but he wasn't waiting to find out. Stevie holstered his gun, then pulled his kerchief off and wrapped it around his arm at the shoulder to slow down the bleeding. He tied it off and continued to ride.

When Stevie arrived at Scotts Bluff, he switched horses just as he usually would have. He ignored his wound and continued his ride to Ficklin's Station. Stevie's arm began to ache as he rode into Ficklin's but switched horses and continued to ride.

Stevie made his relay at each station as if nothing had happened, but he grew weaker as the day proceeded. By the time he finally reached Midway Station, Stevie's shoulder was throbbing; he was becoming feverish and was finding it difficult to stay in the saddle.

Stevie rode into Midway, where he handed off his mochila to the next rider, a boy whom he didn't know. The boy mounted his pony and then rode east to continue the delivery of Stevie's mochila. Stevie saw Samuel Harper walking toward him from the corral as Stevie's eyes went black. He fainted in the dirt.

Samuel called for Elizabeth and scooped up Stevie to carry him into the house. Elizabeth asked, "What happened to him?"

"I don't know."

Samuel checked Stevie's body looking for any indication of why he would have fainted. Then he noticed the bloody right sleeve of Stevie's shirt and the bandana tied around his arm. Samuel looked at Elizabeth and said, "Something's wrong with his shoulder. Take his shirt off so I can have a look."

Samuel removed Stevie's shirt while Elizabeth prepared a pan of water to bathe Stevie's wound. When Elizabeth came back, she noticed the hole in Stevie's shoulder.

"Turn him to see if it went through."

Samuel rolled Stevie over to look at the back of his shoulder. There wasn't an exit wound. The bullet was still inside Stevie's arm. Stevie began to rouse as they examined his wound. He panted through the pain.

Elizabeth handed Samuel a leather belt and said, "Here. Put this in his mouth for him to bite down on while I dig out that bullet."

Samuel did as his wife instructed and told Stevie, "Here, son. Bite down on this."

Stevie bit on the leather and writhed as Elizabeth stuck a knife into his flesh and searched for the lead bullet in his shoulder. Stevie screamed through gritted teeth as the blade moved around in the wound, searching for the foreign body that needed to be removed.

"Got it!"

Elizabeth dropped the bullet into a tin plate on the table, then began dressing Stevie's wound. Samuel moved him to one of the cots and covered him with a blanket. Stevie slept the rest of the day.

When Stevie awoke, he saw a familiar face standing over him, staring at him. Charlie smiled and asked, "Not too good at dodgin' bullets are ya?"

Stevie replied, "Oh, I dodged plenty. They just got lucky with one."

"Did you kill em?"

"I shot two, knocked them off their horses. I don't know if they died or not. The third one got me from above on a bluff in a canyon that runs from Scotts Bluff to Spring Ranch. I'm sure he got away."

Then Stevie asked, "When did you get in?"

Charlie replied, "Couple hours ago."

Stevie said, "I haven't seen you in quite a while. How've you been?"

"Pretty good, I guess. I had a run in with some Kiowa about a week ago."

Stevie replied, "Really? What happened!"

"I had four come after me between Sam Mettache's and Cottonwood as I was headed east. I killed all four of um. Took their ponies with me. One of the ponies had a mochila on its back. One of the Indians had a rifle on him and another was wearing a white man's boots and hat. When I got farther up on the trail I discovered why."

"Why?" Stevie asked.

"They killed one of our riders. Took his horse, mochila, his rifle and every stitch of clothes he had. They beat his head in so bad you couldn't tell what his face looked like. Filled him with arrows. And they scalped him."

Stevie was stunned momentarily, then asked. "Did you ever find out who he was?"

Charlie replied, "Oh I knew! He had a tattoo on his right forearm of a four leaf clover."

Stevie realized who Charlie meant.

"Tom?"

"Yep! Them stinkin' Injuns took everything he had and left him to die. When I come on him, the buzzards was pickin' his bones. I rolled him up in an Injun blanket and took him to Mettache's.

Stevie asked, "Has anyone told his pa?"

"I don't know. I spect somebody in St Joseph probably told him."

Stevie's mind began to race. What would Tom's pa say? How horrible for him. The realization of the dangers of this job began to sink into Stevie's mind. "I need to write him."

Stevie asked Mrs. Arnold for some paper and a pencil so he could write a letter. Elise went to her dressing bureau, found what Stevie had asked for, and brought it to him.

Stevie sat at the dining table and began his letter.
Mr. John Grady General Delivery
St. Joseph, Missouri

Dear Mr. Grady,

I regretfully write to you about the tragic loss of your son, Tom. You may have already received word of his passing by now, but as one of Tom's closest friends, I wanted to inform you of what I know.

Tom and I worked at different routes of the Pony Express, and I haven't seen or heard from him since we parted back in April. Unfortunately, I was informed this morning that Tom died when attacked by a band of Kiowa outside Sam Mettache's Station in Nebraska.

All of us here at the Pony Express are deeply sorry for the loss of your son. If I can do anything for you in the future, please get in touch with me at Ft. Laramie.

Sincerely,
Stevie Watson

P.S. If you see any of my family, please tell them I am safe and doing well.

Stevie then decided it would be good to write his family and let them know he was alright.

Benjamin Watson and Family Parish Place
St. Joseph, Missouri

Dear Ma and Pa,

I wanted to let everyone know how I'm doing out here since I left in April. I love the work. We work long hours and get just a little rest. I am stationed at Ft. Laramie, Wyoming. My route runs west from Ft. Laramie to Sweetwater. On other days I ride from Ft. Laramie east to Midway Station in Nebraska.

It is dangerous at times. I got shot in the shoulder by bandits trying to rob me of my horse and mochila. Don't worry. I'm fine. I can't say as much for those bushwhackers.

I received word today that Tom Grady was killed last week somewhere in Nebraska. At least six Kiowa Indians attacked him. Charlie told me Tom managed to kill two of them before the others got him. I wrote Mr. Grady a letter to tell him how sorry I was for his loss.

Please don't worry about me. If I die out here on the frontier, I will die doing what I love and I will die a happy man. A man can't ask for more than that.

I hope William is doing well at his job. Hopefully, he has changed his mind about working for the Pony Express.

Tell the girls that I love and miss them, and tell Lillian that Charlie asked about her.

Love from your son,
Stevie

What Stevie didn't know was, William had already joined the Pony Express. When he turned fourteen on May 4, 1860, William approached William Russell and told him he had just turned fifteen. When Russell heard that William was the brother of Stevie Watson, Russell accepted William without question.

CHAPTER 33

AUGUST 23, 1860

Jesse Stevenson woke Stevie at four o'clock. Jesse was the station master at Sweetwater Station. He was a bachelor who came west looking for gold but got stranded in Wyoming when his horse died, and Indians stole his mule. He had no choice but to try to make a living in Wyoming. When the Pony Express came along, Jesse was blessed to have been selected to run one of their relay stations.

Slim Wilson had just arrived from the eastern run and was ready for his five-hour layover. After that, it was Stevie's turn to take over. Jesse slapped a biscuit and bacon into Stevie's hand as he headed out the door. Slim handed Stevie the mochila, and Stevie was off.

The morning air was stale on this muggy August morning. Stevie thought it smelled like rain might be on its way. But, since he was riding east, Stevie hoped he could outrun the shower and make his layover stop at Ft. Laramie.

He rode from Sweetwater to Willow Spring without incident. The sun began to rise as he exchanged his pony for another. The area around Willow Spring was green and lush, just as it had been at Sweetwater. However, the closer he got to Red Buttes, the more barren the land became. It was almost desert-like in that the plant life was sparse. The trail was dusty from the dry red sand Stevie's pony stirred as it ran through the plains. Stevie pulled his kerchief up over his nose to filter the dust as the air entered his nostrils.

The closer Stevie rode to Red Buttes Station, the more he saw the tall red rock formations that gave Red Buttes its name. The jagged, flat-topped structures created through centuries of erosion looked like castles in the distance.

Suddenly, Stevie heard a shot fired from behind. He turned to see five riders chasing him two hundred yards back. Stevie kicked his pony, trying to get her to run faster; he thought he might have a chance if he could outrun the bandits long enough to make it to Red

Buttes Station.

Stevie didn't bother drawing his weapon; he needed to concentrate on outrunning the band of ruffians. However, the pony grunted and began to limp just before Stevie heard another gunshot. He knew a bullet must have hit his pony. She continued to run, although the wound impeded her gait. She was beginning to falter in her strides. Stevie moved her closer to one of the buttes, where he could find cover from the gunshots.

Stevie steered the pony to the left and found a butte just one hundred yards away from the trail. The pony grunted as she grew weary until she finally fell into the red sand and died.

Stevie snatched his mochila from her back and slung it over his shoulders to wear like a poncho. The mochila had a slit in the strap that connected the pouches for occasions like this. He ran to the nearest butte and searched for a way to get elevation over the bandits as they approached. Finally, Stevie found a spot twelve feet up that he thought would be perfect as he made his stand. He checked his Colt to ensure it was fully loaded, then checked the extra cylinders in his gun belt. He knew if he were going to outlast these men, he would need to be careful with his shots.

Five bandits rode their horses straight for the butte, where they saw the Express rider hole up. They circled the butte, searching for a way to get to Stevie. Stevie pointed his Colt at one of the riders near the front of the pack. A large burly man who looked too large for his horse. Stevie thought him to be an easy target. He waited for the man to turn his body just right so that he would present the biggest target available. "*Bang!*" Stevie's shot rang true. The big man fell dead to the ground.

The other four riders rode away from where the man died, searching for another way to reach Stevie. Stevie's location allowed him to see three sides of his butte hideaway. Another rider came into view on Stevie's right. Stevie turned to face his attacker and carefully aimed. "*Bang!*" A man with long blonde hair fell to the ground and died.

Stevie counted in his mind, "*Just three left.*"

He sat still on the rock listening for movement. He wiped the sweat from his face with his kerchief. Then, suddenly, he heard rocks tumble to the ground on his left. Stevie turned in time to see a bearded man wearing a red shirt climbing the rocks to reach him. As the man raised his pistol at him, Stevie turned and fired his Colt twice. "*Bang! Bang!*"

The man with the red shirt fell from the rock to the ground twelve feet below with two holes in his chest.

Stevie watched as the remaining two bandits circled the butte. One of them was small, maybe only a boy. The other was tall and slender, and Stevie could see he had a scar that ran across his left eye and down his cheek.

He sat quietly upon the butte. Even though his pistol still held two bullets, he changed the cylinder to one fully loaded. Once he had finished switching out the cylinders, he heard gravel falling down the sides of the butte. Someone was climbing. Stevie made himself as small as he could, pressing his back against the wall of the rock. He looked to the south, allowing his peripheral vision to check movement simultaneously on his left and right sides.

Suddenly, Stevie saw a face quickly appear and then disappear to his right. Stevie waited. His heart pounded in his chest. Then, again, the face popped into view, but Stevie was ready. He fired, "*Bang!*"

Then he quickly turned just in time to see another head coming over the side of the rock. "*Bang! Bang!*" He fired twice and saw the body fall. He turned back to the right and slowly climbed to where he had seen the head pop up. There, on a ledge of the butte, lay a boy who couldn't have been more than thirteen. Stevie had shot him through the head.

Stevie carefully climbed down from the butte, sometimes climbing over dead bodies as he did. Finally, he made his way down to the ground, caught one of the bandit's horses, a big Bay stud, climbed upon it, and rode east to his next station.

When Stevie arrived at Platte Bridge Station, he traded the Bay for one of the reliable Express ponies. Howdy Hicks ran the station at Platte Bridge, and he asked Stevie, "Where'd ya get that monster?"

"I had a run in with five bandits back at the buttes. They shot my pony and killed her, so I traded with them."

"Didgya kill em?"

"Yep! Had to."

Stevie prepared to mount the new pony when Howdy said, "Be careful out there! Watch yer back!"

Stevie replied, "Always!" as he mounted the horse and rode away.

Stevie was thankful for the bridge at Platte Bridge station. It was one less time he had to cross a river or stream without getting wet. Unfortunately, the ride between Sweetwater and Ft. Laramie provided five other times he would have to cross a branch or creek forking off the Platte River. Most of them were shallow crossings, unlike the Platte River, which he had to cross when he took the route between Ft. Laramie and Midway.

An hour after leaving Platte Bridge, Stevie crossed Deer Creek and landed at Deer Creek Station, where he changed ponies again. Stevie made his usual transfer, sliding his pony to a stop, dismounting with his mochila, then making a running mount onto the new pony. Unfortunately, he had no time for conversations; he was already an hour behind schedule because of his run-in with the bandits.

Stevie made three more transfers at Box Elder, La Bonte, and Horseshoe before riding into Cottonwood Station. This was a different Cottonwood from the one run by Ike Slater. The riders referred to this as West Cottonwood and Ike's as East Cottonwood to distinguish one from the other. They did the same with Midway. There was a West Midway and an East Midway.

Daniel Lipman, a man of Hebrew descent, ran west Cottonwood. Daniel seemed quite out of place here in the frontier, but he was a friendly fellow. He always wore his yamaka, which all the riders thought strange. Stevie saw it as a sign that Daniel was a Godly man who could always be trusted.

Daniel and his wife moved out west from Ohio to avoid religious persecution. His wife, Mary, and their three children came out west in 1853; Stevie and his family moved to St. Joseph the same year.

Daniel's older son, Joshua, was thirteen. Joshua met Stevie with the fresh mount as Stevie rode into the station. Stevie took little time to change horses. Instead, he called out to Joshua as he dismounted and said, "Hello, Joshua! Tell your pa I said hi!" Then he was back on the trail.

An hour later, Stevie rode into Ft. Laramie and handed off his mochila to Whipsaw, who began his eastern route. Arnold Reese stepped out of the house to meet Stevie.

"Any trouble?"

"Yeah, I had to shoot it out with five bushwhackers up on the buttes."

"Are you hurt?"

Stevie replied, "No, my horse was killed, though."

"How'd you get to Red Buttes, then?"

"I took one of their horses after I killed them all."

Arnold was impressed with the young man. He seemed so matter-of-fact when he talked about fighting against bandits or Indians who always outnumbered him.

"Well, I know you've got to be hungry. Come on in and eat."

Elise had a stew warming on the stove, ready for whoever might show up throughout the day. Stevie sat down to eat the stew and drink his coffee.

As he sat at the table and began eating, he realized just how tired he was. He slowly ate the stew while conversing with the Reeses. They spoke of Stevie's family, about the things and people Stevie encountered on the trail, and what the soldiers at Ft. Laramie were up to.

Finally, Stevie finished his meal and excused himself to lie down. It was a long, eventful day and Stevie was dog-tired. He lay on his cot and quickly fell asleep.

CHAPTER 34

September 14, 1860

Stevie left Mud Springs Station at eight o'clock, heading east to reach the relay station at Midway. The sun was lowering below the mountaintops behind him as he rode. Crickets and frogs sang to him as he rode down the trail. Stevie rubbed the dust away from his eyes, trying to stay awake.

When Stevie arrived at Midway, he met Billy Tate, who would relieve him on the trail. Billy took the mochila and rode toward the next relay at Fremont Springs. Stevie entered the house, where he found Samuel and Elizabeth Harper sitting in their rockers. Samuel was reading while Elizabeth was knitting.

As Stevie walked into the house, Elizabeth stood and said, "Hello, Stevie! Sit down and let me get you some supper."

Stevie sat at the table and waited as Elizabeth brought him a plate of pinto beans, fried apples, and cornbread. Stevie ate his fill, then retired to the spare bedroom where two empty cots awaited. He chose the one on the right, pulled off his boots, and lay down. Within seconds he was fast asleep.

Three shots were fired in the early hours of the morning that startled and woke Stevie from a restful sleep. He quickly pulled on his boots, grabbed his gun belt, and ran for the door. On his way out the door, he grabbed a rifle that leaned against the wall next to the door. When he opened the door, he heard a commotion outside. Elizabeth stood on the porch watching as several Indians circled the house on horseback. Stevie grabbed her by the arm and led her back inside.

"Stay inside!"

Stevie searched for Samuel and found him in the yard close

to the corral with a rifle in his hand. Samuel fired at the red men as they rode past him, circling the house and corral. Stevie ran to the corral to join Samuel.

Someone else stood inside the corral, using it as a barricade to fight against the attackers, but Stevie couldn't identify who it was. Finally, Stevie decided that the men were after the horses. The air was filled with gun smoke, gunshots, and Indian yells as Stevie joined in to protect the station. Stevie shot a brave as he rode toward Stevie with his war club held high, ready to strike. The Indian fell from his horse and landed with a splash into the water trough next to the corral.

The stranger who hid in the corral used his handgun to fire at the attackers as they rode by shooting their arrows. The stranger seemed never to miss. He emptied his gun as four of the savages fell to their deaths in front of him.

Samuel raised his rifle to shoot at one Indian who rode straight toward him. As Samuel fired, an arrow pierced his left shoulder. Samuel struggled to remain standing but dropped to one knee and continued shooting.

There were too many Indians for Stevie to count, but he estimated there must have been at least twenty. One brave rode up to the corral and looped a leather rope around one of the posts trying to pull the post down to release the horses. Stevie shot the man before he was able to pull the post down.

The stranger in the corral reloaded his pistol and began firing again. Six quick shots and five more braves hit the dirt. Finally, Stevie realized something was familiar with how the stranger fired his weapon.

A brave rode toward the house and jumped from his pony, running for the door. Stevie raised his rifle and shot the man in the back as he reached the door. Another brave ran for the door, and Stevie pulled the trigger again. "*Click.*" The rifle was empty. Stevie dropped the gun and drew his Colt, and began firing. Another brave hit the ground in front of the house. Stevie turned to riders coming from behind the house. "*Bang! Bang! Bang!*" the Colt rang out. Three more fell from their horses and died. The bodies began to pile up as Samuel and Stevie moved away from the corral and toward the house. They stood halfway between the house and the corral as they continued to shoot. Four more braves fell to the ground. Then suddenly, It was over. The remaining Indians retreated and rode away back across the river.

Samuel ran into the house to check on Elizabeth. Stevie walked to the corral to see who he had been fighting alongside. The young man turned and smiled at Stevie as he approached and said, "Hey, brother!"

"William? Is that you?"

They ran to each other and embraced momentarily. Stevie asked, "What are you doing here?"

"I joined up when I turned fourteen. I told Mr. Russell I was fifteen and I was your younger brother. He watched me shoot and hired me on the spot."

Stevie replied, "It's good to see you! How's the family?"

"Ah, everyone's fine. They miss you."

"I miss them too. Come on inside."

William said, "Oh, wait! I forgot my mochila."

William ran back to the corral where his pony was wandering around with the others. He retrieved the mochila and ran back to meet Stevie. They walked into the house and found Samuel trying to comfort Elizabeth, shaken by their ordeal.

Stevie asked Samuel, "Samuel have you met my brother, William?"

"Yeah, we've met. Stevie, you better get a move on."

Stevie said, "Sorry, little brother. That's the nature of the job." William replied,

"So much for family reunions."

William shook Stevie's hand and handed him the mochila, then Stevie mounted a fresh pony and rode away.

Stevie rode to Mud Springs without incident. He was thankful that he had been able to catch his breath. It seemed like every station was under attack. The Kiowa were raiding them, looking to steal the ponies and anything else that appealed to their wants and needs.

Stevie transferred his mochila to a new ride, then began traveling north to Court House Rock. The farther west he rode, the less green the landscapes were, turning to red sand, buttes, and mountainous rock. As the trail turned northward, it moved closer to the North Platte River. Finally, Stevie transferred at Court House Rock, and the path turned northwesterly, leading him to Junction Station.

Stevie felt more relaxed as he rode into the Junction. His nerves had calmed a bit as he slid his horse to a stop at the station and transferred his mochila to the next pony. He continued riding northwest until he arrived at Chimney Rock an hour later. Again, he made the transfer without incident.

Stevie rode into Ficklin's around noon. The station had finally been rebuilt after having been burned to the ground. A new station manager had been hired, James Grover. Grover was born in Wyoming to a couple who wanted to graze their cattle freely. To the locals, they were known as free grazers and were looked upon with disdain. The cattle Barrons didn't want to share their pastures with those who had not legally attached themselves to the land. The Grover's were often attacked by the cattle baron's men or lost many of their cattle to rustlers.

As Stevie dismounted and began to transfer his mochila to the new pony, Grover approached him to meet Stevie for the first time.

"Howdy! I'm James Grover."

"Stevie Watson."

Grover asked, "Have you been riding for the Express long?"

"Since the beginning."

"Where you from?"

"St. Joseph, Missouri. Any news on the trail?"

Grover replied, "It's been quiet so far. How bout you?"

"Midway was attacked early this morning. Kiowa were after the horses. We killed most of them, but about ten of them got away. You better keep your eyes pealed."

"Will do!"

Stevie mounted the new pony and left Grover choking on his dust.

Stevie was most nervous about the next twenty miles of his route. A bluff followed the Platte River along the trail, providing cover for would-be thieves, bandits, and bushwhackers. Stevie kept his pony as close to the ridges as he could while he rode to Scotts Bluff. Stevie was constantly checking his back and looking among the cliffs as he moved through the area along the bluffs. Occasionally rocks would slide down the side of the bluffs startling Stevie and his pony. Stevie's awareness and adrenaline increased each time a stone fell from the cliffs.

Stevie finally made it to Spring Ranch, where he transferred to his next pony. He was relieved that he no longer had to ride below the bluffs. The trail was open from Spring Ranch to Ft. Laramie with only two more transfers.

Around three o'clock, Stevie rode into Horse Creek Station to make his transfer. Horse Creek was a pretty little camp with a small stone cabin nestled between two Boxelder trees. The Platte flowed behind the house and separated it from a 100-acre meadow behind it. The Horse Creek branched off the Platte and turned to run parallel with the Platte River. Stevie loved this station. He thought that when he could afford it, he'd like to find a little place just like this to settle.

Stevie transferred to another pony, then rode toward Bedeau's Station. "*Just two more hours,*" he thought. Stevie was beginning to tire after riding for nearly seven hours. It didn't help any, that he had to look over his shoulder constantly. The mental wear-and-tear was getting to him. Paranoia was setting in, and he was feeling exhausted.

About a mile from Bedeau's, Stevie saw a trail of smoke reaching above the horizon. "*Oh, no!*" he thought. "*Not again!*"

Stevie regretted what he might find up ahead. However, his regret was short- lived as his pony suddenly stumbled, falling head-over-feet and rolling to the ground, propelling Stevie and his mochila through the air. Stevie tumbled to the ground with a thud. He landed on his right shoulder. Stevie lay momentarily, trying to decide if he was injured or not. He was. His shoulder was dislocated. He couldn't move his right arm without wincing in excruciating pain.

Stevie looked around to find his horse, who was struggling to stand. As the pony finally stood, it was evident that he, too, was in pain. The pony grunted, snorted, and whinnied as he attempted to walk. Stevie managed to raise himself to his feet, then walked to the pony to have a look. Stevie felt each of the horse's legs and discovered the pony had broken his right foreleg at the canon bone. Stevie unbelievingly rolled his eyes as he said, "Sorry, old man."

Stevie reached with his left hand and took the Colt from its holster. He clumsily shifted the gun in an unfamiliar left-handed grip and raised the revolver to the pony's temple. Stevie pulled the trigger and a shot echoed through the open fields. The horse lay lifeless on the ground at Stevie's feet.

Stevie slid the Colt inside his belt behind the buckle, then removed his kerchief and loosened the knot making a sling to carry his lame arm. He slipped the sling over his head and gingerly placed his right arm into the sling. Stevie then walked over to where his mochila had landed, picked it up, slung it over his left shoulder, and began walking toward Bedeau's.

The pain in Stevie's right shoulder was nearly unbearable as he walked along the trail. Stevie took quick steps knowing that at his pace, it would likely take him another hour to reach Bedeau's or what might be left of it. He could still see the black smoke rising to the west, and sometimes when a breeze blew into his face, Stevie could smell the burning embers of the station. He only hoped another Express rider might come along and give him a ride.

The summer sun beat down on Stevie as he walked along. He grew wearier and wearier as he walked underneath the blazing sunlight. Finally, Stevie stopped next to the Horse Creek and lay face down to drink from the stream. He allowed his face to linger underneath the water as it flowed over his head. The cooling waters revived Stevie so he could pick himself up and walk again.

As Stevie continued down the trail, he came upon a small grove of Boxelder trees. He decided to take a short rest under the shade of the trees, so he walked into the grove and sat underneath one of the Boxelders.

Suddenly, Stevie heard something whiz past his left ear and imbed itself into the tree. An arrow had narrowly missed Stevie's head and impaled the tree only inches from his ear. Stevie rolled away from the arrow to find shelter behind his tree, but he was too late. Another arrow flew at him and didn't miss. Stevie felt a sharp pain in his back as an arrow pierced him below the shoulder blade and traveled through his left lung. Stevie gasped for air and tried to calm himself as ten riders came out of nowhere, whooping and crying out in their native war yells.

Stevie drew the Colt from his belt and fired with his left hand. The first shot felt awkward and missed its target, so Stevie tried to relax and make his shots count. He fired again, hitting one of the Kiowa braves in the chest and knocking him off his horse. Another brave rode directly at Stevie as he raised the Colt again and fired, "*Bang!*" The bullet hit the Indian in the face, and he fell to the ground.

The remaining braves began riding a circle around the grove of trees, trying to catch Stevie by surprise from behind. However, the trees were growing too closely together, making it difficult for them to find a straight shot with their bows at their target. Stevie continued to fire at the Kiowa braves as they circled him.

Another brave hit the ground eight feet away from where Stevie was hiding. Then, Stevie heard a crash from behind him as a brave on foot ran through the grove of trees surrounding Stevie. Stevie quickly fired three rounds into the Indian's chest and watched as the brave fell on top of Stevie.

Stevie rolled the body off himself and reached into his belt to get another cylinder to reload his pistol. His breathing became more labored as his lung began to fill with blood. Stevie knew he was dying but wasn't ready to give up. He continued shooting at the attackers as they encircled him. "*Bang! Bang! Bang!*" Two more braves died and hit the ground. Only four were left. Stevie coughed blood and spit it onto the dead Indian lying next to him. Another arrow hit Stevie in the left leg as he lay under the Boxelder. Stevie winced as it struck but then tried to ignore the pain.

Another brave ran through the grove, trying to ambush Stevie, but Stevie was ready for him. "*Bang! Bang! Bang!*" The brave fell next to his fallen companion, two holes in his chest and one in his head.

Stevie quickly reloaded the Colt and readied himself for the next attacker. Two more braves rode together toward Stevie, screaming as they flung their arrows toward him. Stevie repeatedly fired, hitting both men and knocking them off their horses.

The remaining brave had had enough. He rode away with several of the riderless ponies following behind him. Stevie was relieved to see him retreat, but his relief was short-lived. Stevie could no longer catch his breath. His lung was completely deflated of air and only held blood that had leaked into it from his wounds. Stevie gasped, trying to fill his remaining good lung so that he might live, but it was no use. Finally, Stevie attempted to cough up the blood filling his lung; he choked and gasped, then died.

CHAPTER 35

SEPTEMBER 15, 1860

Charlie Miller rode his pony into Midway around one o'clock Saturday morning. After eleven hours on the trail, Charlie was ready to hit the sack. As he rode into Midway, Samuel Harper met him with a fresh pony and said, "Charlie, I need you to keep riding. We're missing some riders.

Charlie asked, "Who's missing?"

"I haven't seen Whipsaw for three days. Johnny Sinclair left here heading east, yesterday. Stevie left yesterday going west. Bill Trotter hasn't been here since Wednesday. He should have been your relief."

Charlie dismounted, carried his mochila to the next pony, then mounted and rode away. As Charlie rode at full gallop, the stars were bright in the cloudless sky. Charlie made his transfers at Mud Springs, Court House Rock, and the Junction without incident.

As Charlie reached Chimney Rock, the sun began to peek its light over the tops of the Rocky Mountains that stood far away to the west. Charlie admired the colors of orange and blue as they mixed together, bringing the daylight into sight.

When Charlie changed horses and began riding to Ficklin's, he saw a dark grey cloud forming in the distance, indicating ominous weather was approaching. He hoped he could make it to Ft. Laramie before the rain arrived.

The station managers repeated the same news at each stop along the way. Riders were missing. Henry Scotts at Scotts Bluff told Charlie, "Stevie was through here yesterday. But, I ain't seen nobody else since."

Charlie felt at ease somewhat to hear that his friend Stevie at least was okay, yet he wondered what was happening to all the other riders. Tom James at Spring Ranch gave the same report. Charlie changed ponies and continued to ride.

Around nine o'clock, Charlie rode into Horse Creek. A light rain began to fall as Charlie changed horses and continued down the trail. He galloped his horse but not to its full speed. Charlie was wary of the possibility of slick terrain because of the rain. Several times during the ride, Charlie could feel his pony's feet slip slightly in the mud as he ran.

With only a mile left until he reached Bedeau's, Charlie noticed something odd up ahead in the distance. A dead pony lay on the ground. Charlie stopped his horse to examine the dead animal more closely. First, he saw a bullet hole in the side of the horse's head. Next, he noticed the strange shape of the pony's foreleg. It was broken. Charlie looked behind the pony's saddle and saw what he had hoped he wouldn't, the horse wore the brand of the Pony Express. It was one of theirs.

Charlie remounted his horse and rode toward a grove of Boxelder trees in the distance where something else caught his eye. Charlie saw the body of an Indian lying in the mud. He slowly walked his pony as he drew his pistol and searched the area for any would-be attackers. Charlie could see that the Indian was dead, but scavengers had not yet found it.

Charlie continued to move forward and saw two more bodies lying dead on the ground. Then and another, and another. Charlie searched all around him, wondering if live Indians might be watching him, waiting for him to dismount.

As Charlie grew closer to the grove, his heart sank. He saw the body of what he suspected was one of their missing riders. The body was leaning against one of the trees. Charlie dismounted and walked into the grove. He approached the body until he began to recognize who he was seeing. Charlie stopped in his tracks as tears started to fill his eyes. He couldn't believe what he was seeing. It couldn't be!

But it was. His friend was dead. Stevie had taken Charlie under his wing and treated him like a brother. But now, Stevie was lying against a tree with two arrows in him. His arm was in a sling, and his gun was still in his left hand. Charlie then saw more braves in the grove that Stevie had undoubtedly killed. Finally, he found nine dead Kiowas in all that Stevie had taken down before succumbing to his injuries.

With less than a mile left to reach Bedeau's, Charlie struggled as he raised Stevie's body onto the back of the Express pony. He led the pony down the trail hoping that he could find someone at Bedeau's to help him.

As Charlie approached Bedeau's, he began noticing a burnt wood smell. Even though the rain was falling harder now, the odor still lingered. The help that Charlie had hoped for would not be found here. There were no horses, no shelter, and no one left at the station. He had no choice but to continue walking his pony toward Ft Laramie.

Charlie never stopped. Even though his legs became wiry and limp and his pony began to tire from carrying the load, Charlie never stopped. Finally, at midnight, he walked into the shadows of Ft. Laramie Station. Charlie tied the horse outside the station, then walked to the door and opened it.

"Hello?"

A voice answered him, "Yeah! Who is it?"

"Charlie Miller. Are you the station manager?"

"Yeah. I'm Arnold Reese."

Charlie replied, "I found one of our riders on the trail. He's dead. It's Stevie Watson."

"Stevie? He's dead?"

"Yessir. I found him about a mile the other side of Bedeau's. Bedeau's is burnt to the ground, too. My horse is plum tuckered out, and so am I."

Arnold woke his wife, Elise, and they helped Charlie bring Stevie's body into the house. First, they lay his body out on one of the cots, then Arnold said to Charlie, "I'll get you a fresh horse so you can be on your way to Cottonwood."

Charlie replied with disdain, "I ain't going to Cottonwood!"

Arnold replied, "You have to! There's no one else to take your mochila!" Charlie raised his voice and said, "I don't give a shi. . . sorry ma'am. I don't care about no mochila. Stevie's like a brother to me. I'm taking him home to his folks. I'm fixin' to lay on that cot right there and get some sleep. When I wake up, you better have a wagon waiting for me outside with supplies loaded in it. I'm taking Stevie back to St. Joseph."

Arnold said, "I can't just give you a wagon and some horses

and let you leave. Those belong to the Pony Express."

Charlie replied, "Consider it my wages for the month."

Charlie lay on the cot across from where Stevie's body lay and quickly fell asleep. While he slept, Elise walked over to the fort and asked to see the company doctor. A soldier led her to the infirmary where she was introduced to Captain MacDougal, the post-doctor.

"What can I do for you, Mrs. Reese?"

"One of our express riders was killed and his body was brought in. I want to prepare his body for transport back to Missouri where his family is."

MacDougal asked, "Do you know anything about embalming?"

"No, not really."

"Why don't I come over and give you a hand, then."

Captain MacDougal gathered supplies and instructed one of his orderlies, Private Henry, to come along. They walked back to Elise's cabin and started preparing Stevie's body for transport. They moved the body into the main room and placed it on the table so Charlie wouldn't be disturbed.

The doctor opened the body cavity with a knife and poured powder of myrrh and several fragrant oils into the body. He then stitched the body closed. He used natron, or hydrated sodium carbonate, to dry out the body by rubbing it all over. Once the body was dried, they washed the body, then wrapped it in cotton bandages.

Private Henry was instructed to return to the fort and have the company carpenter build a coffin for Stevie's body. By the time Charlie awoke the next morning, all was prepared for him to take Stevie home to St. Joseph. The coffin had been loaded into the back of a covered wagon hitched to two horses. Supplies had been placed into the back of the wagon for Charlie's six-week journey. Charlie figured he should make St. Joseph if all went well by the first of November.

Driving a wagon down this trail was quite different for Charlie than riding on the back of a galloping pony. He had too much time to think. He thought about his short life and how much he had already experienced at his age. He thought about his family, which he had lost at an early age. They were good enough parents; they cared for and provided for him. But they were nothing like Stevie's ma and pa. During the two weeks he spent with them; he saw they truly loved their children. They were affectionate, gave their kids praise when they did right, and corrected them when they made mistakes without using a switch or a belt. Charlie hoped to have a family like that someday.

He thought about the jobs he had already worked in his short life. First, he rode with wagon trains, working as a messenger boy, riding up and down the wagon line delivering messages from the train master. Then, he worked on a couple of ranches breaking broncs. And, of course, working for the Pony Express. Finally, Charlie wondered what lay in store for him. What would be his next job?

Eleven days into his trip, Charlie drove into Midway. Samuel and Elizabeth Harper met him as he pulled into the station. News of Stevie's demise had already reached them. Someone else walked out of the house when Charlie arrived. It was William.

William's lip quivered and tears ran down his cheeks as he approached Charlie and shook his hand.

"I'm sorry, William."

William couldn't say anything; he only nodded his acknowledgment. Finally, after a long pause, trying to gain his composure, William asked, "Do you know what happened?"

"Kiowa! I don't know how many attacked him, but he killed nine of em. He had two arrows in him, but they didn't get his scalp. I know one thing, the army better do something about keepin' them Injuns under control or there ain't gonna be no Pony Express anymore."

The next morning, Charlie went out, hitched the horses to his wagon, and prepared to leave. William walked out of the house carrying a sack of supplies that Elizabeth had packed. He put the sack in the back of the wagon, then climbed onto the bench behind the horses.

Charlie asked, "You going somewhere?"

"St. Joe."

Charlie smiled and then replied, "Well, alright. Let's get moving."

As they rode together, Charlie asked William, "Are you quitting?"

"No. Just taking a break. I'll come back. You?"

"I ain't decided yet. It's hard to pass up the money, but sometimes I wonder if it's worth it."

Having William beside him didn't make the trip any faster, but to Charlie, it seemed less monotonous having someone to talk to. Charlie asked William, "Do you think your folks know about Stevie yet?"

"I don't know. I wrote them as soon as I found out, but I don't know if they've gotten my letter yet."

"Do they know you're coming home?"

"When they get the letter they'll know. I said I'd be there for Stevie's funeral. I'm sure they'll give me a hard time about coming back to ride for the Express, but I love doing it.'

"Me too. It wouldn't be so bad if they'd do something about them Injuns."

Nine days later, Charlie and William drove into Fremont Springs. They stayed overnight and resupplied before continuing on to Ft. Kearny. Once they left Fremont Springs, they traveled ten more days before they arrived at Ft. Kearny. When they reached Kearny they spoke to a soldier at the fort who told them William Russell and his partners were leaning heavily on the military to increase patrols along the Pony Express route, especially between Ft. Kearny and Ft. Laramie. Five other riders beside Stevie had been killed, and three stations had been burned since the Express began.

Another ten days drifted by as William and Charlie drove the wagon east. William was beginning to think this trip would take as long as his family's journey from Albany to St. Joe had taken. But, at least, it was uneventful for the most part. The biggest headache was having to recite over and over along the trail what had happened to Stevie and hearing how sorry everyone was about Stevie. William was sick of everyone saying, *"I'm so sorry about Stevie"* or *"Sorry for your loss."* And then there was the ever-annoying, *"He's in a better place."*

William wanted it all to be done. He was sure the funeral would be even worse. One after another people would approach his ma and pa and the girls, shaking their hands and expressing their sympathies. It was such an awkward thing for everyone involved. William made up his mind then and there that if he had to say anything to someone who had lost a loved one, he would simply relate a happy moment and a loving quality that the deceased had given him in life.

Charlie pulled the wagon into Rock Creek station on the tenth day. Another ten or eleven days would find them pulling into St. Joseph. Again, they resupplied at Rock Creek and moved on to the next stop. Each night had seen them at a different station along the way. It was safer for the two to stop at a station than to camp along the trail. However, the constant answering of questions and the farewell wishes were wearing the two young men down. They decided to camp just outside of each station for the next few days.

On day forty-nine, the boys drove into Elmwood late in the evening. It was too late to catch the ferry into St Joseph, so they camped on the east side of Elmwood. Other groups of travelers were camping there as well. Several wagons were lined up at the ferry dock, waiting to cross the Missouri River. William remembered when his family arrived at the east bank of the Mississippi and had to wait five days to catch a ferry.

"I hope we don't have to wait here too long to cross. My family had to wait five days when we came out west before we could catch a ferry to cross the Mississippi River."

Charlie stood on the wagon bench to get a better look at the line in front of them.

"I count six wagons in front of us. Maybe we can make it on the first day."

William said, "I hope so. I'm ready to see the family."

CHAPTER 36

NOVEMBER 4, 1860

The weather turned cold that day. The wind whipped across the front of the wagon as the boys waited to board the ferry. Unfortunately, William and Charlie missed the first ferry crossing the Missouri River. Only five wagons could fit on the boat at a time, so they had to wait for the next one.

William took out his jackknife and whittled on a small piece of wood he found lying on the ground. He and Charley sat side by side on the wagon bench, waiting for the boat to return.

At noon, the boat finally returned to dock on the west bank, where Charlie and William were waiting. Charlie drove the team onto the ferry and found a spot near the front of the boat to park the wagon. They waited nearly an hour before the ferry started moving back across the river.

It was a short thirty-minute ride across the river. As the ferry docked at St. Joseph, Charlie drove the wagon off the ferry and moved down the street, turning right toward Kansas City.

Somehow, word had gotten around town that Stevie's body had arrived. Several people who William recognized, came outside their homes and businesses to pay their respects as Charlie drove past them. All was quiet on the streets of St. Joseph. Stevie had made many friends while working for Avery at the livery stable, and they were all saddened by the news of his passing.

When they reached the livery, Avery stepped out and walked beside the wagon and held his hand out to William to shake as they slowly rolled along. William shook Avery's hand and said, "Thanks, Avery."

The boys arrived at Parish Place around two o'clock. Charlie pulled up to the house and tied the horses to the hitching rail at the back of the house. Hannah stepped out the back door and yelled, "William! Ma, its William!"

Abigail quickly came to meet the boys as they stepped down toward the house. She cried as she spoke to them both, "William!

Charlie! You're home!"

William replied, "Hello, Ma! We brought Stevie home."

Lillian and Benjamin heard the commotion from the barn and came running when they saw that William was home. The family hugged William and Charlie for a long while, with tears in their eyes. Then, finally, Benjamin said, "Thanks for bringing Stevie home to us."

William asked, "Do we have any plans for the funeral?"

Pa replied, "We need to dig a grave today. Folks are coming tomorrow to pay their respects at 10 o'clock. We'll have a service, then."

Charlie asked, "Do you need any help?"

"Thanks. I'd like that, Charlie. Although, you've already been a big help to us by bringing Stevie back. I know it couldn't have been easy."

"Don't mention it. Wild Injuns couldn't have stopped me from it."

Charlie drove the wagon to the barn while the family followed on foot. He parked the wagon, unhitched the horses, and then put them in the corral with the other horses. Benjamin, William, and Charlie gathered some digging tools, then walked to a spot on the slope that Ma and Pa had chosen as the grave site. It was a spot underneath an Elm tree displaying its colorful leaves of bright orange. The men dug the grave together while Ma and the girls sat under a Maple tree, huddled together to brace against the wind.

As the sun began to set, the grave was finally finished. They all walked back down the slope together to the barn. Lillian and Heather finished their chores of milking and collecting eggs while Ma walked to the house to start supper.

That night after supper, the family sat in the parlor around the fireplace, telling stories about their favorite memories of Stevie. Ma talked about how smart Stevie was. "I've never seen anyone so good at math before. He could figure things in his head quicker than I could even write the problem down on his slate."

Pa said, "He always wanted to help me. He wanted to learn everything that I could teach him. Hunting, fishing, farming, riding; it didn't matter. He wanted to know everything.

Lillian said, "Stevie always made time for me. He would play with me or take me swimming. I loved him so much."

Heather added, "I love Stevie!"

Charlie said, "Stevie was the brother I never had. Not only that, he was like a pa to me. He helped me learn to read and do my sums, and he bought me clothes when we first met. He wouldn't let me pay him back. He always said, 'I'll catch you next pay day', but he never would."

William struggled to get the words he wanted to say about his older brother. "I always wanted to be like Stevie. But there was no one else like him. Everything seemed to come easy to him, and so hard for me. But, he made me want to be better at everything. I was a better shooter and rider than I would have been if it hadn't been for Stevie. He taught me tricks and encouraged me to do better. The last time I saw him was about a month before his death. We were at Midway Station. Stevie got there the night before and I had just ridden in when about twenty or thirty Kiowa rode in trying to steal the horses. Samuel Harper, Stevie, and I fought together outnumbered ten to one. I don't know how many Stevie took down, but he saved Mrs. Harper at least twice. Stevie was the best brother anyone could ever have."

November 5, 1860

The cold winds died down during the night. The Watsons woke to clear skies and sunshine as they had breakfast together. Before removing the dishes from the table, they heard wagons and horses arriving outside their home.

They all stepped out onto the front porch to see a long caravan of people arriving; they were lined up as far toward St. Joseph as the eye could see. But, then, another line came from the opposite direction from farms and homes along the Kansas City Road.

People got out of the wagons and began setting up make-

shift tables from long boards and saw horses. Then they spread ta-
blecloths and lay out a feast made for a king. Over two hundred
people had come to pay their respects to the Watson family. Ma and
Pa were amazed at the outpouring of love and sympathy to them.

After three hours, everyone had finally settled in. All the
mourners gathered along the slope to find a place near the newly
dug grave. Pastor Sampson of the First Baptist Church of St. Joseph
led the procession from the barn to the grave site. Stevie's family
followed on foot while Charlie drove the wagon carrying the casket
behind them.

When the procession reached the grave site, six men stepped
up to the back of the wagon. They carried the casket to the grave:

• John Grady, the father of Irish Tom Grady.

• William Russell, one of the founders of the Pony Express.

• Avery Johnson, owner of the livery stable where Stevie
worked his first job.

• Cecil Bradley, owner of the local dairy where the Watsons
had purchased their first cow.

• Dr. Trenton Adams, the local doctor who had helped deliver little Heather when they first moved to St. Joseph.

• Paul Wilson.

Paul and his wife, Anna, arrived on the train from Hannibal
only yesterday.

They had received word through Mr. Reynolds at the deed
office about Stevie's death and immediately boarded a train from
New York City. Benjamin was both surprised and delighted to see
the Wilsons.

William glanced over and saw Maria, Angelo, and Lisa
standing next to Maria's new husband, Dr. Adams.

After Pastor Sampson finished his eulogy, he asked if anyone else had anything they wanted to say.

A frail voice spoke out from the crowd and said, "I do!"

It was Mrs. Amanda Taylor, long-time widow of St. Joseph.
She was eighty- four years old and could barely walk, but she had
caught a ride with some of the ladies from her church to come to the
funeral.

"Stevie Watson was the finest young man I have ever met

in my eighty-four years of living on this earth. I met Stevie when he first started working for Mr. Johnson at the livery stable. Stevie saw me coming out of the general store carrying some packages and offered to carry them for me. Ever since that day up until he went to work for the Pony Express, Stevie would come by my house and offer to do my shopping for me. He also kept me supplied in firewood and anything else I needed. I tried to pay Stevie, but he would never take money from me."

John Grady walked forward and said, "Stevie and my boy, Tom were good friends for years. They started riding for the Pony Express at the same time. When Tom was killed, Stevie took time to write to me and tell me about it. Stevie always thought about others."

Avery then said, "Stevie was the best friend I ever had. I gave him his first job, but he was doing me a favor. He was smart as a whip! He showed me how to make money from my business. He even taught me to read and do arithmetic. No offense to you, William, but there will never be another Stevie Watson. He was the best of the best!"

Paul stepped forward and said, "My name is Paul Wilson. My wife and I live in New York City. We met the Watsons years ago while they traveled from Albany to make their home in St. Joseph. While at Niagara Falls, my wife accidentally fell over the edge of a cliff overlooking the falls. Benjamin and Stevie, who was only eight years old at the time, came to her rescue. Stevie let Benjamin down over the cliff's edge on a rope tied to Stevie's horse. Once Benjamin reached Anna, he grabbed her and held onto her while Stevie pulled them both to safety. Even at a young age, Stevie was brave and skillful."

Benjamin finally stepped forward and began to speak, "Abigail and I want to thank all of you for coming out today and showing us your love and admiration for our son, Stevie. We will all miss him dearly. But, although I am saddened by his death I know that he died doing what he loved."

Benjamin took out the letter Stevie had written so many months ago and read from it:

Dear Ma and Pa,

I wanted to let everyone know how I'm doing out here since I left in April. I love the work. We work long hours and get just a little rest. I am stationed at Ft. Laramie, Wyoming. My route runs west from Ft. Laramie to Sweetwater. On other days I ride from Ft. Laramie east to Midway Station in Nebraska.

It is dangerous at times. I got shot in the shoulder by bandits trying to rob me of my horse and mochila. Don't worry. I'm fine. I can't say as much for those bushwhackers.

I received word today that Tom Grady was killed last week somewhere in Nebraska. At least six Kiowa Indians attacked him. Charlie told me Tom managed to kill two of them before the others got him. I wrote Mr. Grady a letter to tell him how sorry I was for his loss.

Please don't worry about me. If I die out here on the frontier, I will die doing what I love, and I will die a happy man. A man can't ask for more than that.

Benjamin looked up from the letter and closed by saying, "Stevie was right. Although his mother and I tried, we couldn't help but worry about him. However, we take comfort in knowing he died doing what he loved, and we as men and women we can't hope for much better here on this earth than to die doing what we love. If we do that, we will die happy people, and we can't ask for more than that."

Notes from the Author

I have always loved westerns. My favorite author as a young man was Louis L'Amour. I know westerns have faded in popularity over the past years as stories about dragons, witches, wizards, vampires, and the such have taken over. But, the old west is a huge part of our history. Although over dramatized much of the time, men of the west carved out what would some day be the civilizations we now know and love.

Although given the name of my college friend from years ago, Stevie Watson is fictional. However, many of the other Pony Express riders mentioned in this book truly existed although fictionalized in this story by the author.

Bronco Charlie Miller was one of those men who actually rode for the Pony Express at an early age. Charlie's parents moved to California to find gold during the gold rush years of the 1840s. Charlie was born in 1850 and was said to have ridden for the Pony Express at age eleven. He worked for Teddy Roosevelt on his horse ranch breaking broncs while a young man. He then became a performer with a Wild West show performing as a rider and knife thrower. He joined the Canadian Army while in his sixties so he could fight in World War I. He offered his services again while in his nineties wanting to fight in World War II, but was turned down. He died January 15, 1955.

Several books of fiction have been written about Bronco Charlie and others of the Pony Express riders mentioned in this book. I hope you have enjoyed reading this book as much as I have enjoyed writing it.

Michael L. Clark is author of **The Shimmering Trilogy**. This series allows the reader to explore what it might be like to live on the Natchez Trail in the early 1800's His latest book, "Ambush at Horse Creek" has been highly anticipated by Clark's loyal readers. His next book, "Blood Sails" is expected to be released in late 2023.

A long time resident of Middle Tennessee, he spends much of his free time exploring historical places throughout the Southeastern part of the country. With each journey, he discovers new intriguing material to research for upcoming books. Clark has recently retired from the United States Postal Service which allows him more time for writing and researching his next projects.

www.author-michaellclark.com
Subscribe to get notification of new releases from
Michael L. Clark

Don't miss *The Shimmering* trilogy by Michael L. Clark